REDNECK REBELS

A WMBW REVERSE HAREM ROMANCE

JAMILA JASPER

JAMILA JASPER ROMANCE

ISBN: 9798201825409

2nd edition.

Thank you to my Patrons:
Join the Patreon Community.

Visit deniadesign.com for more information about the cover design and cover design services used for full-length Jamila Jasper romance novels.
Contact: denia@littledipper.com

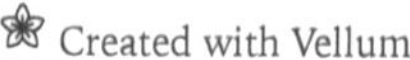
Created with Vellum

DESCRIPTION

"The three of us men are kin. We share everything... especially her — Caroline Coulson, the woman we ain't s'posed to love..."

3 alpha male country boys...
1 Black intellectual woman...
A segregated town that isn't ready for interracial love.

Exposing town secrets & scandals threatens all four lovers in this interracial reverse harem.

Can Caroline keep the quad together, or will she have to choose between the strapping men who love her, and her career in politics?

Stay Alert! The hottest scenes are in Chapter 4 and Chapter 8. If you aren't ready for Caroline to get ridden like a bronco by three beefy, strapping, muscular, and rock hard country boys, hop away from this searing hot interracial romance.

Book #1 | Redneck Rebels Trilogy

THE COMPLETED SERIES

Redneck Rebels
Redneck Rebellion
Redneck Retribution

1

TRAVIS MONTGOMERY, TOTAL HOTTIE

TRAVIS PULLED a hairpin from Caroline's head. Thick black curls draped down over her chest, covering her small, perky B-cup breasts. He'd parked his cop car beneath a magnolia tree a mile away from the town's well. Here, it was quiet enough and isolated enough that no one would notice a dirty beat up police car parked beneath a tree with the windows up and the air conditioning blasting to stave off the summer heat.

Caroline was naked, sweat pooling at her brow despite the air conditioning, and for the first time in weeks Travis was finally alone with her. He took his pale hand and pressed it to her sepia colored cheek, drawing her in for a kiss. Magnolias bloomed around this time of year and flurried to the ground like hail during a storm.

Their pink and purple petals fell to the ground beneath the trees, littering every inch of the sidewalk and the earth with these sweet scented reminders of the springtime. Old Town breathed with life again, and the Southern winter was finally officially over.

A fresh southern breeze blew across the town, past the

white Evangelical Church and over the train tracks past the Black Baptist church where Caroline's mother sang every Sunday. That woman could have been a star, people in Old Town said.

Old Town was always going to be quintessentially American. Each house hung a large American flag, the stars and stripes floating in the breeze and marking Old Town as a home for true patriots. There would always be two sides to the town. Even as they sat intertwined in Travis' car, both he and Caroline were painfully aware of the differences.

There would always be the side with large houses, old antebellum mansions with their pillars and acres and acres of old plantation land. On that side of town, sometimes the flags hanging from balconies were decorated with the stars and bars instead of the stars and stripes. Southern pride, they said.

Caroline knew different.

Tufts of cotton floated on the breeze at the height of growing season, landing on the porches and cars of the townspeople. The train tracks would always be in the same place, cutting the town in two.

On the other side of those train tracks, Old Town was different. There were no more columns or large swathes of land that stretched out for acres and acres. Small wooden houses were built not too far apart from each other and on the other side of the tracks, the houses centered around a deep well that had watered that half of the town for decades.

That morning Caroline Coulson had twisted her long kinky black hair into a top bun. While the other girls in her office could get away with "messy buns", Caroline did not share that privilege. Using stiff black hair pins, she pinned down every strand of hair lest she be accused of being unkempt. It was the first day since Buchanan's inauguration as mayor, and the most important day Caroline would have in the office. The new administration would probably be making changes to the staff and getting rid of anyone unfriendly to Buchanan's leadership.

Caroline ate a small bowl of oatmeal her brother Caleb made her for breakfast that morning before meeting Travis, drowning out the noise of her family members, all of them crowded into their small house. Nobody noticed how quiet she was at breakfast. They were all busy and in a rush to get to work. Only Caleb seemed to notice. And he didn't say anything until after he watched her put her bowl into the sink. Caleb chased after her and offered to walk Caroline to work.

"Travis is already giving me a ride," She said to her brother, reassuring him that she would make it without his help, even if the factory was past the mayor's office and they usually walked to work together.

In the car, with Travis, Caroline began to regret not leaving with her brother that morning. Travis looked at her with that worried look in his eyes.

"I hate when you look at me like that," Caroline complained.

Travis' eyes as blue as a prairie sky softened. He leaned in and kissed her cheek, then her lips.

"I can't help it, Caroline."

"Find a way to help it. I wasn't worried about today before, but now I am with all your staring and ogling."

Travis pulled her in for another kiss. His lips were soft and Caroline swore she could smell magnolias on his skin. His cropped blonde hair was just wet from a shower and he smelled like cinnamon and Axe deodorant. Caroline straddled his lap and ran her hands over his head and his neck, burned red from the strengthened sun on his morning run before work.

She didn't want him to stop kissing her but they had already wasted enough time. These morning romps had become their morning ritual of late. They were just old friends, going for a small drive in his car. That was how it started at least. Now, they kissed and kissing lead to other things. Caroline slipped into her clothing, hoping that her bun could be twisted into its former glory. Travis stuck the last hairpin in.

"Before we leave, let's just have one more round," Travis suggested, his eyes wandering to her breasts as he helped her fix her hair one last time.

Caroline succumbed easily to his suggestions. He kissed her and then pushed her back up against the seats. The door handle dug into the middle of her back, but Caroline didn't care. Travis spread her legs wide and undid the zipper to his cop uniform, pulling his hardness out again. His member was large and thick, throbbing with anticipation before he even pressed the tip up against her silky dripping entrance.

Even if this was their third round for the morning, heat never subsided between them. Travis thrust every inch between her legs with one stroke and Caroline moaned as she accepted his firm pulsing cock between her legs. He pinned her hands over her head, pressing them into the window. He plunged into Caroline deeply, making love to her in the back of his police car until she screamed in pleasure and the windows fogged up.

Her toes, raised in the air, traced the fog on the window and pressed up against the back window, sliding across the condensation as Travis grunted while pounding her. It was a good thing no one really came to this part of town. Travis knew all the good spots — chalk it up to him being the starting quarterback at their high school and having plenty of girlfriends to take out into these abandoned fields.

Once Caroline finished in a loud, euphoric climax, Travis erupted between her legs causing her to shake and tremble as his seed filled her slippery honeypot.

Once they finished for the third time that morning, Caroline buttoned his shirt and help him tuck it in his starched blue pants. Travis Montgomery grinned. He loved their morning ritual. And Caroline? Well he had always loved her. Since they were teenagers, they had been best friends. When Caroline went to college, Travis was convinced that she would never come back. Now, he worried that Caroline was trapped in this town, like he was, and he regretted ever wishing that this smart brown-skinned beauty would return. Old Town didn't deserve a woman like Caroline, Travis thought. He kissed her forehead again, unable to resist giving her one last nervous peck despite her warnings.

"You're way too pensive in the morning. Lighten up. I'm already going to have a hellish day at work," Caroline complained, smacking Travis's shoulder with a teasing expression on her face.

Travis grinned and rolled his eyes, countering her complaint with one of his own.

“I'm going to have an even more hellish day.”

“What, the Old Town hooligans going to egg another old lady's house?”

“You know what I mean, Caroline," he said.

"Right. It's our dear mayor's first day on the job."

"Speaking of which, I had better get you to work. You button up that shirt,” he commanded.

Caroline liked when he made demands like that. As a police officer, Travis was used to to telling people what to do. And since he became an officer, it was a welcome change. When they were kids, Caroline ran the show. It was nice that Travis grew up to be such a good leader. People really looked up to him — and not just because his daddy was sheriff Montgomery. Travis carved out his own respect in town.

Caroline had an ulterior motive for asking him to drive her to work. It wasn't just that their morning romps were some of the few things she still looked forward to. It wasn't just because Travis was smoking hot with a perfect toned body that he diligently maintained. It wasn't even the fact that his sky blue eyes were filled with such soul, and that his Southern manners made her feel like all hope wasn't lost.

There was something else that she wanted from him today. It was almost hard to admit to herself that she needed anything from Travis. When Caroline first left for college, she was convinced that she didn't need anyone in this town, least of all Travis. Now, Caroline needed her old friend more than ever, especially since she had taken that job in politics hoping that she would be able to make a difference in Old Town.

Travis drove Caroline from the black side of town, the only safe place they could meet and canoodle like that, across the train tracks to the center of town where the mayor's office stood with the imposing dominance of a castle in a feudal kingdom. To be a mayor of a town that small may not seem to be such a big deal to you or me. In towns like Old Town, the small town folks with the gumption for it find power and cling to it with the tenacity of despots in small foreign nations.

Travis offered to stop at *Dunkin' Donuts* for coffee. Caroline declined. She'd been trying to quit coffee for sometime now with limited success. Travis stopped anyway and the smell was tempting enough that Caroline ordered a decaf. Travis was amused with her latest attempt at good health and he teased her about her "water coffee". He noticed that Caroline didn't seem to be her usual chipper self. She was still outspoken, true, but there was a faraway look in her eye, like she had something on her mind. It must be something going on at work. Ever since the mayor won the election, Caroline had been acting strangely.

"Are you going to bother telling me what's on your mind or will I have to guess?"

"I need your help, Travis," Caroline confessed.

"I know. That's why am driving you to work."

"I need more than that. You know my opinions about Mayor Buchanan. It's a total mistake to let him assume power. We have to do something."

"Buchanan won the election fair and square, Caroline. I don't know what you expect me to do."

"Ask your daddy for help," Caroline insisted.

Travis continued, "Daddy helped Buchanan's campaign. He worked on it as sheriff! He's not going to help you prove the man cheated his way into office. I don't think my daddy would be involved in a conspiracy this big, quite frankly."

"Well, I know that there has been wrongdoing and I'm going to prove it no matter what it takes."

"Ever heard of the phrase you catch more flies with honey than with vinegar?"

"I'm not trying to catch any flies. I'm trying to get rid of them," Caroline replied stiffly.

"You know what I mean Caroline. This town is old-fashioned. Traditional."

"You mean it's segregated and racist?"

"There you go again with that race stuff."

"It's not a race stuff, Travis. It's my life. And Buchanan is going to make that life and the lives of other people like me way worse when he assumes power."

"How can you know that for sure? All that stuff on the campaign was just him mouthing off. He's a proud, old

Southern family. You are judging him before getting to know him," Travis replied.

Caroline's cheeks changed color to a deep mulberry, something Travis only recently started to notice. Caroline's cheeks only changed color when she was upset. She had been struggling with this new job at the mayor's office and Travis knew that. The past few weeks had only gotten worse as the inauguration date approached.

From the moment Buchanan won the election, Caroline had it out for him. She believed that he cheated his way into office, but Travis couldn't tell if this were one of her liberal notions gone rogue or if there was actually something to it. She had proof, she said — skewed polling data and mysterious envelopes disappearing as the unbiased reviewers counted votes.

Travis tried to reason with her at least, "If you want to make a real change in politics, you have to work from the inside, Caroline."

Caroline didn't answer him and scowled. Travis offered her an apologetic smile which did nothing to wipe the frown off Caroline's face.

Travis put on his hat and sunglasses before continuing, "Don't be angry with me. You know I'm trying to help you."

"If you were trying to help me, you would prove that Mayor Buchanan cheated his way into office."

"Come on, Caroline. You can't ask me to do that. I took an oath. I'm a police officer."

"I used to think that not all cops were gun toting idiots, but I'm starting to see that I was completely wrong," she snapped, knowing it would hurt him.

Caroline got out of the cop car outside the mayors office and Travis knew that it would be foolish to follow her when she was that angry. She would have no problem making a scene and then of course he'd be standing there screaming at her in the middle of the street and people would see and then tongues would wag.

As Travis said, the town was traditional and there was nothing traditional about the sheriff's son getting involved with a brown-skinned girl from the wrong side of the tracks.

"Have a good day at work!" Travis called to her.

Caroline flipped him off and went inside, her perfect shape hugged in by her pencil skirt and her bun piled high on her head without a strand of hair out of place. Travis couldn't stop staring at her slim waist, and her nice big butt. That woman really was something.

2

CAROLINE'S HUGE MISTAKE

CAROLINE'S FACE twisted into a perfect scowl as she stomped up the stairs to her office. The morning light on Travis' tanned shoulder and the mischievous look in his eye as she kissed him and touched him in the back of his car could almost cause her to forget that he was a cop. Travis! A cop! The entire idea was unfathomable.

As the star quarterback and valedictorian for his year — he was two years older than Caroline — he'd had so much potential. Caroline always thought he should have gone to college. His daddy gambled away his college fund and Travis kissed dreams of Ole Miss behind in favor of the police academy.

Travis had no idea what he had done to upset Caroline as she walked away from him. If she had his help, that would at least have made things easier on her. Today would not be an easy day. Before Mayor Buchanan, Caroline had the notion that working at the mayors office would allow her this great grand opportunity to change politics in her town.

She believed what Travis did at first. Caroline, through her work in the mayor's office, got the well on the other side of the tracks cleaned up so the water that she and her family members drank was no longer toxic. Still, there were plenty of problems within her community and one of the biggest ones was that the factory in town refused to pay black workers the same amount as the white workers.

Just when her department had been well on its way to some semblance of equality, an election year sidled over the hill. Caroline was so certain that Mayor Alexander would win another term that she'd never considered the impossible. Along came Mr. Buchanan with his landslide victory unheard of in Old Town's entire history. Caroline was shocked and shaken. She suspected foul play but of course, she was the only one. Most people in the office were only mildly disappointed, if not outright gleeful.

Caroline suspected that they didn't even mind Mayor Buchanan despite all the liberal notions many of them professed. *Of course* they didn't want off the books segregation, but no one in her office lived on the "wrong side" of the tracks and none of them would let their kids date a black person. They just *believed* in equality, they didn't do anything about it.

None of the changes Mayor Buchanan made would affect them directly. It was her people she had to worry about, the people on the wrong side of the tracks who drank dirty water from a contaminated well for decades before Caroline stepped up and made it a priority.

All the work Caroline had done would be completely unraveled by Mayor Buchanan. And Caroline couldn't have that. She took action that any normal principled person would take. There was no telling how her boss would react to what she had done. It was only a matter of time before everyone found out. Only a matter of time...

Caroline organized her desk during her first hour at work.

Then she replied to text messages from Chase Owens and Bud Landry, two more high school friends. Most of Caroline's old girl friends had kids now and they cared about three things: Bibles, guns, and babies — none of these issues concerned Caroline as much as clean water for her people, fair pay for the factory workers and the future of all the people in Old Town, especially the black people.

As the blondes and brunettes piled into the office, no one bothered to stop into Caroline's office to see how she was doing. She emptied her cup of decaf in the bin and walked over to the coffee machine to strike up some casual conversation with Shiloh Reid and Loretta Calloway.

As soon as Caroline entered the room, they stopped their conversation and plastered uncomfortable smiles across their faces. Loretta squeaked in a suspiciously high voice, "Hey Caroline."

"Hey, how was your weekend."

"Oh, it was okay."

"How's Anna-Mae doing?"

"Same old, same old."

"Great."

"Uh huh!"

Shiloh finally chimed in, "Caroline, can I ask you a question?"

"Yeah. Sure."

Caroline filled her "Girl Boss" mug with some coffee as she waited for Shiloh's question.

"Do you wash your hair?"

"Huh?"

"I heard a rumor that black people don't wash their hair. Is that true?"

"Shiloh!" Loretta hissed.

"What? I want to know if it's true or not. My daddy says that ni— black people don't wash their hair."

"I do wash my hair. Thanks for asking."

Caroline's jaw clenched. She hastened out of the room, a flush of anger rushing to her cheeks. She had to deal with "innocent" little inquiries like that at work all the time. First, it was folks saying she was so articulate, meanwhile she was one of three people in the office to have a degree! Then, there were comments on her hair, her body, her ass, and her skin tone. She had to field questions about whether she tanned, why her butt was so big and whether or not her hair was clean. The nerve!

Caroline was sick of having to educate people. Most of them lived in the same town as black folks all their lives but they'd gone out of their way to be separate. Now, they acted as if Caroline owed them an explanation, as if she was the one who had chosen to be an outsider. Caroline hated that urge to feel as if she had to prove them wrong about her.

Why did she have to be the representative for all black folks everywhere? Why couldn't she just be *Caroline Coulson?*

After her failed attempt at reaching out to her coworkers, Caroline braced herself for Mayor Buchanan's arrival and the arrival of her department head, Augusta Abernathy. Caroline sighed and sipped her fresh cup of coffee. So much for quitting. A message from Chase popped up on her phone.

Chase* 🔨*: Hey, how's work?
Caroline: Shitty. Ready to start the revolution.
Chase* 🔨*: Haha. Hope I can see you later.
Caroline: After work drinks?

Before Caroline could wait for Chase's reply, the familiar sound of Augusta's heels clicking across the linoleum sounded throughout the office. Caroline gulped another swig of coffee and smoothed her shirt, subconsciously checking her bun in anticipation of her boss's arrival.

Caroline could hear her boss getting closer. Augusta stopped Loretta and asked her to bring a copy of the building lease downstairs to accounting, then she asked if we were out of coffee. There was still plenty, Loretta said, and that bought Caroline some time as she waited patiently for her day to get a whole lot worse. Augusta stuck her head into Caroline's office after filling up on coffee. Her Southern drawl filled the room with its sonorous depth.

"Why hello sweet heart, how are you?"

"Doing well, Mrs. Abernathy."

"That's good to hear. Don't forget to drop by my office this afternoon for that sweet tea recipe I promised."

"Yes, Mrs. Abernathy."

She winked and Caroline let out a sigh of relief. She hadn't seen it yet then. Either she hadn't seen the paper yet or somehow she was okay with what Caroline had done. Wishful thinking, Caroline.

She tapped her worn heel anxiously against the ground and clicked open the *New York Times* to try to distract herself with an article about immigration in America. Caroline heard Augusta asking Shiloh to get the newspaper downstairs. Her minutes were numbered now. Caroline sighed, staring at the mustard yellow walls that had surrounded her since she started working in politics.

The wall color hadn't been changed in over forty years, much like everything else in the office. This isn't where Caroline thought her career in politics would end up, and now she might have put an end to it before she even started. Maybe Travis was right and work was better done from the inside. But inside, the wallpaper was peeling, and standing up for the truth could put you at risk of getting fired.

Caroline watched Shiloh walk past her office and called her name.

"Shiloh, wait!"

"Yes?"

She raised an eyebrow as if to say 'how dare you' and tapped her heels in frustration in my doorway.

"Are you going downstairs to get the paper?"

"Yes."

"Before you do that… could you…um… could you help me fax this."

Caroline picked up a random piece of paper off her desk.

"You want me to fax a letter from Crazy Eye Jim?"

"Uhhh yes. I need to fax it to… The Standard."

Shiloh picked up the paper as if Jim's conspiracy theories were contagious.

"Sure. I'll fax it over. But there's a reason we call him Crazy Eye Jim. What could the paper want with this letter?"

Caroline shrugged, desperate to look aloof, "No idea."

Shiloh took the letter to the fax machine and Caroline peered out of her office and snuck to the stairs so she could run down and get the paper first. She couldn't keep Mrs. Abernathy's eyes off of it forever, but Caroline figured she could at least stall. Before she made it down the steps, the office building cleaner Josefina stopped her. Caroline always made time to talk to her.

"Why good morning Meez Coulson," she said with her heavy, Puerto Rican accent.

Caroline sighed and leaned against the railing. She couldn't be rude to Josefina. Josefina made her this spicy soup when she was sick last winter that cleared her flu right up. Caroline grabbed her shoulders and hugged the portly Puerto Rican cleaner.

"Good morning, Josefina, how are you?"

"My back is hurting but you know, I thank God everyday for my life."

"How are the kids?"

Caroline's heart sank as Shiloh passed them on the stairs, on her way to grab the morning paper with her ponytail bouncing merrily behind her. Caroline missed her chance to get ahead of Mrs. Abernathy. Josefina noticed Caroline's distracted gazing and she asked, "Are you okay?"

"Yeah. Yeah, I'm okay."

"Miss Coulson, I know you have difficulties in this office but you are the only girl here who bothers to say hi to me. You may be the only one to know my name. Don't worry if you don't get along with these people. They are not good people."

How did Josefina always know what to say to cheer her up? Caroline thanked her, spoke about her kids for a second and snuck back upstairs to her office. She just reached the door when Mrs. Abernathy called, "CAROLINE!"

Her shrill voice rung out throughout the office. Caroline held her breath hoping that she had misheard her. Then, Mrs. Abernathy called her name again and there was no mistaking the sound.

Sheepishly, Caroline walked through the door of her office and Mrs. Abernathy slammed the newspaper on the table, removing her reading glasses and scowling before she spoke.

"Do you have an explanation for me?"

Caroline couldn't bear to look directly at the headline. She knew what they wrote about the mayor, and knew that the so-called anonymous source would be easily traced back to her.

"Mrs. Abernathy, you have to believe that I didn't do this on purpose."

"Caroline, I've known you long enough to know that you aren't thrilled about Mayor Buchanan. But to do this... You leave me no choice."

"Are you sure? I'm sorry. I'm really sorry this time. I took it too far and I realize that now."

"You should have never leave this information first place. What were you thinking?"

"I was thinking that nobody was going to do anything."

"Nobody was going to do anything because you have no evidence of these claims."

"It's obvious isn't it? The polls were never in his favor. All of a sudden he wins by a landslide."

"What you're suggesting is some kind of conspiracy theory and it's unfounded. Caroline, you've done a lot of great work around here but I have to wonder... Do you still want to work at the mayor's office or are your politics going to keep getting in the way?"

That was how it always was in the office. Either Caroline's politics were getting in the way, or she was doing the bidding of everyone around her. Mayor Buchanan's victory had turned everyone.

Before, they were liberal and ready to be activists for the community. Now, they were content for Old Town to return to tradition — a tradition they'd claimed to want to change. Caroline balled her hands into fists and responded to her suggestion sternly.

"Mrs. Abernathy, I don't want to stop working here. I've made a real difference around here. I'm valuable to this office."

"Miss Coulson, my dear sweet doll, you and I both know this shift in power will be a big change for you. This newspaper article doesn't inspire a lot of confidence that you can keep your head on your shoulders while working here."

"With all due respect Miss Abernathy, I believe I can keep my head on my shoulders. If I leave, there's not another qualified person in Old Town who can do my job."

Her green eyes widened as she pursed her lips and sighed.

"Well sweetheart, what do you think I ought to do? Word will get out that someone in the office leaked this story, and Mayor Buchanan will want to know who."

"You don't have to tell him it's me."

"I can't lie to my boss, Caroline," Mrs. Abernathy gasped, her hand rushing to the silver locket around her neck.

"Can't you edit the truth?"

"It's too late. You've already showed that you won't be loyal to the office. How can I ask the other employees to trust you with classified information after this?"

"Are you firing me, Augusta?"

"Bless your heart, dear. I'm not *firing* you. We're discussing the status of your employment. Like I said, the mayor will be expecting me to do *something.*"

"By something, you mean firing me."

"Sweet heart..."

"Fine, Mrs. Abernathy, I'll go."

"Bless your heart dear, I'm sorry to hear that you're quitting," she said, much too quickly before standing up and wrapping Caroline in a hug that smelled like moth balls and Werther's Original candy.

Caroline's arms hung limp. She pulled away from Augusta Abernathy and with head held high, walked out of her office. Loretta and Shiloh were waiting on the other side of the door and they pretended like they weren't listening in.

"Hi Caroline, is everything alright sweet heart?" Shiloh asked.

Loretta kicked Shiloh and she squeaked, but didn't pursue her line of questioning. Caroline walked past them with her head held high, fighting back tears. They'd heard all of it. They knew she was getting fired for what she'd done and despite Shiloh's fake concern, Caroline could sense they were overjoyed.

Travis warned her that all my attempts to make this town better would only stir resentment. Caroline didn't want to believe him. She looked around at the mustard walls and an odd pang of sadness coursed through her. She'd always known getting fired was a possibility, but not so unceremoniously.

Caroline thought we were all better than that. Loretta brought her an old box with a missing panel on the bottom, taped together by duct tape, grinning from ear to ear as she asked, "Do you want me to help you pack, darling?"

"No. I've got this."

"Suit yourself."

Shiloh chimed in, "Caroline, I know the *black* church might be hiring an accountant. Maybe you'd like a job better on your people's side of town."

Loretta nodded, her smile still plastered on her face.

"Shiloh's right, sweet heart. I mean, this job is kind of complicated."

Caroline slammed her box on the desk.

"What's wrong sweetheart?"

"Stop. Calling. Me. Sweetheart."

"Bless her heart, I think you've offended her, Shiloh," Loretta said, although it sounded more like a sneer to me.

"I'm not offended," Caroline grumbled, fitting a photo of

her and Caleb into the box and stacking her Howard University paperweight on top of it.

Shiloh reached into the box and grabbed the paperweight.

"Howard University," she said snickering as she placed it back in the box, "Where the hell is that?"

"It's a school for colored people," Loretta said, "It ain't very good, ain't it?"

"Please, keep my university's name out of your mouth," Caroline breathed.

She'd be out of here soon and there was no need to take Loretta or Shiloh's cruelty to heart anymore.

"I'm sorry, what did you say Caroline?"

"I said, don't you talk bad about Howard University, thank you."

Shiloh shrugged, "I was just being accurate. I mean, it's not a good school."

Caroline the handles of her box and tried to leave the office.

"Uh uh, not so fast," Loretta said, a smile on her face.

"I'd like to leave, Loretta."

"You can't leave," Shiloh chimed in, "'Cause we've heard a rumor and we don't know if it's true."

"Please, just move out of the way."

Loretta leaned in, her eyes glimmering with twisted delight as she asked, "Is it true you've slept with Travis and his friends — all of them at the same time?"

"I asked if I could leave," Caroline replied, raising her voice.

Unfortunately, her attempts to be assertive only attracted the attention of other folks in the office, which hadn't been her intention exactly. Two other girls gathered around, pretending not be listening and then Corbin peeked out of his office, peering behind his coke bottle glasses and watching the scene unfold.

Shiloh and Caroline moved to block the door. Caroline dropped her box, her cheeks flushed a deep mulberry color.

"We aren't going to let you leave until you tell us the truth. Did you *fornicate* with them?"

"I don't believe it," Loretta sneered, "Travis is much too smart to shack up with a girl from that side of the tracks."

"Loretta? Can I ask you something?" Caroline asked in a saccharine voice.

"Sure thing, sweetheart."

"Why are you such a raging bitch?"

Loretta gasped and Shiloh stepped in front of her, fists balled up.

"What the hell did you just say to her?"

"I asked why she was such a raging bitch. Do you have an answer?"

"You watch your mouth you dirty little charity case!"

Caroline heard Shiloh gathering the wad of spit in her mouth but by the time she opened her mouth to respond it was too late.

Pthewww!

The ball of spit flew out of Shiloh's mouth and directly into Caroline's as she opened her mouth to protest. Caroline spat the nasty wad of spit on the ground and screamed.

"You bitch!"

A rage unlike any other came over Caroline. She screamed and reached for the Howard paperweight. Caroline lobbed the heavy object at Loretta's head. Loretta ducked. Caroline swung hard at Shiloh next.

"You spat in my mouth you dirty little hoe!"

Caroline grabbed her hair, yanked it out of Shiloh's perfect, tight bun, crunching the hairspray as it unraveled and pushed her up against the wall, slapping her hard. Shiloh had brothers and she knew how to brawl better than any of them.

She pushed Caroline off and kicked her in the shin, her heel causing a run in Caroline's stockings that ripped them off her legs. Caroline screamed and Loretta grabbed her hair, pulling her down to the ground. It was two against one now.

"Get off of me!"

Shiloh dug her knees into Caroline's chest and balled up her fists ready to punch Caroline in the mouth. Loretta pinned her arms down and Corbin finally yelled, "Someone call security!"

Augusta Abernathy heard the commotion and came out of her office.

"Mighty Jesus, what in heavens name is going on here!"

She fanned herself but never told Loretta or Shiloh to stop. Shiloh punched Caroline in the face. Her jaw throbbed and she wrestled her way out of her ex-coworker's grasp. As Caroline fought Loretta off, Shiloh grabbed her hair, ripping it out of its bun. Then she grabbed onto Caroline's blazer and ripped the seams down her spine. Surrounded at all sides, Caroline's attempts to stand up for herself quickly proved futile.

Her heart fluttered with relief when building security approached.

"Help! Help me!"

The security guards walked straight up to her and linked arms beneath Caroline's as her legs thrashed out in front of her.

"Hey! Why are you holding me down! They attacked me."

"Be quiet, ma'am," one guard said in a heavy, Southern drawl.

Caroline thrashed again and the guards lifted her off the ground, dragging her out of the office without her box of things.

Caroline could already hear the gossip before the security guards even set her on the ground outside. Tongues would wag about everything under the sun. The guards set her down outside and Caroline screamed at them, "What about my stuff upstairs?"

Loretta and Shiloh emerged outside the mayor's office holding Caroline's box. They tipped it upside down onto the sidewalk and dropped it outside.

"Oops," Shiloh taunted with a smirk on her face.

"Good luck finding a job, sweetheart," Loretta called.

They laughed and turned around, entering the Mayor's office. Humiliated, Caroline got on all fours and picked up her pictures, documents and paperweight, stuffing whatever she could in a haphazard pile in her box. The new mayor's car pulled into the lot as she finished packing her box. Buchanan exited his car, dressed in a white suit with his silvery blond hair slicked back with gel. He puffed his chest and stepped over her possessions, entering the office without acknowledging the fact that she was on the ground.

Caroline picked everything up and stared up at the large columns and giant oak double doors. Fired. She'd been fired and Travis would probably only say "I told you so".

3

BIG BEEFY FACTORY BOYS

THE OLD TOWN Whiskey Plant was on the white side of town, two miles away from the mayor's office. From the mayor's office, you could see the pillars of steam and smoke rising from the stacks. Bud and Chase both worked at the factory and since they'd moved to the day shift for the week, Caroline could go see them during lunch.

Now that I have no job, she thought morosely, I have plenty of time to see Bud and Chase in the middle of the day for lunch. It was a mediocre consolation prize.

Caroline hated being on this side of town when she didn't have to work. She'd lived here for most of her life, except the years she'd gone to college, and she still didn't feel at home on Bud, Chase and Travis' side of the tracks.

Caroline walked down the street from the mayor's office into the residential area. The Buchanan's lived in an old white plantation house and hanging from the flagpole was a large confederate flag flapping ostentatiously in the breeze, a proud declaration of Buchanan's slave-owning heritage. Caroline shuddered as she walked past the new mayor's house.

Rich and poor white folks alike lived on this side of town. That's how Bud and Chase came to live so close to the mayor. Their parents had as much money as Caroline's — maybe less. But they were allowed to buy on this side of town. Caroline's parents would have never been permitted the same privileges.

Caroline remembered admiring their homes when she was a little girl and didn't know any better. Back then, she was *so* easily impressed by their towering houses. She always used to wonder why nobody on their side of town could have a big house like Sheriff Montgomery or Mr. Buchanan, who at the time had only been a small business owner, and not the mayor.

Now that Caroline was older, she no longer admired towering antebellum houses. She wasn't envious of these people, she was angry.

As Caroline stared at the Buchanan house, paying not one lick of attention to where she was resting her feet, she tripped on the raised part of the sidewalk and her box flew through the air as she screamed and landed knees first on the pavement. Her Howard paperweight rolled into the street, underneath one of the cars parked street side. Caroline got up, dusted off her pants and winced. Her knee hurt *badly*. She leaned against the giant magnolia tree whose roots had pushed up the sidewalk and caused her to trip. Caroline exhaled sharply, catching her breath as pain surged through her knee. Then a loud screeching sounded near her ear.

Caroline screamed and pulled away from the tree as she noticed the giant cicada sitting on the trunk, buzzing merrily in her ear. Her surprise knocked her over again and this time, Caroline landed on her butt. A gust of wind blew most of her papers out of the box and she scrambled to her feet, racing after what she could. It was too late for most of the papers and Caroline couldn't even get her hands on the paperweight that rolled beneath the car. She raced for the box. There was still about a mile and a half to go until she got to the factory and without a car, Caroline would have to trek down there carrying her stupid half-broken box.

As she passed the library, the houses started getting smaller, and smaller. Caroline passed the Owens house, where Chase, his brother Zachariah and their family lived for three decades. Mrs. Owens was home, working in the kitchen with her auburn hair in a right mess around her head. Caroline's box gave way about 3/4 of a mile away from the factory. The bottom split and everything from her desk fell into the street.

"Damn!" She hissed.

There was nothing she could do about the box or her possessions. Caroline let out a defeated shriek. Her possessions were strewn everywhere and there was nothing she could do about it. Racing after the remaining papers and letters from constituents wouldn't help. Pleading with God for mercy wouldn't help either.

Caroline slumped her shoulders and continued her walk towards the factory. As she got closer, the smell of toxic waste filled Caroline's nostrils. Old liquor, worn leather, and chemical exhaust filled the air. The boss met Caroline at the entrance and hollered over the sound of machinery in the back.

"CAN I GET YOUR NAME AND ID MISS?"

"Miss Coulson."

"AH! ARE YOU HERE TO SEE CALEB COULSON?"

"Not today, I'm here to see Bud Landry."

"Bud Landry? I'll go look for him."

When the boss heard Caroline's name, his attitude changed. His face turned into a downright scowl when she said that she was looking for Bud. He wasn't as friendly and helpful anymore. He wandered off to the back of the factory and Caroline could hear him yelling nondescript words followed by Bud Landry's name.

The boss returned to the front desk and informed Caroline that Bud was out back having a cigarette. Caroline thanked him and wandered around the back of the factory. She heard Chase's distinct laugh first, and as she rounded the corner, both boys were leaning up against the corrugated metal walls of the plant. Caroline hadn't expected to see both of them together, but it was just as well that she did.

"How you doing sweet cheeks?" Bud called, with his low, Southern drawl.

Bud was the biggest of the boys. He was 6'3" tall with thick brown hair that he always wore down to his shoulders because he was too lazy to get it cut. Bud had a big linebacker's body that was surprisingly toned. In high school, they'd called him "Beefy Bud".

Buds's work boots were covered in mud and he wore camel colored Carhartt pants, a stained white t-shirt and a Carhartt jacket. He flicked his cigarette butt into the mud and stomped it out. Chase still had half of his cigarette to go. Caroline coughed and gave him a stern look as she approached.

"What are you doing here?" Chase followed. His hair was a light mousy brown color, and it was cropped short. Chase's eyes were cornflower blue. Chase had a big beard for a country boy that was a copper color on account of his Irish grandma.

"I got fired today. Travis was right. I shouldn't have stuck my nose where it didn't belong."

"Whaddyou mean they fired you?" Bud said, slow and lumbering as he scratched his head, "You done went to college and everything."

Chase widened his stance, adjusting his cowboy hat and flicking his cigarette out.

"C'mon over here and give Chase some sugar," he said, widening his arms for Caroline to give him a hug.

She was reluctant at first, but resisting Chase was pointless. He'd only tease her and tickle her and get her in a hug anyway. He'd wipe the frown off her face like he always did. Caroline nuzzled into Chase's embrace and buried her head in his chest so his beard prickled against her forehead.

"Why I oughta punch the bastard who fired you," Bud threatened, "Now tell me who it is."

"It's Mrs. Abernathy!" Caroline said, "You can't punch her."

Chase glared at Bud and shook his head. Bud loosened his fists and sighed.

"Fine. If I can't punch Abernathy, then I oughta get somebody."

Caroline pulled away from Chase and before she could move and inch, Bud yanked her over, lifting her as if she were weightless and setting her on the ground after giving her a big old Bud Landry squeeze. When he set her down, Caroline pressed her fingers against Bud's chest.

"No, no, no. Don't punch anybody. It's my fault. I spoke to the paper and Mrs. Abernathy saw today's headline."

Chase's eyes widened, matching the sky so perfectly, as his cheeks turned scarlet.

"Does Travis know what happened?"

"I tried to warn him this morning but he didn't listen."

"Jesus Christ, Caroline. He's going to be madder than a wet hen when he hears it."

"I know. I know. I'm an idiot."

"Wait what does the paper say?" Bud asked, scratching his head again, his cheeks turning as red as his neck.

Chase and Caroline exchanged awkward glances. Bud couldn't read. He'd left high school after freshman year to work at the factory and help his daddy on the farm and if he'd ever known how to read before, he'd forgotten.

"I told The Old Town Standard that there was reason to believe Buchanan bought his vote and I shared poll statistics that our office was never supposed to release."

"You really think that bastard won from cheating?" Bud asked, leaning in curiously.

"Yes, I do. I know it in my heart, Bud."

"Well you was doing the right thing."

He yanked Caroline in for another one armed hug that nearly squeezed the life out of her.

"Thanks, Bud."

"I don't want to talk about getting fired anymore. When Travis finds out, it's going to be a shit show."

Chase pressed his hand to Caroline's shoulder and a shiver traveled down her spine.

"That's fine."

"Oh... There's one last thing I guess," Caroline said reluctantly.

"What is it?"

"Something Loretta and Shiloh said."

"Did those uppity princesses say anything to you?" Bud asked, his hands balling into fists again.

"No... I mean... Yes. But don't you get me in any more trouble than I'm already in," Caroline replied.

"Oh, I'm going to lose my temper," Bud growled through gritted teeth.

"Calm down, Bud," Chase replied, calming down his oldest friend, "What exactly did they say to rile you up?"

"They asked if all four of us had done it — you, me, Bud and Travis."

Chase and Bud exchanged worried glances.

"What did you say to 'em?" Bud asked, turning brighter red than before.

"I didn't say anything, I'm not stupid!"

"We shouldn't listen to rumors around town," Chase mumbled.

"I agree, we shouldn't," Caroline whispered, "But... did either of you tell her."

"No!" Bud and Chase answered together.

"Cross your heart?"

"Cross my heart," they replied in unison.

Caroline released a sigh of relief and relaxed the tension in her shoulders.

"Nobody knows."

"Unless Travis talked," Bud suggested.

"Travis is more likely than any of us to keep it quiet," Chase defended his absent friend.

"We have to be careful from now on," Caroline insisted, "I took a risk and now I'm pretty sure I'm on the mayor's black list."

"We wouldn't want anyone using this against you, or Travis. Got it," Chase replied.

"If they don't keep quiet, I'll deal with them."

"Right. Well, what's new? I don't want to keep talking about this," Caroline sighed, exasperated from her awful day at work.

"Can't talk for much longer, sweet cheeks. We gotta get back to work."

"How's the union coming along?"

"We're making progress," Chase said.

"I wish you boys luck. I'd better go back home and tell my family we'll be eating grits and sugar every night for the rest of the year."

"Caleb's still got this gig, don't worry, Caroline. Everything will be okay."

Caroline wished she could believe Chase. She said goodbye to the boys and agreed to meet them after the factory shift and after Travis got off work — around 8 p.m. Caroline walked home, remembering what happened the last time the four of them got together.

The experience had been wonderful, terrifying, shocking... and had changed the way she thought about the three men entirely. They'd become her boys then... her redneck alphas...

4

GUESS HOW MANY INCHES?

CHASE AND BUD watched Caroline as she disappeared out of sight, her hair falling out of its bun and draping down her back in a mess of thick black curls.

"That girl's got gumption," Bud declared.

"Does your dumb ass even know what that means?" Chase teased.

Bud punched him in the shoulder and Chase pretended it didn't hurt. Bud's hands were the size of a trashcan lid, thick and callused from chopping wood since he was big enough to hold an axe up.

"I know what it means," Bud insisted, "She's also the prettiest girl I've ever seen."

"I reckon you're right about that. C'mon let's get on the floor before the Boss pitches a fit."

Bud and Chase walked back onto the factory floor. Earplugs. Safety glasses. Gloves. Then they got to work lifting, sanding, pushing buttons, moving bottles, hammering open old oak casks of whiskey and doing whatever it was the boss needed from them until their shifts were over.

It was always dark by the time the day shift ended. The night shift came through, skinnier and more doped up than the day shift. These days, around half the workers had track marks on their arms and more than half of those didn't bother cleaning up the blood that spilled out when they missed a vein. Old Town hadn't always been that way and Chase wasn't happy with the way it was now.

He wasn't the type of guy to like stuffy office politics though. Chase organized from the ground up and in the factory, he was fixing to organize a union of workers — the first union that allowed both black and white folks to join.

Bud was the union's first member and even if he couldn't read and his understanding of politics wasn't too good, Chase thought Bud was a great member to have since everybody liked Bud Landry, and the guy had a heart of gold anyway. He'd defend those he loved with his life — including Caroline, who all of them loved, especially Chase.

She was the one who'd given him the courage to learn about organizing the community, activism and working class power. Chase didn't realize that he wasn't doomed to repeat the life his daddy had until Caroline. Part of why he was doing all of this organizing and union making was for her.

After work, Bud went home to help his daddy on the farm for a couple of hours and Chase drove from the factory to the station where Travis sat down doing paperwork at his desk.

"Officer Montgomery!" Chase boomed, "May I talk to you for a second."

Travis rose, a smile plastered on his face, his blond hair still neat and slicked back from the morning. The old friends hugged each other and Travis ushered Chase into the back room. The sheriff was out on duty and Travis used his father's office when there were conversations he wished to keep private. Considering what happened the last time he saw Chase, Travis sensed privacy would be important, and he was right.

"What brings you over here so late? I thought we weren't meeting 'til 8."

"It's about Caroline."

"What's she gone and done."

"Nothing... nothing... Only, she got fired today."

Chase hoped to mitigate Travis' reaction. If he got too upset, he'd tell Travis to cool it and spare Caroline his reaction. Travis didn't understand their need to always be stirring up trouble in Old Town.

"Fired?! Did she go ahead and do what I specifically asked her not to do?"

"I know you're mad at her, but it ain't her fault completely."

"It's Caroline. Of course it was her fault. She can't just leave well enough alone," Travis uttered in frustration.

Heat rose to Chase's cheeks.

"Hey, watch the way you talk about her."

"Sorry. Sorry, I'm just frustrated. I know how much that job meant to her."

"She asked for our help," Chase pointed out, "and we didn't give it to her."

Chase was surprised he was the even-keeled one in this conversation. Usually, he left that up to Travis. Chase was the firecracker; Travis was a soothing campfire. Travis sat on his father's desk and tapped his fingers against a stack of papers.

"She's going to get us into trouble, isn't she?"

"Ain't she worth it though?" Chase replied with a grin.

Both men thought of the last time all four of them had been together. They thought of Caroline, naked, shared amongst the four of them, heaving and moaning in the throes of pleasure as they caressed her skin, touched her cheek and kissed her as they made love in a filthy, twisted pretzel of passion.

"Damn right, she's worth it," Chase replied, a grin spreading across his face.

"We've got to think of a way to help her out, okay? Whatever she asks," Chase insisted, noticing that Travis had gone off into his own world again.

"What if we can't give her what she wants? You ever consider that?"

"Nonsense."

"I'm serious Chase. Caroline likes to stir the pot. She could piss off someone dangerous in this town and then what? Do you really think the three of us can protect her if she gets on the wrong side of Tommy Lee Buchanan?"

"We have to protect her," Chase insisted, getting closer to Travis and staring his friend right in the eyes.

Chase could get frustrated with Travis' obsession with playing by the rules. He could look injustice square in the face and he'd still have that reasonable, calm look on his face. Chase thought Travis might be suited to be president one day — if he could ever get to college.

Travis would always rub his chin and run his hands through that golden blond hair of his and he'd say something infuriatingly rational and pragmatic. Chase was a firestorm compared to Travis, who was an immovable wall of both strong morals and aggravating conformity.

"I'm not saying I won't protect her," Travis answered, stewing in frustration of his own with Chase's insinuation that he cared about Caroline any less than he did, "I'm simply saying that not everything that happens is in our control."

"You know Caroline, she won't let this go. So what do you say?"

"Fine. I'll do what I can to help. Whatever she wants."

"Good. Thank you."

"Why didn't Bud come with you?"

"He's getting drinks and smokes for tonight."

"8 p.m. right?"

"Yes," Chase replied with a nod, "8 p.m."

If there was one time Travis could break out of that rigid cop brain of his and actually unwind for a second, it was when it came to Caroline and the dangerous game the four of them had just started playing. At least Chase could be reasonably certain that Travis wouldn't mess things up for them tonight. Caroline could just as easily close herself off to the whole arrangement if she thought they weren't on her side.

Sweet Caroline...

Chase tipped his had to Travis and left him at the station. He drove over to Mr. Landry's plot of land, two miles past the factory. Bud Landry's father owned a lot of land which he would have farmed better if he hadn't fallen prey to the pills like half the fathers in town. He could still work at least, but he was behind in maintaining some of his land, including the place where the four of them met.

Chase pulled out his flashlight and trekked across the field to the large barn which all the farmers would be repairing later in the summer. Chase pulled the barn door open and the scent of hay, dust and mulch filled his nostrils.

"Hello? Bud?"

"I'm up here!"

Bud raised the lights in the barn even higher. He sat up on the barn loft, a lit cigarette between his lips as his feet dangled off the ledge.

"You talked to Travis?"

"Yes, I did."

"Is he gonna help?"

"He says we'll do whatever Caroline wants."

"You reckon she'll ask for much?" Bud asked.

"Naw, knowing Caroline, it won't be much."

"I brought beer and blankets," Bud chimed excitedly.

"Get down here you big bastard and we'll sort it all out. I want it to look nice for when Caroline gets here."

"This barn ain't exactly the Motel 6," Bud commented.

He jumped down from the loft, landing on both his feet with a loud thud that shook the floorboards.

"It ain't the Motel 6 but we can do our best to make it pretty."

Bud directed Chase toward the blankets and he pulled out the old Apache blankets, rolling them out so they covered the floor. Bud lit two kerosene lamps since the generator could only sustain an hour or so of light before everything would go dark again.

"Hand me one of those beers."

Bud handed Chase a beer and cracked one open for himself.

"Goddamn, it'll be good to unwind tonight."

"Caroline might not be up for it," Bud pointed out, "You know women. If she ain't happy, we ain't getting laid."

Chase chuckled, "You really think Caroline is like other women after last week? Shit. She's special."

"Yeah. She's special. You think one day she's gonna choose one of us?" Bud asked.

"Not unless we make her."

"You don't think any of us would do that, right?"

"I think we've made it perfectly clear we're okay with sharing," Chase replied, patting Bud on the back.

"Now don't you worry," Chase added.

Travis showed up at the barn next. He hadn't changed out of

his uniform and he was overdressed compared to Bud and Chase who wore their clothes from the factory — muddied boots, Carhartt pants and plain white t-shirts. Bud's neck was scarlet from his evening work in the sun with his daddy.

"You boys getting started drinking without me? I ought to put you under arrest."

"Heyyy! Travis! Come over here and join us," Bud slurred.

He could handle his liquor better than most but it hit him quicker than most too. With flushed cheeks, he handed Travis a beer and they toasted to their second meetup as they waited for the guest of honor to walk through the door.

Caroline was never late to meet up with Travis and the boys, but after dinner she had to explain what happened to everyone in her family which meant everyone had a million and one questions for her about the job, why she'd been fired and what she'd done to provoke it. They didn't know Caroline had leaked the information to the press.

Caroline skirted around their answers as best she could. She felt too guilty to sit around talking about this stuff all night so she made an excuse to leave as soon as she could.

Trudging across the Landry fields to the abandoned barn alone, Caroline used her cellphone for lighting and tried to avoid stepping on a field mouse or a grass snake or some other horrifying nighttime critter that might be lying in her way.

Caroline smelled beer before she could see anything. Thrusting the barn door open, she found all three men drinking beer, sitting on barrels or on Apache blankets spread on the ground. Kerosene lamps illuminated the barn with a soft glow and the smell of hay and old wood warmed Caroline from the chilly night.

"Hey boys, hope you didn't have too much fun without me."

The intense energy of having three men lusting after her

and loving her in equal amounts affected Caroline in the most peculiar way. Where she lacked confidence, she found it. Where she was a nervous, anxious and overworked mess, the men transformed her into this beautiful goddess. At least they treated her like a goddess.

"We saved you a beer," Bud Landry replied, handing Caroline a chilled and open can.

She didn't much feel in the mood for beer, but she accepted the can anyway.

"Thank you, Bud."

Emboldened from his drinking before his arrival, Bud leaned in and kissed Caroline on the cheeks. His kiss was friendly, and Caroline mightn't have read anything into it until Bud's hand slid all the way down to the small of her back where he pulled her in for a hug.

Travis sat on a barrel, five crushed beer cans at his feet, his cop uniform unbuttoned exposing the white undershirt beneath, crisp and clean in stark contrast to Bud and Chase who wore their factory work on their clothes and on their skin.

"Why don't you come over and have a seat," Chase suggested, patting the seat next to him with a mischievous glint in his eye.

Already? Caroline wanted to stop herself from succumbing to them so soon, but then again, why stop herself. After the day she'd had, Caroline could use a seat and a beer. She sipped her beer and sat next to Chase. After a couple of sips, Chase's hand eased over Caroline's shoulders and he started to massage Caroline's shoulder, nice and slow. His palms eased into the large muscle on her back and tension unraveled slowly. By the time Caroline knocked back her beer and by then Chase worked out all the kinks in her back.

"Another beer?" Bud asked, tossing Caroline another can. How could she turn down an offer so tempting?

Before Caroline could get half the beer down, Travis approached her shoulder and lowered the strap to Caroline's shirt. He planted a soft, special Travis kiss on her shoulder that sent a shiver running down her spine. Chase's hand snaked around her hips where he squeezed Caroline's flesh. She turned to face Chase as Travis kissed her shoulder and Chase Owens put his other hand up to her cheek and kissed her lips long and slow, thrusting his tongue in her mouth.

Bud hopped off his seat and positioned himself between Caroline's legs. She took a break from kissing Chase and spread her thighs wide to accommodate Bud's large thick torso between her thighs. Bud hitched her legs up and Caroline squealed as she pressed her hands to his firm beefy chest for balance.

"C'mon cowgirl. Let's get you down on these blankets."

Before Caroline could protest, Bud lifted her off her seat with one hand and gently laid her back on the carpet. By the time Caroline's back was on the Apache blanket, the three men were all at her side and each one of them planted different kisses on her body as they peeled back her clothing without removing it.

Travis kissed like a Southern gentleman with puckered rosebud lips tenderly pressing against Caroline's soft brown arms and shoulders as his lips sought permission to pleasure her. Chase was firm and slow, like he took sick satisfaction from teasing Caroline with his tongue. Chase liked to use teeth too, just slighting grazing over her flesh as he worked his lips down Caroline's neck and lifted her shirt so he could kiss her tight stomach. He liked it nice and rough.

Then there was Bud, the thick brutish wild man who was

rough and controlling and feral. He didn't care if his beard scratched Caroline's neck or about sticking his tongue into her ear, into the crevices of her collar bone or even into her navel. Bud fumbled with the buttons and zipper on Caroline's tight pants which clung to her coltish legs.

He was in such a rush to disrobe Caroline that he didn't care about ripping fabric. His large hands worked Caroline's pants off as Chase and Travis unbuttoned her work shirt. Caroline arched her back as Chase moved from her shoulders to her lips, the warm scent of beer on his breath drove her mad. He was every bit the man she wanted. That was the problem, wasn't it? All three of them were the man she wanted. Bud was rough around the edges, a salt-of-the-earth guy who worked with his hands. Travis was the perfect Southern gentleman, and Chase was the complicated blue collar guy with a secret poetic side and a fire burning inside him constantly.

Caroline moaned as Travis' tongue tickled her nipple through her bra and Chase's hand traveled to unhook her bra and release her bosoms to the warm, humid Southern night. Kerosene lamps flickered as Caroline's bra fell to the hardwood floor. Bud hiked her legs up and rolled her pants over her voluptuous hips and her homegrown booty. Bud's touch was hot like fire and as Caroline jerked her legs away from his strong grasp, Bud held her down firmly and spread her legs apart.

As Chase worked on Caroline's nipples, Travis moved back to her lips. He grabbed her cheeks and looked her right in the eye, only the way Travis could with his summer sky eyes.

"I'm sorry I didn't help you," he breathed, before diving back in for another hotter and deeper kiss.

Caroline thought that was all she needed right then, only a few words and then back to tongues tasting her flesh, back to

Bud spreading her open and pressing his giant fingers to her entrance through the fabric of her underwear.

She needed him to whisper, "She's so wet..."

As he said it, her tightness throbbed in anticipation. Caroline moaned and closed her eyes, wishing she'd found some other way to joy that wasn't so taboo. Two men and one woman was unheard of. But three? If anyone found out the black girl in town was here between these three good Southern boys, they'd call her a jezebel...

Bud peeled her underwear off and spread her legs wide so her juices dripped out of her dampness onto the blanket.

... a whore...

Tongues would wag about the girl from the other side of the tracks who had turned the sheriff's son into the kind of man who would line up alongside Bud Landry to pry her thighs open wider.

...a harlot...

Bud dove between her legs, his tongue lapping at the full length of her damp puffy lips, shaved smooth as butter. Travis kissed her thighs and mound as Bud made swift work of the slit between her legs.

...maybe even Lilith herself...

Caroline moaned as she climaxed long and hard. Chase sucked on her nipples as Bud's tongue slipped over every raw inch of her pussy. The mixture of sensations along with Travis kissing the top of her mound pushed Caroline over the edge. Bud grasped her thighs as Chase kissed her neck and Caroline writhed in their arms, finally allowing herself to lose control.

It doesn't matter what they call me, she thought to herself. Any label in the world would be worth the heaven between her thighs. Bud stiffened his tongue and pushed it deep inside her honeypot. Caroline cried out again, her deepest fantasy unleashed as Travis joined Bud and their tongues alternated between her legs, pressing deep inside her and rubbing her engorged clit with each passing stroke of their strong masculine tongues. Bud was the messier eater and the two and when he pulled his face away, he was coated in Caroline's juices.

As Bud moved from Caroline's pussy to her lips, Chase took his place between her legs, kissing her stomach as Travis drove his tongue into her honeypot. Caroline gasped. Her chest rose and she grabbed the wool blanket to brace herself, arching her back to allow Travis greater access between her legs. Caroline moaned as she squirted all over Travis' face, her pussy throbbing with euphoria and desire for more as she thrashed about.

Six hands held her down, keeping her still as they kissed her and caressed her. They weren't even close to finished yet and Caroline still had three red-blooded men with voracious sexual appetites to satisfy. Bud pushed his tongue down her throat, forcing her to taste her juices on his lips. His kiss was rough, controlling, and his hand traveled down to her neck where he held her still without squeezing, kissing her like she belonged to him.

Travis and Chase raised their heads from between Caroline's legs and Bud lifted his lips away from hers. They were at a crucial point in the night. They could stop fooling around, pack up their cans of beer, blow out the lamps and go home, to humid nights in their separate houses after walking Caroline back to her side of town.

They also had the option of finishing what they started. It was quiet, except for knees shuffling across the wooden floor as all three men lined up in front of her, chests heaving with arousal as they waited for Caroline, the one who held all the power, to make the decision for them.

Their eyes burned with hunger for her. Caroline had never

felt so wanted… Not even her first boyfriend, that guy she'd met at Howard with the glasses and the smooth talking, made her feel this way.

"Say the word and we're yours," Travis breathed.

The lamp flickered warm orange light off his face. All three of their cheeks pinked with arousal and Caroline said the two words they were all desperate to hear her say.

"Take me…" she breathed, "All of you…"

The boys didn't give Caroline a moment to regret or have second thoughts. Before they started, the three of them would have to decide who went first. Caroline left the deciding up to them. The three men had been such good friends for years. They had shared everything from a football team to Travis's first car. Now, they shared Caroline too. They looked from one to the other and Travis spoke first, "Chase why don't you go first."

Travis flashed Caroline a wink in reference to their morning together. Down here, he might let someone else go first but He enjoyed romps that he could share with Caroline alone just as much. This whole situation didn't exactly have rules. There was only one rule – Caroline came first.

Bud didn't mind Chase going first. He liked to be the last one to have her anyway when she was all sweaty, when her clothes stuck to her skin and when she was whimpering shivering mess beneath his firm grasp. He loved unraveling her and pushing her to her limits as she writhed and moaned in his firm grasp. Bud grinned and moved out of the way.

All three men were shirtless, each of their bare chests telling a different story about the man who bore it. Travis' chest was clean and bare, paler then the rest. Bud had the tattoo of a bald eagle and American flag on his chest with the word's "BY THE GRACE OF GOD" in cursive across the front. His chest was thicker and meatier than the rest 'cause he'd been working the fields longer than anyone. Chase had a hairy chest with flecks of oil on it from the factory and grease from working on his car in his spare time. Chase had a tattoo on his shoulder of a large C. Only Caroline knew that the "C" was for her name and not his own.

Even before this, Chase loved her. He'd loved her even when he took someone else to prom. He'd loved her all the years she'd gone away and he'd spent long nights on the phone with her as she cried over her first break up. He'd helped her study for her tests at school, even if he could never hope to afford to go. Caroline was his world because she'd given him the courage to cross a boundary in this town that few white boys ever had. Chase knew he was lucky… especially now.

Chase moved forward between her legs, his member bulging from his pants already. Caroline flopped down on her back, ready to take him between her legs ready to take Chase's endowment between her thighs. She scrunched up the Apache blanket between her fingers as Chase hiked her thighs up and pressed the fabric of her pants to her bare cunt.

"I can't wait to put this thing inside you, beautiful," Chase drawled, the liquor bringing the nasty freak out of him. He licked his lips and a naughty twitch fluttered between Caroline's thighs. Chase turned redder than usual when he was inebriated and as he ran his hands from Caroline's hip to her knee, he murmured, "I just want you to know, even if I was sober, I'd be doing this…"

He reached for his pants and got himself completely naked. Bud and Travis switched their attention to Caroline's naked breasts and her lips which were now unoccupied. Chase felt up her soft stomach and pressed his fingers to her mound to experience just how wet she was as he slipped two fingers inside her. Caroline moaned and her tightness clamped hard around

Chase's fingers, desperate to be filled by thick pulsing man flesh.

Chase pulled out of her, a trail of Caroline's juices squirting out from between her thighs. Bud's tongue teased across her nipples and Caroline moaned as Chase licked every last drop of her juices off his fingers with nothing but pure satisfaction written across his face.

Caroline peered over her heaving chest to catch a glimpse of Chase's throbbing cock before he finally plunged the whole thing between her legs. All eight inches of Chase's thick, pulsing man meat stuck out proudly erect. His desire oozed from the engorged pink mushroom tip and the giant, meaty thing looked practically delicious to Caroline. She squeezed her eyes shut as he braced himself against her hips and she felt the ticklish cool sensation of his precum dampening her lips as he pushed the head past the pink elastic flesh of her entrance. Caroline shuddered as the tip slipped past the tight hole, widening it to accommodate the full length of his member.

She cried out as he widened her entrance again and thrust another inch inside her. Chase grunted and pushed the rest of his eight inches in. Chase's cock was a respectable eight inches and thick... he was at least the width of a glass coke bottle and even taking four inches forced a mixture of pleasure and pain out of Caroline. She moaned and tossed her head back, hair tickling the middle of her back as Chase thrust inside her even deeper. His thickness forced her juices to drip out of her wetness and coat his cock in her desire to ease his way inside her.

He thrust his full length between her legs. Caroline cried out and pulled Chase into her with her heels, unconsciously driving him deeper inside her even as she cried out in pain. Chase grabbed her buttocks and plunged his length into her deeper. Caroline was stretched so wide, she could hardly take it anymore. She whimpered and thrashed about, but Bud and Travis held her still so Chase could work between her legs.

Chase couldn't hold himself back with her. He couldn't take it slow, he had to move swiftly between her legs, driving into her with deep strokes that drove Caroline to a heaving, sopping wet climax within a few short minutes. Chase pumped between her legs, spreading her wider with his thick cock until his ab muscles tensed, flexing his perfect body, chiseled by hard factory labor.

"C'mon baby, take it," Chase grunted, thrusting deeper. Caroline gripped him closer, running her hands down his pale spine as he pummeled inside her. Caroline came one last time and Chase eased to the edge of a climax. He buried himself deeper and deeper and groaned as he released thick spurts of his seed between Caroline's legs.

He pulled out of her, coated in sweat, giving her only a second to remember before Travis positioned himself between her thicks. Travis' member wasn't as thick as Chase's but he more than made up for it with the extraordinary length of his pulsing member. At 11 inches, Travis had nothing to be shy about.

His cop uniform lay in a crumpled pile on the ground as Travis positioned himself between her legs. Travis kissed her stomach, taking his time with her before he readied his tumescent cock to enter her. Travis' blond hair hadn't moved an inch from its combed position over his head. The reflection of the flame from the kerosene lamp illuminated his gorgeous blue eyes. Making eye contact with him like this was too intense. Caroline squeezed her eyes shut, ready to feel Travis inside her again — her second big hard cock for the night.

Travis ran his hands down over her stomach and his lips

followed. Then he pressed his unsheathed eleven inch cock against Caroline's entrance and thrust his way in nice and slow. Chase was urgent, masculine and intense, but Travis liked to make love... It was always making love with him. Like he'd taken all his ideas about sex from a historical romance. Even when it was urgent for him, he would move his hips into her slowly, paying special attention to Caroline's pleasure and adjusting based on her breathing, the way she licked her lips or the way her perfect brown breasts heaved before him.

Travis leaned forward, caressing Caroline's cheek as he pushed another inch inside her. As he watched her moan, he stuck a finger into her mouth and she instinctively wrapped her puffy lips around it, sucking on his hand as he pushed another inch inside her.

She was soft, and hotter than before since she'd just taken Chase, but the way she moaned just for him would never get old to Travis. He slid another inch between her perfect thighs, as brown as a walnut and smooth to the touch. Caroline had perfect homegrown Southern curves. She was a well-fed woman and that good eating contributed to her feminine softness that he craved so much.

Travis drove the rest of his hardness deep inside Caroline. His cock penetrated her so deep, she could feel a round knot beneath her belly button and surges of intense pleasure emanating from her core and spreading to her fingers and toes. Travis moved his hips out of her and she moaned, ready to have an instant climax.

Travis slowly plunged back in and he pumped between Caroline's legs nice and slow, easing out of her so her juices could drip around the shaft of his cock. Every slow thrust pushed Caroline until she couldn't take it anymore and she climaxed long and hard, exploding on Travis' big dick as he slid into her at a slow, romantic pace. His hot hard man flesh spread her lips wide and tightened her tummy again so another climax quickly followed Caroline's first.

Travis squeezed her hips and stared into her eyes as she climaxed and her mouth formed a perfect O-shape. As Caroline writhed beneath him, Travis gripped tighter and he couldn't contain himself any longer as he watched the beautiful woman writhing in his grasp. Travis grunted and plunged deeper inside Caroline with one final thrust and a shuddering groan as he released thick spurts of his seed inside her. As he pulled his cock out of Caroline's tightness, the mixture of cum and juices squirted out of her and spilled down her thighs as euphoria surged through every part of her body.

Despite having climaxed and climaxed again, she was still hungry for more. When Bud and Travis switched places, Caroline didn't notice. Caroline was so lost in an orgasmic high that she hardly noticed until Bud's large, rougher hands grabbed her and yanked her closer.

Bud made love like a wild man, uninhibited by care for Caroline. He was the perfect end to Travis' sweet and tender lovemaking. He was rough. He was firm. He took control the way every woman desperately needed from a man. Bud grunted as he pulled his monster cock out of his pant. Bud's dick was raw, uncut, twelve inches long and as thick as a thermos.

He'd been shy the first time she'd seen it, warning Caroline that she might not be able to handle what he packed between his legs — few women could. When Caroline faced that impressive, oversized member the first time, she'd been terrified. But then she'd closed her eyes and allowed the pain and pleasure and total submission to override her better sense. She'd cum so hard that she couldn't walk for a weekend.

This time, Caroline couldn't help but think that this time she wouldn't have the fortitude to take Bud's big buddy between her legs. Bud stroked her stomach, his rough hands contrasting her soft brown skin as he soothed her like a brood mare. Having worked with animals his whole life gave Bud an instinctive edge. He could sense fear and he could assuage it just as easily.

He also hated taking Caroline while she was on her back and just as soon as she was soothed, he flipped her onto her stomach, ignoring her squeals and pinning her down with one of his large hands. Travis and Chase stroked her back, forcing her spine to arch and her buttocks and pussy to remain exposed for Bud's entry. This would hurt — a lot. After the pain, there would be nothing but a mad and desperate euphoria.

Caroline inhaled slowly as Bud ran his hands over her buttocks and spread her cheeks to expose her oozing entrance. Caroline felt the soft, sensitive head of his uncut cock probing her sopping entrance, already soaked with the cum of two of her other lovers. She bit down on her lower lip so hard she tasted metal. Bud pushed his head in slightly, enough to spread her lips and legs wide. He was testing her, seeing how much she could handle before he thrust the entire length between her perfect thighs.

"Easy girl…" he whispered, the twang on his voice soothing her as Caroline arched her back further.

"Take daddy's cock," he whispered, "I want you to take daddy's big white cock like last time…"

He could have been reciting the Lord's Prayer for all she cared. Bud's voice was deep, sultry and soothing, exactly the way Caroline liked it. She moaned as he thrust the rest of his hardness inside her with one swift stroke. Caroline cried out.

He spread her legs so wide and filled her so deeply and with so much pleasure…

Her eyes rolled back in her head and she went blind for a moment as Bud thrust between her thighs for the first time that night, filling her with pain, pleasure, lust and love, and everything in between all those feelings. Caroline broke out in a sweat as Bud pumped between her legs, going slow at first so she could accommodate his massive, monster cock. As she moaned and wriggled her ass cheeks, he grabbed her ass with his rough palms and pulled her closer to him so he could impale her more deeply on his powerful uncut cock.

Caroline whimpered as he plunged into her deeper and Bud moved his hips so he could pump between her legs faster. As Bud pounded her, Caroline grabbed the Apache blanket and moaned. The kerosene lamps shook and shuddered as Bud thrust between her thighs. Chase and Travis alternated kissing her lips and kissing her back so her body exploded in pleasure as Bud took her from behind.

"Ohhhhhhh," Caroline moaned as Bud's big cock touched the most sensitive flesh of her entrance. She thrust back against him, her ass slapping against his chiseled workhorse torso. Travis and Chase kissed her and soothed her as she took Bud deeper and deeper and climaxed hard all over his cock. One climax wasn't enough and Bud pummeled between her legs over and over again until Caroline came and came, her juices squirting all over Bud and the blanket so everyone was soaked by the time Bud was nearly finished. Bud grabbed her hips and buried himself deep inside her one last time as he came.

Thick spurts of cum erupted from his hardness, plunging deep inside her tight pussy and pushing all the other cum out as well as Caroline's own juices which streamed down her legs in an incredible mixture. The barn no longer smelled of beer, but of sweat and warmth, and love. Bud pulled out of Caroline and she collapsed onto her bosom, spent from the incredible pounding she'd received from all three men.

After making love to her, Travis, Chase and Bud huddled around her, each one touching a part of her body with their hands. Travis' grasp was gentle and loving. Chase was firm, but soothing. And Bud's hand was possessive and his grasp tighter than any of the others. None of them would let this beautiful woman go — no matter the cost.

All they had to do was keep these four-way romps a secret. If no one found out, nobody could get hurt.

5

BUD CAN'T READ

THE FOUR OF them lay together for over an hour. Travis's radio woke them out of their euphoric reverie. He sprang to his feet and searched the pile for his clothes. Travis got a call about an accident on the highway and all available units were required to respond. Bud, Chase, and Caroline sat up with sleep fresh on their eyes and attempted to help Travis find his things. They were still all exhausted, and recovering from the insanely erotic experience they'd just had. Three men, one woman, the ultimate taboo, yet the only thing the four of them found satisfying.

As he dressed in his cop's uniform, Travis was visibly nervous.

"Can you smell the beer?" He asked Caroline as he made his way to the barn door, the gun in his holster and his uniform so crisp and clean, she could forget he'd been naked and tangled with her on the floor only moments before.

"Nope. Not really. I can smell the barn, though."

"That'll be easy enough to explain at least," Travis muttered.

He said goodbye to Caroline, leaving her with a kiss and the memory of his touch as he hastened across the field back to his car.

Chase groaned and rose to his feet, cracking his back which still ached from a long day at the factory.

"I'd better get out of here," he said, "I've got to go home before Zach starts asking questions."

"It's best if we all leave separate," Bud replied.

Chase said goodbye to Caroline and after Travis was gone, Chase followed across the fields. Bud rose, dusting off his legs and slipped back into his boxers. Caroline bit down on her lower lip as she stared at his body. He should have *so* not been her type. I mean look at him... Bud was a thick, muscled redneck from the heart of the south who had grown up his whole life in a segregated town. Caroline should have hated him.

But she couldn't help it. Bud couldn't read, she could. Bud might have been country as a Cracker Barrel, but he cared about people. He was poor. He understood what it was like to eat hopes and dreams for dinner. Once they were alone, Caroline rushed to his side and rested her hand on his shoulders. Bud grunted.

"You gotta rush home?"

"No. Not without you walking me there, at least."

"I'll walk you home but you gotta promise to help me learn how to read tomorrow, okay?"

"Okay."

"I don't want to tell the guys about it."

"There's nothing embarrassing about not knowing how to read, Bud."

His cheeks went red and his giant hands clenched into a powerful fist.

"Bullshit."

"I mean it," Caroline whispered, kissing him on the cheek.

"I don't need your pity, Caroline."

"You think I pity you?"

"Yeah. I kinda do."

"You're wrong. I don't pity you, Bud. You had the same opportunities as all the other boys in this town but you drank beer, chased tail and now you can't read. So what? I'll only pity you if you give up. So make sure you're there tomorrow, bright and early."

"Will you be pissed if I come with a hangover?"

"Be sober," Caroline replied.

She linked arms with Bud and rested her head on his shoulders, "Now it's time to walk me home."

"I'll drop you at the end of the street. I know the deal."

"Good," Caroline nodded, "And come 'round out back in the morning. I don't want my parents to see you."

"What? They don't like the idea of you hanging around a white boy?"

"No… but they know your father won't like the idea of you hanging out with a girl from the other side of the tracks."

Bud blushed again.

"My daddy don't make my decisions for me."

"I know, but they don't know that and I don't want them involved."

"It ain't fair. None of this color stuff matters. I like to think I'm colorblind."

Caroline folded her arms and popped her hips. Bud could tell she was real angry when she did that even if she never yelled and only pursed her lips when she got upset. She was a lady, after all.

"What do you mean color blind?"

"I mean, I don't see color."

"Bud, I know you mean well but that doesn't make sense. Color matters. I'm black, you're white."

"It shouldn't matter."

"I know, but it does. And if things are going to change, I don't want any of this color blind nonsense. I'm black, and there's nothing wrong with loving me because of that, not in spite of it."

"You got a way with words, Caroline," he murmured, twirling his finger around a strand of her hair. Caroline sighed and pushed him away. If she wasn't careful, she'd let Bud have her again on the barn floor and her thighs ached enough as it was from the three massive cocks.

"C'mon big boy," she whispered, "Take me home."

Bud linked arms with her and walked Caroline all the way to the end of her block. They were in public and didn't want to risk being seen by nosy neighbors so they said goodbye without kissing and Caroline snuck into her house and across the living room.

"Where are you coming from so late?" Caleb asked.

Caroline's hands flew to her lips and she stifled a screech.

"Sorry, didn't mean to scare you."

"I was out."

"With Travis?"

"No."

"Good. I don't like the idea of you hanging out with that guy."

"What's wrong with Travis?"

"He's a cop, Caroline. I don't need to be the one to tell you that all cops are bastards, do I?"

"Not *all* cops."

"Yes, all cops. You aren't safe with that guy."

"There's no law that says I'm not."

"There's no law but the white folks in this town have other ways of enforcing traditions..."

"You worry too much, Caleb."

"With good reason. Ever since you came back from the city, you've been different. You've been reckless, like these newfangled notions of yours are getting in the way of common sense."

"I'm fine, Caleb. I promise, I can look after myself."

"Just make sure you remember to look after this family too. You owe Ma and Daddy."

"I know. I haven't forgotten."

"Good. Now good night."

"Good night, Caleb," Caroline said, hurrying to her room and struggling to silence her racing heart.

Caleb was wrong about Travis. Cops might have been horrible in other parts of the country and certainly the sheriff and his cohort were up to no good more than half the time. But Travis was different. He was a cop because for him, there was no better way to make a living. He was a cop because he had no choice except the military. And wasn't it better for him to stay home and look after his sister?

Caroline couldn't stop thinking about Caleb's warning until she finally fell asleep. She woke up with the sun, before anyone in her house. Caroline slipped into her robe and slippers and made a flask of coffee before heading out onto the rickety back porch. Bud leaned up against the wall wearing a flannel shirt, with a few buttons undone so his chest hair peeked out, and a cowboy hat balanced on his head, covering his eyes.

"G'morning, cowgirl," he said, raising his hat and stuffing his hands in the pocket of his mud-stained jeans.

"Ready to learn how to read?"

"Yes'm."

"I brought coffee."

"Perfect," he sighed, rubbing his hands together from the cold, "Let's get started."

They sat on the steps and Caroline pulled out the newspaper. They might as well start there, even if it meant going over that embarrassing headline again and remembering every event that lead to her getting fired. Bud struggled over the letters, but he was doing a bit better. Caroline wondered if he were in a richer town, if he could have gotten treatment for his dyslexia, or if someone better could have at least helped him. Big ole Bud had always been "slow" and labelled the class clown before any teachers got a chance to know him.

No one had given him a chance 'cause he was too big and beefy and poor and dirty — not worth their time. Mr. Landry's well known on-again-off-again relationship with Vicodin didn't help either. Caroline guided his hand over the page and after an exhausting hour punctuated with a lot of "shits" and "goddamns", their lesson was finished. Bud was beet red.

He stood up and thrust his hands in his pockets again.

"Thanks for taking the time, Caroline."

"No problem, Bud."

"I could just kiss you for being so patient."

"Don't..." she whispered.

It was too late, Bud leaned in and stole a big kiss.

"You've got a good heart."

"So do you, Bud. I wish you could be mayor of this town."

Bud laughed.

"In your dreams. A mayor who can't read? No way in hell."

He pulled out a cigarette and lit up as he walked away from Caroline's back porch. Caroline sighed and pressed her fingers to her lips, relishing the taste of his rough but grateful kiss.

6

WHITE MAN IN WHITE CLOTHES

Tommy Lee Buchanan always wore white. His wife bleached his clothes and if there was a stain left on them, Mrs. Buchanan would have hell to pay when he got home. He cured her of her lazy washing right quick and slapped her one good time when she dared ask for a maid as if he'd *pay* one of these lazy blacks to lay their dirty hands on his clothes.

Tommy Lee grunted and sidled into the chair in his new office. It was old and uncomfortable and stank of liberal filth. This town would be finished of liberal filth if he had his way. There were some who wanted to have those people from the other side of the tracks spilling into his side of town and Tommy Lee would die before he let one of the blacks be his next door neighbor.

He'd have to wave to 'em and smile and pretend like he gave a shit about their low, worthless lives. Hell no. Tommy Lee's great grand-daddy fought a war to protect him from that sort of thing and Tommy Lee held his great grand-daddy in high regard.

Mr. Oswald Buchanan owned the Buchanan house many

years ago and back then he'd owned 100 slaves. In his shame, Tommy Lee's father sold the house. What an imbecile, tainted by his fanciful yankee notions. Tommy Lee wasn't ashamed of his heritage. He wasn't *ashamed* that his great grand-daddy had been a war hero or that he'd owned 100 people. He was a businessman and he'd earned all his wealth, damn it. Just like Tommy Lee earned the mayor's office. Yes, he'd earned this. Tommy Lee put his feet up on the desk and leaned back.

"I earned all of this," he whispered to himself, chuckling with true satisfaction.

The two officers came to Tommy Lee's office with starched blue uniforms, haircuts worthy of proud old Southern men. Tommy Lee invited them in with a gruff, "C'mon in gentlemen." He didn't budge from his seat as Sheriff Montgomery and junior officer Zachariah Owens entered the room.

Chase Owen's younger brother looked nearly exactly like him but his eyes were stern and mean compared to his brother's. They even had the same reddish beard, except Zach kept his face clean-shaven during the spring, only growing out his tufted red beard during November.

Tommy Lee liked Zachariah. He understood Southern values, just like the Sheriff did. He was a good boy, and Tommy Lee enjoyed the stiff no-nonsense way Zachariah carried himself. He was young, but by God, he hadn't forgotten tradition. Sheriff Montgomery approached the desk and gave Tommy Lee Buchanan a firm handshake.

"I have to say, I'm awful flattered the mayor called me in for a private conference on his first day," Atticus Montgomery gushed, overstating his excitement.

"At ease, Atticus. This is an informal meeting. Everything here, off the record. Got it?"

"Yes, sir," Atticus Montgomery and Chase Owens spoke at the same time.

"Good. Good. I want to talk about a former employee of the mayor's office. I believe she keeps company of folks you're familiar with."

"What has this young lady done to get your attention if you don't mind me asking? Does Mrs. Buchanan know about this?"

Tommy Lee waved his old friend off.

"Oh it ain't nothing like that, Atticus. Do you read the paper?"

"No, sir."

"Mr. Owens?"

"No, sir."

"Hmph," Tommy Lee Buchanan grunted.

"We can get the paper and read it later, sir, if that's what you'd like," Zachariah followed up.

Sheriff Montgomery rested his hand on Zachariah's shoulder, encouraging him to be a little quieter and listen a bit more before opening his mouth and allowing drivel to slither out

"That won't be necessary Officer Owens," the mayor replied patiently.

Mayor Buchanan leaned back.

"Heard the name Caroline Coulson before?"

Sheriff Montgomery scowled.

"You running into trouble with her?" He grunted.

"I'm afraid I am, Atticus. She's gotten it into her head somehow that this election was bought and paid for."

Zach and Atticus Montgomery exchanged looks.

"We can't have that, sir," Zach replied, eager to please and earn his place amongst the mayor's chosen elite.

"No, Mr. Owens, we can't."

"Say the word, Tommy and we'll take care of her," the

sheriff offered, leaning in with an earnest expression on his face.

"There's no need for anything drastic, Atticus. I need you and Mr. Owens to keep an eye on little miss Caroline."

"My brother keeps her company," Zachariah offered, "We ain't close these days but it's never too late to reconnect with family."

Zachariah offered a pleading, dopey grin that caused Tommy Buchanan to return his smile with a pleased nod.

"Why thank you, Zachariah. Atticus, think you can keep an eye on young Travis?"

Young Travis wasn't quite so young anymore, and Atticus Montgomery didn't know how much he'd be able to keep an eye on his son. Travis had been getting testy lately, questioning too much and obeying too little.

He wasn't a little boy anymore, Atticus new that, but he also sensed his son getting lured in by these newfangled liberal notions that seemed to be infecting everybody. He didn't like that very much either.

"I'll keep an eye on Travis, Tommy. You can count on it," the sheriff answered without betraying his uncertainty about keeping an eye on his son.

"Good. Miss Coulson can't spread her fake news theories further than this office. We did what we had to in order to keep this town safe and traditional. Let's not have that uppity woman ruin three years of hard work, boys."

"Yes, sir," they replied in unison.

Buchanan dismissed Zach Owens and closed his eyes, content that Atticus and the young Owens boy would take care of this little mess for him. Caroline Coulson. He scoffed at the idea that a girl from the other side of the tracks thought she could uncover some great conspiracy and take him down. It was the typical liberal idealism at work. Buchanan scoffed.

If there was one person he trusted to get that woman to back off, it was Atticus. He had a way of maintaining order around here that Tommy Lee admired. Hell, if it weren't for Atticus, he would have never have been *certain* that the citizens of Old Town would accept his victory.

This place was quiet. People didn't like making a fuss. Except for that Caroline Coulson of course with her fabricated evidence and overzealous reporting. If she didn't back off, well, there were other ways of keeping folks quiet. Some methods were more permanent than others. Buchanan had few enemies and he liked to keep it that way. Fewer people to crawl out of the woodwork and make trouble for you.

"Atticus, I've got something to ask you privately."

"Sure thing, Tommy."

"Take this. Burn it."

He slid an envelope across the desk. Atticus tucked the envelope underneath his arm and nodded.

"Make sure Zachariah doesn't find out about the affair, or Miss Coulson. That's sure to come up in her little investigation if she digs deep enough."

"Don't worry, Tommy. You got nothing to worry about with Miss Coulson. I'll keep an eye on her."

"I know I can count on you, Montgomery."

7

OH BROTHER.

CHASE'S brown hair stuck to his neck after his shift at the factory. The back of his neck ached and tightened into a knot. He couldn't lift his arms above his head if he tried and his chest withered with each painful breath. Factory work was hard but organizing the boys at the plant was even harder.

They didn't see why they should team up with the colored folks for better wages. As Jack Wilkinson said, "Why should I join hands with the colored man when he's the reason they don't pay us so good?"

Chase's head hurt when he thought about the stupid arguments like that he had to counter. Try blaming the boss instead of your fellow worker, he'd say, or maybe if the guy was particularly stuck on stupid, Chase would make a stick figure diagram to explain it. The whole integrated union thing was a huge project, and Caleb Coulson was luckily up to the task.

They disagreed on many things. Caleb was more of an anarchist, untethered by structure and tradition. Caleb knew that they'd make no good progress in town without at least paying mind to tradition. They argued, but at the end of the day, Caleb was a good man, and so was Chase.

They walked after work to the Owens house and shared a cigarette. Caroline hadn't told Chase anything about her and the three boys, so Chase kept his mouth shut when it came to Caleb's sister. It's not exactly the kind of conversation you bring up with your coworker anyway.

"Seen Caroline lately?" Caleb asked eventually.

"Can't say I have. She stopped by the factory the day she was fired and that's it."

"Hm. I was wondering how she's holding up. You know Caroline. She plays her cards close to the chest. It's hard to know what's going on in her mind."

"Ain't that true."

"If she says anything, will you let me know? She's got it in her head that Mayor Buchanan is up to something and I don't want her to do anything stupid. That guy is dangerous."

"What makes you say that?"

"Trust me, Chase, he is."

They stopped outside the Owens house, a blue house with white shutters and Mrs. Owens hydrangea bushes blossoming out front.

"I'll keep an eye on her as much as I can, but you know Caroline."

"Stubborn," both men said at the same time. That was what Caroline was known for after all. Once she got her teeth sunk into something, she couldn't let go.

Caleb said goodbye to Chase and he kept going toward the train tracks, whistling an old country tune as he left Chase Owens front porch. Chase sat on the front steps, reaching into his pocket for another cigarette. Nasty habit, smoking, but when you work all day in the factories and when your bones hurt after a sixteen hour shift, you'll do whatever you can to take the edge off.

No sooner had Chase lit the cigarette than he heard footsteps coming down the stairs. He'd recognize his brother's heavy tread even if he were blind and deaf. He could feel Zach in the floorboards. The door swung open and his heavy set brother with his cornflower blue eyes popping against his police uniform came out onto the porch.

"Sitting outside in the cold enjoying a cancer stick. Why can't you drink beer like the rest of us?"

"Shut up, Zach."

Chase wasn't in the mood for Zach's moralizing. From the minute Zach put on that uniform, Chase considered him a traitor. Mr. Owens, their father, had been in jail for six years on account of a minor drug charge. Sheriff Montgomery himself had picked him up and now Zach stuck around the sheriff like a lost puppy, sticking his nose so far up the officer's butt he looked like a damn fool.

Travis was one thing. Being a cop was in his DNA. Zach? He had a choice, and he'd chosen to be a traitor rather than doing honest factory work like they father had done before he'd been injured and dabbled in darker money.

"Hey, just trying to make friendly conversation."

"I ain't in the mood for friendly conversation," Chase grunted, "Sit on the porch and shut up. And bring me a beer."

A flash of rage surged across Zach's face which was immediately replaced by a more mellow smile. Chase was too fixated on the upcoming union meeting to analyze his brother's every mysterious glance. Zach brought out a beer and sat on the porch, spreading his stance and clinking his can against Chase's.

"Don't you have work right now?" Chase asked.

"Just making time for my big brother."

"Why's that?"

"No reason."

"Hm."

Chase flicked his cigarette and continued to stare at the hydrangeas. This wasn't like Zach at all.

"You watching the ballgame tonight?"

"Don't think so. I've got a big meeting coming up."

"Meeting at the factory?"

Chase grunted.

Zach continued, "Is this some kind of subtle way of saying you've got a date?"

"No. I don't have a date."

Zach smirked.

"What about Caroline Coulson? You two are pretty close?"

"Shut up, Zach."

"What? You mean to tell me you've been hanging around Caroline all these years and you've never wanted to stick it to her once? I know she's the wrong color for that but any red-blooded man's gotta love an easy lay."

Chase crushed his beer can with one hand and slammed it on the ground.

"You shut your mouth about Caroline."

Zach kept smirking, his cheeks reddening. Chase realized he hadn't had a sip of beer and his suspicions about his brother's sudden friendliness and questions about Caroline heightened.

"What's the real reason you're talking to me, Zach?"

"Ain't no reason," he stood and thumped his brother on the back, "I s'pose it's a good thing you haven't done anything to bring this family any more disgrace. Daddy took care of that a long time ago."

Chase's cheeks reddened but he didn't say anything to Zach

as he walked away. Let him go. Let him insult their father's legacy. If he were less of a pig, he'd appreciate all their father had done for them. He'd sacrificed everything and now he paid the price. He'd spend years behind bars. By the time he got out, Chase would be an old man...

Chase tossed his beer can onto the porch and went for a long walk. As he meandered down the streets, past Buchanan's mansion, he didn't think he'd end up anywhere in particular. The flag hanging from Buchanan's pole pissed him off. He would have gone over to pull it down, but he could see Mrs. Buchanan in the kitchen from the sidewalk.

As the crickets screamed into the night, Chase kept wandering until he found himself at the Montgomery house. The lights were on and he smelled a pot roast cooking inside.

He rang the doorbell and Sheriff Montgomery answered.

"Mr. Owens! Good to see you," he boomed, "I expect you're here to see Travis?"

"Yes, Sheriff. Thank you."

Chase flashed him a smile. It was all he could do to hide how utterly he despised the man who put his father in jail. After all the football games they'd watched together, all the tailgates, all the ways he knew Chase's dad struggled, he'd still locked him up like an animal without giving him a chance.

Atticus Montgomery shuffled off into the house. Chase waited on the porch until Travis showed up in just his wife beater and a pair of basketball shorts. He was unperturbed by the cold. Chase's legs ached, but he'd been troubled since his brother spoke to him on the porch.

"Can we take a walk? I got something to ask you about."

"Sure thing. Let me get a hoodie."

Travis threw on a hoodie and walked outside with Chase down the block.

"What's going on, man?"

"It's Caroline. I'm starting to worry about her."

Travis thrust his hands into his pockets.

"Why do you say that?"

"Zachariah approached me tonight and started asking all these questions about her. I don't know. I kinda got the feeling something was going on."

"Hm."

"That's not the answer I expected."

"I know. It's just that my daddy was asking the same thing. If they're up to something, I ain't got the faintest idea what it is."

"We'd better find out, Travis. You know Caroline. She has a way of getting herself in trouble."

"You're right. I hope it's nothing," Travis replied.

8

A-E-I-O-U

BUD CUSSED ALL MORNING.

$#%^@#^!

###!@%$^!

%^$!

@%$^#!!

They'd gone over vowels and diphthongs again and while Bud laughed plenty at the word "diphthong" and even made Caroline repeat it again, they weren't making much progress without him cussing and hollering. Caroline couldn't believe how far he'd made it in school without knowing this much. It paid to throw the pigskin, apparently.

Just as Caroline was losing patience with him, Bud dropped the newspaper.

"Is that Zachariah Owens coming up here?"

Caroline squinted across the field.

"I don't know. You sure it ain't Travis?"

"Naw. He's got the walk of Zachariah."

Bud rose and his face reddened even more.

"What the hell is that weasel doing over here?"

"Calm down, Bud," Caroline urged, rising to her feet and smoothing out her dress. She even fixed her hair. Bud raised an eyebrow.

"Fixin' your hair to see Zach Owens? Ain't that a bit twisted?"

"Shut up, Bud. I'm only doing it 'cause I don't want to look all unfinished."

Bud rolled his eyes.

"Well don't you go getting the hots for him."

Yes, it was clear now that Zachariah Owens was crossing the field over to the back porch.

"Hi Zach!" Caroline called.

Bud stuck his hands in his pockets and glared suspiciously. Zach Owens wasn't one of those folks you caught on this side of town too often. He wasn't the type of fella to hang out with the "wrong crowd". Caroline was a good girl but Bud knew Zach's type. All his book-learning and he was still a bigot. Bud bristled at Zach's bright smile which was out of character for the sour lug, who was about Bud's size.

"Good morning, Miss Coulson. Bud."

Bud grunted. Caroline glared at him.

"What brings you over here?" Caroline asked with a smile.

"I was wondering if you could help me out, Caroline. Everyone knows you're the smartest girl in town given you went to college and everything so I was wondering if you could help me study for the entrance exams."

Caroline beamed. Bud was still suspicious.

"I'd love to help."

"Are you sure?" Bud grumbled.

"Bud, you mind your manners or I'll swat you! No problem, Zach. We can get started whenever you'd like."

"Why Caroline, this means the world to me."

Zach took her hand and kissed it. Caroline looked away bashfully, her eyelashes fluttering. Bud felt his temper rising. Why couldn't Caroline see through this slime ball? He was sleazy, no good... Bud's fists balled up. Caroline rested her hand on his shoulder and he relaxed.

"We could start next week if it's alright with you."

"Yes, ma'am."

Zach tipped his hat, thanked her and walked off across the field. Bud turned to her, red-faced.

"What the hell do you think you were doing?"

"Don't tell me you're jealous that I talked to Zach..."

"Jealous? You think this is about jealousy?"

Bud grabbed her hips and pushed her up against the wall brash and sudden. He kissed her, long and deep and then pulled away.

"I'm not jealous. I know who you belong to Caroline. I share you with two other men. It's not about sharing you. I can handle that. It's Zach I can't handle. I don't trust him."

Caroline stammered, thrown off because of the kiss, "I didn't know you felt so protective of me."

"Damn right I do. All of us do. Be careful with Zach. Chase will tell you that more than anybody. You shouldn't trust him."

"He's not trying to get with me. He's asking for help on an exam."

"I just want you to be careful."

"Fine. I'll be careful."

Bud pushed her up against the wall again and kissed her. This time, Caroline pressed her palms to his chest and thrust him away.

"You have to be careful! What if someone saw you do that?"

"I don't care anymore. I just want you to be safe. I want you to know that I ain't gonna let anyone hurt you. Got it?"

Who knew Bud could be so passionate? Caroline licked the taste of him off her lips and nodded.

"Yeah. I've got it."

After Bud left, Travis called Caroline's house. They had to meet in the barn again, he said. His voice was urgent and Caroline worried that something had gone wrong. Or maybe Travis discovered something about Buchanan. That would be welcome news. If he had, why was he acting all strange? That kind of behavior wasn't exactly typical for him.

Caroline made dinner for her family and after Caleb got home, she knew the shift at the factory was over, so she told her brother she was headed out for a walk and not to wait up for her. Before she left, Caleb warned Caroline to be careful. It wasn't usual for him to worry like that. Caroline promised she could handle herself and she walked to the unfinished Landry barn alone.

Flickering lights on in the barn and the dull throbbing raucous chatter from the boys warmed Caroline's expression as she approached. Tonight, they'd stayed away from the beer but they'd set out a blanket with a thermos of hot chocolate which Bud poured into metal camping mugs. For ages, the boys tried to get Caroline to go camping with them. She'd always refused.

"What would people think if they found out?"

She'd turned them down every time so the boys found a way to bring the camp to Caroline. She couldn't help but feel… flattered. The three of them were already warmed up with hot chocolate, and Travis brought Caroline a mug as soon as she entered.

"What's all this about?"

"Thought you might enjoy some hot chocolate," Bud said, "It's my ma's special recipe."

"Does this have liquor in it?"

"Not tonight. We thought it best if we all kept a clear head," Chase replied, a smirk easing across his face.

Caroline accepted her mug of hot chocolate, knowing that the boys must have been up to something, and not caring that they were. Bud was right about his ma's recipe being something special. Smooth, rich, thick chocolate with a dash of sugar and a large helping of whipped cream slid easily down Caroline's throat.

"Where should I sit?" She asked after one sip.

The boys exchanged glances. She was teasing them, they were sure of it. It didn't matter. It wouldn't be long before they managed to have Caroline on her back, eagerly accepted the three of them between her legs. They'd been waiting for this moment far too long and as the day went by, each of them longed for a taboo night in the barn — the summer breeze, hot sweat as their sticky aroused flesh pressed together, and of course the kisses were incredible.

Caroline sat between Chase and Travis on the blanket. She'd spent plenty of time with Bud that morning, and Caroline had to admit that she worried about Bud spilling the beans regarding Zach Owens. She didn't want Chase to get angry that she was spending time with his brother. It was old news that the two boys didn't get along.

Chase wrapped his arm around Caroline and kissed her forehead.

"Heard you spent all morning with Bud. What were you two up to?"

"We were—"

"FORNICATING!" Bud interrupted.

Caroline glared at him.

"Bud!"

He flashed her a pleading glance. He hated that he couldn't

read and he didn't exactly want the other fellas to be laughing at him and joking about it. Caroline let it go.

"Fine. We were fornicating."

"And you didn't think to call us over?" Chase teased.

Travis shook his head, "To think you two could keep such a secret."

Caroline stammered but Bud interjected before she could get far.

"Don't tell me y'all are jealous," Bud goaded.

"Why the hell would we be jealous of you?" Chase snapped.

Bud shrugged, "Maybe y'all are afraid Caroline likes me better."

Bud smirked. Chase laughed. Travis pretended to shrug it off but his face settled into a decidedly envious scowl. Caroline shot Bud a stern look.

"What are you getting all mad for, Travis?"

"I ain't mad."

"Yes you are," Chase added, grinning from ear to ear, "Don't tell me you're actually jealous of that big idiot."

"Who you calling an idiot?"

"Boys!" Caroline shrilled, "Can you three let me enjoy this drink?"

"Sorry," Chase muttered, kissing her on the cheek, "I guess we all got a lot of pent up energy."

Chase flashed her his mischievous smirk and Caroline's heart fluttered. What she would give to feel his beard prickling across her bosom as his tongue licked around her nipples. She'd have to be patient for that. Too patient.

"I'll drink to that," Travis grumbled, and he relaxed, apparently over whatever surge of jealousy that had coursed through him.

With mugs of hot chocolate polished off, the four waited

with bated breath for whoever would make the first move. Caroline never wanted to be the one to do it. Even if she could give herself to these men completely, there was still a part of her that felt dangerously taboo opening up to three men like this.

She hugged her knees into her chest until she felt Bud's large hand press into the small of her back.

"Relax, honey pie," Bud whispered, "We'll take care of you tonight."

Travis lowered Caroline onto her back and he kissed her, pressing on top of her as Bud and Chase took their positions on either side of her. Travis' kisses were firm and urgent. She wanted him to fuck her badly, to spread her legs and get between them with his throbbing man cock and get her nice and wet.

Caroline wrapped her arms around Travis, running her hands through his blond hair, which was messier then usual. He spread her legs wide, his cock straining from his pants and ready to escape and slide into her tight slippery sleeve. Bud and Chase writhed beside her, spreading kisses up Caroline's arms. Their lips blazed with their fiery hunger for her taste.

"We're going to fuck you so hard tonight," Travis murmured.

Chase's tongue flicked across her ear and she moaned, bucking her hips upwards to press against Travis' growing cock.

"I can't wait to fill you up, pretty girl..."

Then he ripped her clothes off fast. Caroline hardly noticed what happened. As Travis' rough hands worked her pants off, Bud and Chase joined forces to unbutton her blouse. One of the buttons popped off as Bud eagerly ripped at her shirt. Bud pulled her face away from Travis for a moment and he thrust his tongue down her throat, enjoying her delicious taste and stripping her down to her underclothes.

Caroline reached back for her bra but before she could get her hands into the hooks, Bud flipped Caroline onto her stomach and ripped her bra off with her bare hands. Caroline moaned and found herself on all fours with her back arched. Travis ran his hands down her spine and hooked his thumbs through the waistband of Caroline's white panties which were soaked through with her juices already. Travis enjoyed the warm, sweet smell of her pussy that already wafted through the air. He pulled her panties down over her ass cheeks and inhaled her fresh scent.

He'd been waiting to get a taste of her for far too long. Everything that happened that week with his daddy and with Zach Owens drifted a million miles away as Travis spread Caroline's legs wide and drove his tongue into her slippery puffy brown lips. Chase sucked on one of Caroline's nipples and Bud sucked on the other one, his beard bristling over her flesh and tickling her as Travis' tongue drove between her legs… *deep*.

Caroline moaned and bucked her hips backwards as her pussy squirted all over Travis' tongue. He gripped her thighs, flesh spilling between his fingers as he sucked on her engorged flower until Caroline couldn't handle another minute of his pleasure and she came long and hard all over Travis' lips and mouth.

Travis sucked on her pussy like a ripe mango and ran his tongue between her slit, lapping up every drop of juices and slurping between her legs so Caroline couldn't help but climax again…

"Yes… Oh yes…" she moaned.

Travis' clothing fell away and he kneeled between Caroline's legs as her tight pussy dripped like a faucet. The tiny slit before him held the power to provide so much pleasure. Travis' cock oozed with excitement as he pressed the tip outside of Caroline's tight, eager sheath. Her heart rate quickened as Travis' controlling palm spread her wide and he started to work his lengthy member between her legs.

He began by thrusting the mushroom head past her entrance, sending Caroline into a fit of squeals and moans. Her fluffy black hair draped across her back and her sepia-colored cheeks flushed a deep mulberry as Travis thrust between her dark, erotic thighs.

He pushed inside another inch and before she knew it, Travis was making love to her nice and slow, driving his long hardness between her legs nice and deep and squeezing her ass cheeks with slow massaging motions as he pumped between her legs.

"Ohhhh," she moaned, "Don't stop, Travis…"

"I love it when you say my name," Travis drawled.

Caroline thrust her hips back to meet his dick and she climaxed as his length pleasured every inch of her tightness. She climaxed again and again, stimulated into waves of intense orgasm from Travis' slow strokes. When the pleasure from her tightness clamping hard around his member grew too intense, Travis came hard.

His seed spurted between Caroline's legs and she climaxed as his juices streamed down her legs and he slowly removed his hardness from its sheath. Before Travis could collapse from exhaustion beside her, Bud gave up licking and sucking at Caroline's nipples and took Travis' place behind her.

Given the way he'd kissed her earlier, Caroline knew she was in for a while ride. Bud would have her bucking like a bronco and he'd enter her so deeply and forcefully that she'd have no choice but to cum for him and submit herself totally to his pleasure.

"C'mon Caroline," he murmured, "Get nice and wet for Bud..."

Caroline's pussy dripped like a faucet. Her legs were soaked and glued to the fresh blanket the boys lay out on the barn floor. The smell of hay and hot chocolate soothed her completely. She could smell Bud's intense delicious musk as he stripped down to nothing between her legs. As he pressed the tip of his hardness on her wetness, Bud did the unexpected...

He took a mug of warm hot chocolate and as he slid the tip of his cock inside Caroline's tight heat, he dripped hot chocolate all over her back and butt. The hot chocolate spread down her thighs and coated his cock and her pussy as Bud slid one inch between her legs. Caroline moaned. He was bigger and harder than she remembered and his cock was searing hot as he split her wide and shoved his girth between her legs.

Caroline cried out and Bud rode her hard from behind, keeping her legs spread wide as he plunged his monstrous hardness fast and deep between her legs. He poured hot chocolate over her body and thrust into Caroline deeply. Travis and Chase stuck their tongues out and cleaned every drop of hot chocolate off her body with their tongues as Bud thrust into Caroline hard and deep. He groaned as he plunged deeper inside her. The tickling sensation from the tongues teasing and licking the chocolate off of her body and the intense pleasure from Bud's monstrous cock spreading her thighs drove Caroline to another more intense climax.

By now, she was soaked with hot chocolate, sweat and juices from their romp. Her hair stuck to her neck and tufts of it stuck up towards the sky from the humidity that built in their private barn enclave.

"Come to daddy," Bud groaned, "Cum all over daddy's big hard country dick."

Bud breathed heavily, his words shuddering out of his mouth as he kept pumping into her. He was rougher than she remembered, taking her from behind vigorously.

Caroline moaned and writhed as he pressed her head down so her back arched even more and Bud took her deep, forcing her into total submission as she came for him. Her juices squirted all over his cock and landed with a splash on her back as Bud kept thrusting away. When Bud finally climaxed, Caroline didn't have a second to recover before Chase took his position behind her.

Chase's thick cock oozed with desire and he didn't wait a moment before thrusting his thickness between her legs. Caroline came instantly. From the hard pounding she received, she couldn't hold herself back one bit. She moaned and collapsed onto her stomach. Chase held her down and as she squeezed her thighs together, he plunged between her chocolate covered thighs and fucked her hard and deep.

Chase picked up the can of whipped cream and squirted it all over Caroline's back. She was too aroused to care about the mess. And the mess didn't matter. Bud and Travis armed with eager tongues danced their way across her flesh, licking all the cream off their chocolate princess' body and worshipping at the altar of her unleashed female sexuality.

This was the hottest romp they had yet and as they played together more often the four found themselves in sync . Chase grunted and gripped Caroline's hips as he approached his own climax. He slid his cock between her tightness which only clamped harder around his cock as she grew more aroused. He moaned and Caroline moaned and the two of them entangled in ecstasy together as Caroline climaxed and

Chase followed, lying on top of her spent once he was finished.

It took ten long, slow minutes for Caroline to catch her breath. Her chest heaved and pulsed as she lay betwixt all three men who couldn't stop pawing at her and kissing her and occasionally licking some of the remnants of their lovemaking off her skin. They were enjoying this more than she was, she thought. They took pleasure out of sharing someone, out of having another way to bond their band of brothers together.

Once they cooled off, Bud got his clothes on. His father called him back home 'cause one of their cows was about to give birth. Chase offered to go help and Travis offered to stay behind with Caroline to clean up. Alone with Travis, Caroline could feel his eyes on her, as if he were holding himself back from saying something.

She buttoned her shirt as best she could, although the missing button from the top she'd have a hard time hiding from Caleb. Her brother picked up on *everything,* even the smallest details like a missing button. Caroline would have to come up with some excuse.

"Care, can I talk to you?" Travis asked, scratching his head nervously.

"What?"

"I gotta ask, you noticed anything funny recently? Anyone following you, something like that?"

"Why do you ask, Travis?"

"I worry about you, that's all."

"Should I be worried about me?"

"Not yet. It's just that, I've had kind of an odd experience and I thought we should talk."

"Okay. What happened?"

"It ain't my intention to scare you, little lady."

"I'm a tough cookie, Travis. So stop beating around the bush."

Caroline folded her arms and popped her hips which Travis knew meant business. He couldn't keep this away from her for long.

"I think Mayor Buchanan may be after you. I don't have evidence exactly but I get a bad feeling about him."

"A bad feeling? It's not like you to get all worked up over a bad feeling."

"It's true. It's just that I think my daddy might be involved."

"Atticus?"

"Yes."

"C'mon Travis, your daddy wouldn't do anything to hurt me."

"You know he's not into the way the town's getting more integrated. He's a traditional man and he has his flaws."

"It's *Atticus.*"

"C'mon Caroline. Take this seriously. He's also got Zach Owens involved. I think."

"Zach? Oh."

"Has Zach talked to you?"

"He stopped by today. I thought Bud was going to throttle him!"

"Maybe he should have."

"Travis!"

"Sorry," Travis mumbled, "I just don't trust what those two are plotting."

"I'll be careful."

Caroline approached the door to the barn and Travis jumped in front of her, stopping her from leaving.

"I'm serious, Caroline. I need you to back off from whatever it is you're doing. I know you. Don't poke the bear."

"I'm not going to poke the bear."

"So you've given up trying to find proof that Buchanan bought the election?"

"Not exactly..."

"That's what I mean. You need to stop this. Stop before you get hurt."

"I won't get hurt."

"Please, Caroline. I'm begging you."

Travis' blue eyes bore into hers as he made her promise.

"I don't believe Zach Owens would do anything to hurt me, okay? I'll back off, but it's *Zach*. If nothing else, he won't want Chase to kill him. Trust me."

"Chase doesn't trust him."

"Chase doesn't trust anybody."

"Caroline..." he pleaded.

"Fine. I'll back off."

"Promise?"

"Sure."

"Care..."

"I promise..."

9

BROTHERS IN SPIRIT, BROTHERS BY BLOOD

"WHAT ARE you doing here so early?" Chase grumbled as he came out onto the front porch where Caroline sat, her wet hair slicked back into a tight bun, and a white dress hugging her curves.

"I needed to talk to you."

"It's early."

"I know. It's also the one day you've had off all month."

"Fine. Fine. Let's go for a walk. I don't want to wake the whole house."

"Fine by me."

Caroline and Chase walked down the street together keeping a respectable distance from each other. The last thing either of them wanted to do was attract any kind of attention.

"Travis told me you think Zach is involved in some kind of conspiracy with the Mayor."

"Jeez, Caroline. That's what you wanted to talk about?"

"Is it true?"

"I don't know. Zach's a weird guy but I don't think he'd hurt you."

"I didn't think so either. You were still suspicious though."

"At first. But I've been keeping an eye on him and maybe I was wrong. He's been trying to get his life together."

"He told you he was applying to college?"

"Yeah, and apparently he's getting lessons from the best."

Caroline giggled.

"If you want, I can talk to him and find out what he's up to. I'll even ask him to help on your little project to dig up dirt on our dear mayor."

"About that… Travis told me to drop it and I promised him I would."

Chase laughed.

"Yeah. I probably shouldn't have promised."

"You never let anything go, Caroline — never."

"I know. Shit. I'm such an asshole, aren't I?"

"Maybe. How would I know?" Chase replied with a wink.

"Will you help me then? Don't tell Travis I asked you to do that."

"Don't worry princess, I can keep a secret."

"Princess? You've got to stop hanging around Bud."

"What can I say," Chase teased, "I kind of like the sound of it."

"Zach might be a cop, and I know you don't like that, but as far as I know, he's always been loyal to you."

"Loyal to me, not loyal to my dad."

"Your dad went to prison. Zach was young. He probably blames him for abandoning your family."

Chase grunted.

"Will you ask him for help?"

"Sure. I'll ask," Chase sighed, "You have a way of getting under my skin, Caroline Coulson."

"I'll take that as a compliment, I guess..."

"It is a compliment. Not many women can get me riled up the way you do. Not many women would be willing to be...shared."

"Now is *that* a compliment?" Caroline asked.

Chase shrugged.

"It is if you want to be. I'm happy. Travis is happy. Bud is happy. All we care about is that you're happy too."

It was nice to be cared for like that. Caroline liked having all three boys fawning over her. If they were worried about her being content, they didn't have to be. Chase walked Caroline around town and then back to her house. The sun was coming up and neither of them wanted rumors to start about the two of them being an item.

"I guess I'll have to look for a job soon," Caroline sighed as Chase brought her to her front porch.

"Chin up, something will come along soon."

"What are you going to do today?"

"Sleep. Get drinks with Travis later. Nothing much."

"You boys have fun. But not too much fun."

Chase tipped his hat and left Caroline on her front porch. She'd assuaged his suspicions about Zach for the time being. She made a good point about the man turning over a new leaf. Didn't everyone deserve a second chance? From what Travis said, Caroline couldn't believe the Sheriff would hurt her either. Considering what happened to his dad, Chase wasn't so sure.

Chase crawled into bed and slept all day. He missed the sound of Zach arguing with his mother. He missed the man from the dairy coming to the front doorstep to drop off their empty bottles.

He missed Bud Landry stopping by to borrow his copy of "Shane" to struggle through it. He missed Zach heading out to work and his mother sitting on the stairs clutching her handkerchief and the last picture she took with their father.

By the time Chase woke up, he had a knot in the middle of his back from work at the factory and the sun was just setting. He hobbled down the stairs to find his mother in the kitchen.

"Hey, ma."

"You've been sleeping all day I thought you were damn near dead."

"Not quite."

"Do you have the money for the light bill yet?"

"Not yet. They're paying us late this month."

"Dang it."

"I know. We're trying to get something organized, ma."

Her thin lips pursed and she nodded.

"What's that look for?"

"You sure you ain't given that money to Caroline?"

"Ma, how could you say that?"

"Nothing. I know you boys are loose with your wallets when you're sweet on someone."

"I ain't sweet on Caroline, ma. We're friends."

She tutted and shook her head.

"Ain't no such thing as a man and woman being friends. You're old enough to know that by now."

"I didn't give her the money. That's all you need to know."

"Alright. I believe you. Now come over here and try this casserole."

Chase tasted the casserole.

"Delicious."

"Good. Now you go on out and have a life tonight. You can't stay here cooped up in the house."

Even now, she still mothered him, even if Chase was far from needing it and despite his small income, he only stayed at home to take care of her. There were some things Zach didn't care to do that Chase always took the time for when it came to his ma.

"Where's Zach?"

"He left hours ago."

"Why? He ain't working today."

"Yes he is. He said he was meeting the *sheriff*."

Chase's heart sank when he saw the proud look in his mama's eye. Despite everything, Zach was her golden boy. She was proud of him for becoming and officer and for doing something that wasn't backbreaking labor. Chase felt a pang in his chest. If only his ma knew what he was planning at the factory. Maybe then she'd realize how much her son cared for her.

"I'm meeting Travis in a bit. Want me to fetch anything for you on the way home?"

"No, no. You go out and have fun. And stay out of trouble!"

"Sure thing."

Chase met Travis a block from the bar. For once Travis was out of that stiff, infuriating cop uniform. Chase was more forgiving with his oldest friend than he was with his brother. Travis had real pressure to join the force. His daddy had all but done his police academy exams for him. And even then, Travis always wanted out. He was saving for college now. Atticus made sure the man would be trapped in town and understandably, Travis was a few years behind the typical college age. If there was anyone Chase trusted to do it, it was Travis. And hey, maybe he'd be great in politics someday like he'd always dreamed.

"Did you tell Caroline we were meeting up?"

"Yeah. I did. She thinks we should back off from Zach and Atticus."

Travis grunted and stuffed his hands in his pockets. Even out of uniform, he dressed more crisply than Chase, who never went anywhere without a little dirt on his boots.

"We'll back off if they give us a reason to trust them."

"I dunno Travis. Maybe we're being a little harsh. I mean if *Caroline* trusts them."

"Maybe you're right. She does have decent judgment about people."

"Yeah."

"But she's not perfect," Travis finished.

His statement hung in the air. No, Caroline wasn't perfect. But wasn't that why they loved her? It was why Travis turned down wheat-haired Shannon and why Chase had allowed his relationship with Claire-Marie to fizzle out. Caroline was everything to them and if she asked her boys to heel, she was the only one who could ever get them to do so.

Travis pushed the door open and the scents of beer, sweat and salt wafted into their faces. Travis and Chase slid into the first seats they could find at the dark bar. It wasn't the busiest day of the week, but the country music was still too loud to hear yourself think.

"Ay Officer. Off-duty tonight?" Jim Beam (yes, that was his real name) the bartender asked.

"Two shots of tequila," Chase called, a mischievous grin tugging at the corners of his lips.

"No way, Jim. Ignore that. Two cans of PBR."

"Cans?" Chase smacked Travis upside the head, "I ain't come all the way down here for you to wuss out. I said two shots of tequila. Let's go!"

Jim gave Travis a look that asked "are you okay with this?"

Travis gave up. That was why he'd gone out with Chase that night, right? Chase could get you to forget all your problems and he'd push you right to your limit.

Jim slid over two shots of tequila. Wild-eyed, Chase grabbed his and egged Travis on.

"After that we're gonna do another one. Ready? Ready? Jim! We want two more shots ready to go. C'mon, Travis. Let's do this."

ONE.

TWO.

Chase gestured again for Jim to pour them another shot.

THREE.

By then, the two of them had a little buzz going on and Travis could feel the weight of his suspicions lifting. He stopped worrying about Caroline and whether she'd find a job. He stopped worrying about someone in town finding out he was sharing a woman with two of his closest friends. He just felt... good.

The country music rocked and a pretty girl who was tits on toast came walking up to them in cowgirl boots, Daisy Dukes with a chicken cutlet booty hanging out and the biggest fake boobs they'd ever seen.

"How'd you boys like to dance tonight?" She drawled.

Chase and Travis exchanged glances.

"No thank you ma'am. We're awfully sorry but we're..."

"Married!" Chase finished for him.

"Aw shucks. Why do the good ones always have to be gay?"

As she stomped off disappointed, Chase and Travis couldn't help but laugh to themselves.

"Think she bought that a little too easy, officer," Chase slurred, "C'mon. Let's go shoot some pool 'fore more tongues start wagging."

Travis shrugged and followed Chase to the pool table. The dance floor was still crowded, and Hannibal had just finished playing a game with his new girl, a redhead from out of town. Chase chalked up the pool cue and stared across the way. He dropped the chalk.

"What's wrong with you? You look like you've seen a—

Travis turned around instead of finishing his sentence and peered through the parting of bodies in the dance floor that Chase stared at. They two men were huddled at a table in the corner, talking in hushed voices to Tommy Lee Buchanan with hats tipped over their eyes so at first they were hard to recognize. You couldn't miss Tommy Lee's white suit though, which rendered their attempts at disguise laughable.

"Sonuvabitch," Travis hissed.

"Let's get out of here, Travis. I don't want 'em catching on."

Travis nodded and followed Chase out the door.

"What the hell was Zach doing with my father?" Travis hissed once they were outside.

"I dunno but it looked like they were up to no good."

"Caroline was wrong."

"Think we should tell her?"

Travis thought it over for a bit. For Chase to ask his opinion on it meant Chase didn't have a clue what to do either. Travis bit the bullet and shoot his head.

"No, sir," he said, "We'd better keep this between you and me for now. Let's just tell her to be careful. We don't want to worry her and we can look into it on our own."

Travis added, "And let's not tell Bud. You know he can't keep a secret from Caroline."

"Alright. You know best."

"Yeah. I'm drunk as a skunk right now though."

Chase laughed and through his laughter he suggested,

"Let's get another drink at the Dark Horse instead. Then we can figure out a plan for how we're gonna catch these bastards."

Chase swung his arms over Travis' shoulder and singing an old factory tune, they drank at the tavern until late into the night.

10

FINDING A JOB? IN THIS ECONOMY?

"WHERE ARE you going dressed up like a funeral director?" Caleb asked.

"Is it that bad?" Caroline groaned.

"It's horrible... Don't you have anything that fits?"

"I've been gaining weight lately," Caroline complained, "I can't help it."

"Uh huh. Well maybe you'd better buy some clothes."

"With what money?"

Caleb reached into his pocket and handed Caroline a twenty.

"What am I supposed to buy with this?"

"I dunno."

"This won't get me half of a shoe!"

"You've got to lower your standards, Caroline. This ain't the big city."

Caroline rolled her eyes and grabbed the twenty.

"Fine. I'll get new clothes. But I still have a job interview today."

"Where?"

"Peabody Elementary."

Caleb snorted.

"What?"

"You're looking for a job on the white side of town?"

"Segregation is over, Caleb. Peabody pays better than our school and there's no law saying I can't teach there because I'm black."

"C'mon Caroline. You know as well as I do that the law don't matter. They'll do whatever they want and you can't prove it was discrimination."

Caroline turned her nose up haughtily.

"Not everything is about race like that Caleb."

"Yes, it is."

"Can you stop being so 'woke' for a second? Some white guys are nice. What about Chase..."

"I never said Chase wasn't nice!"

"Stop being so paranoid then," Caroline huffed.

"Jeez Caroline, it's not paranoid. I just don't want anything to happen to you. That's all."

"Oh."

"Yeah. My fault for caring I guess."

"I'm sorry, Caleb."

"That's okay. I'm a bit stressed is all. All that union planning wears down on you."

Caroline squeezed her brother's hand.

"You be careful. I can handle myself."

Caroline kissed her brother on the cheek and walked to her job interview. She made it on time to Peabody Elementary and when she arrived at the school doors, the thought crossed her mind that she'd made a mistake.

Did she really have to shoot for the highest salary? Shouldn't she be helping her people? Caroline bit on her lower lip as she thought about her parents. They needed money now more than ever. She had to do what was best for them. Politics aside. This was the only place in town that paid as well as the mayor's office.

As Caroline walked into the interview room, her stomach sank. Something here didn't feel right.

She tried to calm that feeling and tell herself that she was exaggerating about the hostility coming from her interviewers. At the end of the interview, the women were so quiet, you could hear a pin drop.

"Bless your heart, Miss Coulson. Maybe you'd do better finding work at the *other* elementary school. We want to make sure our new hire *fits in* at Peabody. You understand, don't you sweet heart?"

That was it. No chance. Caroline cursed herself as she stormed toward the factory, tears running down her face. Caleb tried to warn her and she'd walked in there guns blazing actually expecting these women to be impressed by her credentials, work experience and dazzling cover letter.

They'd only seen one thing: the color of her skin. And because of that, they turned her down. Caroline was one tough cookie but damn, how tough does a girl have to be? When can a black woman just break down and admit getting treated like dirt hurts like hell?

By the time Caroline made it to the plant, she could hear from the sound of the machinery and the foreman yelling at the top of his lungs that the boys weren't on their break yet. She sat outside beneath the magnolia tree and hugged her knees to her chest.

Before Chase and Bud were on their break, Travis' police car pulled up to the curb.

"Hey, what the heck are you doing there?" Travis called out

the window.

Caroline rose and dusted herself off, sniffling and wiping her nose clean.

"Waiting for Bud and Chase."

"So am I. Care to join me?"

Travis got out of the car and opened the door for Caroline, so she slid in and leaned back.

"Another shitty day," Caroline sighed.

"You get puked on by a meth head?"

"No!"

"Happened to me at 9…"

"Please tell me you changed."

Travis laughed.

"Of course I changed. What happened to you though?"

"I tried to get a job at Peabody."

"Oh. Did you get it?"

"C'mon, Travis."

"Those women are friends with Mrs. Buchanan. That's probably why you didn't get it."

"Among other reasons," Caroline grumbled.

Travis thought it was a little awkward sometimes when Caroline brought up racism. It made him feel a little guilty and foolish, even if he hadn't done anything, he felt like it was his fault when some asshole treated her like crap because of her skin tone. He wanted to protect her from those types, and to tell her that this white man loved her, and he always would.

Instead of saying all that, Travis reached over and held Caroline's thigh. His hands were warm and made her feel safe. She closed her eyes and leaned her head on Travis' shoulders.

"You always know just what I need," she whispered.

Travis kissed her forehead and then pointed to the entrance of the factory.

"They're on their break. Let's go have a quick chat."

"Okay."

Travis let Caroline out first and she walked to the back where Chase and Bud staked out their secret spot. No one saw her go back there and five minutes later, Travis followed, looking clean and sharp in his uniform. Travis smelled like cologne and junior mints, which he sucked on like crazy in his car. Chase and Bud smelled like whiskey and hard work. Caroline loved the mix of them together.

"Caroline? What the heck are you doing down here?"

"Job interview didn't go so well."

"Shit. I'm sorry."

Bud wrapped Caroline in a big, warm hug. She pressed her head to his chest and sniffed. Bud's chest was so warm and safe that she almost started crying again. Chase tugged on her arm and wrested her from Bud's grasp.

"Cheer up. We've got you. Okay?"

Caroline nodded and stiffened her upper lip. Bud and Travis were great for comfort but Chase never stopped encouraging her to take action and to face her problems head on.

"Chase and I made a decision last night," Travis said.

"We're going to help you look into the mayor. We think it's about time we did a little digging."

"Do you guys mean it?"

"Listen, Caroline, if you think he cheated his way to the top, it's only the right thing to do."

Bud nodded, "Cool. You boys need my help?"

"Sure thing. Ain't nobody more well liked than Bud Landry. We'll see if Bud can distract the front desk and I'll take a visit to the mayor's office tomorrow," Travis whispered.

Caroline's expression brightened. Travis' promise meant more to her than he could have realized.

"Thank you," she said, "It means a lot to me."

"Hey, maybe then we can clear your name and you won't have so much trouble finding a job."

They wrapped Caroline in a big group hug and then Chase and Bud returned to work. Travis drove Caroline home, kissing her goodbye before she ran inside. Caroline always got a thrill when he kissed her like that — in broad daylight where anyone could see. She felt special when any of the boys did that. She felt like she *belonged* to them.

Caroline was happy that the boys finally changed their minds. She knew that what she believed about Mayor Buchanan was true. It didn't matter who else believed her really. She knew he bought the election and all Caroline needed was proof. Caroline knew in her spirit that man was up to something and with the help of the boys, finding the proof should have then become easy.

After a day or two, Caroline met up with all three of them at Chase's house. Chase, his mother, and his brother Zachariah were both out of town.

Zachariah was apparently taking this college thing quite seriously. According to Chase, he hoped to get into politics one day. Caroline thought he was doing well in their tutoring sessions. Although Zachariah unnerved her, he really gave her no reason to suspect him of anything. Caroline might have suspected Mayor Buchanan but she was far from paranoid. The way Caroline saw it, paranoia could easily turn ugly. That was the last thing she wanted.

Caroline showed up at Chase's house in the middle of the night. Caleb noticed her leaving but he didn't press her when she fed him an obvious lie about where she was going. Caroline wondered if her brother Caleb had noticed her changing relationship with the three boys.

The three had always been close. These days, they had been closer than ever before and Caroline couldn't stop thinking about each one of them. How had she ended up here? Caroline never thought she'd fall for any man.

She had never actually been able to picture herself just being with one man. In the past, Caroline thought this meant she wanted to be single forever. After all, she was in a town full of country boys and rednecks and she was a career woman where most women only wanted to stay home and have babies.

One man had never fit into her dream. But three? Caroline had been unable to predict that either.

Pushing the door open to the Owens house, quiet blues music greeted Caroline. She wasn't a huge fan of the blues, but Chase was always going on about how the blues were the ultimate soundtrack to a working class man's life.

He always said funny deep things like that even if he'd never gone to college. Caroline still thought he was the smartest person she knew. Back in her university days, she hated how everyone thought you could only be smart if you had gone to a prestigious school. They'd never known Chase Owens, or Caleb, or any of the other folks stuck in town, pinned down by their circumstances, not their lack of intelligence.

In Old Town, Caroline saw that sometimes the smartest people simply didn't have the opportunities to go to college. Chase for example had taken care of his mother and brother from the day he turned 18. His father had been arrested a year later and he had become the man of the house overnight. Caroline couldn't blame him for not seeing college in his future. She still thought he was stinking smart.

Bud was already a little tipsy. He took her by the hand and spun her around the room rocking her back and forth in a hilarious dance that was some mixture of a foursquare and a line dance. Travis sat beneath a lamp on the couch nursing beer in a glass bottle. He was brooding again.

Travis was always thinking. He was always the big protector out of all of them. Even if Bud was about twice Travis's size in elementary school, Travis had the quick wit to realize when others were taking advantage of Bud's likability, and he'd fought off bullies and grifters who were quick to take advantage of the weak. He wore the uniform because of his idealism. Caroline flashed Travis wink that he didn't catch.

Chase eventually cut in and as he held Caroline close and swayed back and forth, he sung the blues tunes to her in his deep bass voice. She could stand there listening to his voice forever and feeling the protective gaze of her other two men. This was bliss.

This was a bliss she never thought she deserved. Could one black woman really be so beautiful and so enchanting to attract three strapping young white men? Maybe in the past, Caroline would have questioned her worth. After all, her town wasn't forward thinking and she knew how certain people thought of her would never change. With Travis, Bud, and Chase, she never had to question whether or not she was worthy. Each of them loved her deeply and even if they had not said it yet, Caroline knew that it had always been true.

After watching Caroline and Chase dance together for a while, Travis determined it was time to cut in. He took her hand and he swung her around the hardwood living room floor that Chase had installed himself, keeping Caroline at just enough of a distance so he could stare into her beautiful deep brown eyes. Travis loved brown eyes. Everyone in his family had eyes the color of the summer sky and so he had always been entranced by the opposite — a deep enchanting almond brown color that stirred something deep inside him.

"I've been waiting all day for this," Travis whispered and he kissed Caroline slow and deep.

That was how the tone of their nights often changed. Someone would planted a kiss on Caroline's lips and then they would quickly descend into a sex romp unlike any other. Dancing, and laughing and then holding onto each other, grasping at pleasure in each other's arms...

As far as Caroline was concerned, there was nothing wrong with that. She closed her eyes and allowed Travis to kiss her neck. As he kissed her, she could smell Bud approaching behind her with heavy footsteps, his sexy man musk wafting into her nostrils.

Chase came up on her other side and he kissed her neck as Travis kissed her cheeks. Bud ran his large hands all over her body, squeezing the firm and soft bits with equal amounts of pleasure and desire. He enjoyed owning her like this. All of them did. These boys were so bonded together but they would really share anything — even love.

"We are all alone for the night. And, we can be as loud as we want as long as we crank up the stereo."

"Fine. But play something other than blues," Caroline whispered.

Bud knew what she wanted. He switched to an old R&B CD. Back in high school, Caroline had made the "mix tape" when it was popular to burn CDs for your friends. She made one for all three of the boys to share before even knowing how all four of them would end up. There was a track that made her think of Travis, his sky colored eyes and his blonde hair. There was a track that made her think of Chase, with his fiery passion, copper-colored beard, and his quick tongue. Then there was a song that reminded her of Bud, his enormous body, and the way he made love to her as if it were the last time he would ever have such a chance.

"Maybe we should slow down," Caroline pleaded. She didn't mean it and the boys knew it. They ran their hands over her and soon she was naked and six hands roamed all over her body. As one hand pinched her nipples, another tongue swirled around them and Bud's firm hand spread her ass cheeks apart and he dipped his finger deep into her tightness.

"I think it's about time we take her last hole," Bud grunted in his thick southern drawl.

Caroline became instantly wet but her common sense overrode her body's pure physical reaction to Bud's suggestion.

"Are you crazy? I've never done that!"

"I think you're ready," Bud suggested.

Chase and Travis stared at her intensely now. Hovering under all three of their gazes, Caroline felt her cheeks turn a mulberry color. For all the ways they spread her apart, licked at her flesh and pawed at her, she was still the one in ultimate control. She was still the one who decided whether or not to let them inside her. She could stand having all three men make love to her and push their massive members inside her tight pussy, but what about her ass? That forbidden tight puckered hole was completely pure. It was the one place where Caroline was still a virgin. No man had spread her almond ass cheeks apart and entered her there.

Could she really give them that? Could she really commit to belonging to all three of these men in such a powerful and painful way?

"Can you promise me it won't hurt," Caroline breathed.

"We can be careful Caroline. None of us would do anything to hurt you," Chase chimed in.

All three of them were practically salivating with desire for her. If there was anything that turned Caroline on, it was all three men all madly in love with her, and more than that, all three of them utterly devoted and faithful to her. All three of them were loyal to her the same way she was loyal to them. Faithfulness isn't only about being honest to one person. It was about being honest to all of them. And honestly? Caroline was totally smitten. And, she was finally ready.

"Be careful. I don't know if you three will be able to fit in a hole that tight," Caroline whispered.

Despite her appearance of protest, more to protect the last shreds her remaining virginity, Caroline craved what they suggested more than she could admit. She wanted three men between her legs.

She wanted them to rebel against everything Old Town wanted for them. She wanted to turn them into *her* alphas. No woman in this town could say she had the three hottest, most eligible bachelors completely smitten with her.

Caroline stuck her butt out so Bud could grab it and squeeze her cheeks. A shiver ran down her spine as Caroline gave up control to all three men. All three of them could fuck her in the ass and own it. She was finally ready.

Travis led Caroline to the couch and bent her over the arm. Chase went to get the lube. Bud brought Caroline a shot of tequila. What better drink is there for when you're about to put three big dicks up a virgin asshole? Caroline took the shot gracefully. This wasn't what she prepared for but when it came to her boys, Caroline had a knack for finding her way into trouble.

Travis kneeled between Caroline's legs. She dripped love honey like a ripe papaya. Caroline moaned as Travis pressed his tongue inside her pussy lips getting her nice and wet. As she stood, he could lick all the way from her clit to her asshole in smooth strokes. Caroline moaned and then Travis focused his attention on her back door, pressing his tongue against her clean, sensitive and forbidden hole.

He ate her ass like soup, slurping at all the right crevices and using his tongue to make slick every last inch of her flesh. He sucked on her skin and dove back down to her pussy eventually bringing his tongue back to lick at her sensitive asshole.

Caroline never experienced primal lust like this and as Travis' tongue went places no man's tongue had gone before she couldn't help but explode. She moaned, gripping Mrs. Owens' decorative pillows as Travis thrust his tongue inside her tight little booty hole. Juices dripped down her thighs and Travis rose to his feet just as Bud got down on his knees between her legs. He roughly spread her thighs apart and moaned, "Don't move."

Some men are born to eat ass. Bud was one of those men. He licked his lips like he was about to dive into the Applebee's full rack of ribs and drool slid down his beard as he pushed his head between Caroline's thighs, burying them there as his tongue went buck wild between her legs. When he wasn't sucking on her pussy lips his tongue was buried two inches inside her ass and he licked at the puckered sensitive flesh surrounding her hole which was lubed up and pulsing open and closed with anticipation of three fat hot cocks stretching her wide.

Bud dribbled and vibrated his lips, motor boating Caroline's homegrown ass cheeks as she moaned and arched her back. This backwater redneck loved nothing more than eating black pussy and pounding her big black ass. Caroline climaxed as Bud added two fingers into her pussy while he buried his tongue in her butt. She came so hard that for a moment, points of light flashed before Caroline's eyes.

She collapsed over the arm of the couch as Bud lifted his head, his beard soaked with the creamy juices from her tightness. Chase positioned himself behind Caroline and pressed his crotch against hers. She moaned and arched her back as he taunted her with what was coming next…

As Chase stripped behind her, Bud squirted lube over her ass and pussy although Caroline was so wet she almost didn't need it. Caroline squeezed her eyes shut and prepared to be stretched by Chase Owen's thick cock. The girth of Chase's cock would split her pussy wide and prepare her for the onslaught of thick pulsing man meat. Chase took his head and probed at Caroline's entrance before sliding inside her tight sleeve. There was no need to be careful now. Her pussy gushed like an ocean and he groaned as her tightness clamped hard around his cock gripping him like a vice.

"Please…" Caroline whimpered, "Harder…"

All the teasing from all the tongues she encountered drove Caroline over the edge. She was terrified by how horny she was and how badly she craved all three of the readied cocks between her thighs. She needed all three men to satisfy her filthy urges and to awaken the sex goddess trapped just beneath the surface. Chase thrust deep inside Caroline and moved his hips hard and fast within her tightness and in a few short strokes, Caroline couldn't help but explode, cumming all over Chase's mighty, thick cock. He groaned and pumped into her harder, his hands slipping over her lubed up ass cheeks as he drove deeper and deeper inside her.

"Yes, oh yes… give it to me Chase…"

Caroline collapsed onto her stomach as she climaxed again and her juices squirted out of her pussy all over Chase's cock. He pulled out only after Caroline had cum so many times her voice was hoarse and only after he dropped head to toe in sweat. Chase pulled out without cumming. He saved his load of white seed for Caroline's perfect, untouched ass.

As Chase moved away from her pussy, more juices dribbled down Caroline's slit and Travis took his place behind her. While he hadn't suggested what would happen that night he had fantasized about getting deep inside Caroline's ass for years. The tight satiny heat sandwiched between the full voluptuous cheeks of her booty drove him wild. This was his kink — having this pretty, sexy black woman bent over and spreading her tightest, tiniest hole for his pleasure.

He pried her asscheeks apart and Caroline shuddered with anticipation. This was madness. Just when Caroline thought she couldn't surrender more completely to the three men, she slid deeper into rebellion. Travis pressed the tip of his cock to her entrance and he could feel Caroline's thighs tending nervously.

"Easy princess," Travis murmured. Bud stroked her spine and Chase pushed the hair out of her face, kissing her as Travis eased the head of his cock past her entrance tenderly. Caroline moaned and arched her back as Travis pushed his lube-covered cock head just past the tightest muscles of her asshole. It hurt less than she expected. Travis stroked her back as he slipped another inch past her tight sphincter. That was when the pleasure started — an intense and taboo euphoria.

She moaned as Travis buried himself between her legs inch by inch. Caroline arched her back and allowed him to spread her cheeks with his monster cock. She moaned as Travis reached the hilt of his cock and his full length was buried inside her. Caroline never felt so *full* before. Travis' cock throbbed in her ass and stimulated every inch of not just her ass but her tight, dripping pussy.

Bud thrust his tongue down her throat as Travis moved his

hips and started pounding Caroline's ass from behind. Caroline's pussy dripped as Travis' pounding made her cum so hard. Her juices squeezed out of her pussy like a summer peach as Travis' anal pounding brought Caroline to a climax.

He thrust into her deep and hard, claiming her ass as his own and completing his fantasy of watching her big beautiful brown butt cheeks bouncing around his engorged white cock. After Caroline's third climax, Travis couldn't take it anymore. He groaned and released inside Caroline's tight ass.

As his white seed spilled out of her puckered hole, Chase took his position behind Caroline. Bud continued to fondle her nipples and kiss her while Travis fell into the armchair, covered in sweat and red-faced from euphoria. He'd never been inside something as tight as Caroline's asshole. She was tight succulent perfection… in every sense of the word.

Chase had never lusted after the chocolate starfish. What he liked was sex where he could take control. He loved sharing women, and his kink was watching a woman experience as much pleasure as he'd allow. Now that Caroline's gaping asshole presented itself to him, Chase saw another way he could dominate, another way he could feel that surge of arousal and control he got when he took charge in the bedroom.

His cock stiffened at the sight of cum seeping out of Caroline's hole. That would make her nice and slick and she'd be putty in his arms just the way he liked it. Chase cleared his throat and growled, "I hope you're ready to cum hard as I fuck you in the ass princess…"

Caroline moaned as Chase slid his immense cock into her tight puckered hole. They both groaned as he buried his cock up to the hilt in one stroke.

Chase pounded into her tight hole nice and slow, taking advantage of how tight her asshole clamped down around his thick cock. Her bubble butt jiggled around his hardness as he slid inside her and pleasure mounted in Caroline's core before she exploded in a hot climax. As she screamed and moaned, Caroline could barely hold her balance. Bud held her up as Chase pummeled her deeper and then groaned as he planted his seed deep inside her tight ass.

He pulled his cock out slowly and Caroline shuddered as he moved out of her ass and left her bare, gaping and ready for another one. When Bud left his position on the couch, Caroline's heart raced even faster. She'd forgotten that the last cock she had to take was Bud's. Bud's enormous dick would stretch her even more and push her even more to her limits.

Caroline gripped a throw pillow and her legs shook as cum from two men spilled down her thighs. Bud's belt came off and she winced, her legs trembling faster. Bud's hand touched Caroline's back, and her troubles melted away. His touch traveled down her spine and Caroline exhaled slowly.

"There, there, you ain't got nothing to be scared of. Bud's gonna take care of you."

Caroline squeezed her eyes shut as she felt the engorged tip of Bud's enormous uncut cock pressing at her slickened back door. Usually Bud was rougher, wilder and more untamed than the rest of the men. Caroline finally found a way to get him to slow down: allow him access to her tight asshole.

He plunged inside nice and slow so Caroline barely felt any pain, only pleasure as his massive cock was buried up to the hilt inside her ass. As Bud's big dick was buried in her ass, Bud took one of his rigid thick fingers and plunged it inside Caroline's juice pussy.

Then Bud moved his hips, easing out of Caroline's tight asshole as his fingers massaged her dusky pussy lips. Caroline whimpered and moaned as Bud eased his hardness back into her and rubbed her with his hands. Sensations from both her holes stimulated Caroline to cum hard…

After she'd cum for the first time with Bud, he plunged between her legs faster. He was wild again and as he pumped his enormous cock between her legs, Bud thrust his finger into her dripping wet pussy. Caroline climaxed again and Bud unleashed his full potential, grunting and groaning as he pounded her ass from behind and as Caroline screamed in pleasure.

Her pleasure intensified when Travis and Chase attacked her breasts with their tongues, sucking the pleasure out of her tits as Bud used her ass well with his big hard redneck dick. Caroline came again and again and Bud roared as he climaxed inside her. As his cock throbbed Caroline moaned in pain. The giant member pulsing and throbbing between her legs stimulated her sensitive skin and as Bud pulled out of her, the two of them collapsed in a heap of arousal and desire. Chase and Travis pulled their lips away from Caroline's tits and they threw a blanket over her.

That night, all of them slept together on the floor in a heap of blankets and pillows and euphoria.

Travis left early in the morning to meet his daddy at the gym. Once a week, Atticus Montgomery spent one on one time with his son, pumping iron and getting details about Travis' life. These days, Travis had been far too quiet and brooding. Atticus always knew he had a serious child, one who saw it as his God given duty to care about everyone and everything under the sun.

Atticus was proud of the boy but concerned. This whole business with Tommy Lee and that colored girl was giving him plenty pause about Travis' judgment. You can't save everyone, Atticus thought to himself. That Caroline woman was no different. Sure she was smart and all, and he knew Caroline like a daughter.

But messing with politics was well out of line. I mean, what did she really expect? The town had a way that things always were and it was called tradition for a reason. It's not like Atticus hated progress. Hell, he'd let Caroline into his home, hadn't he? He just didn't think it made sense for colored folks to be governing the town. It just wasn't right. They'd be petty leaders and they'd probably all try to get revenge on the white man. Atticus had limits. I can't let this town go to hell in a hand basket, he thought to himself.

Travis was late to the gym by 30 seconds.

"I would've never got away with that in the Marines," his father chided.

"Sorry. Got caught up this morning."

"Ain't any excuse."

"Sorry, dad. I'm ready to go. C'mon."

They started on the treadmill, working up a sweat after a hard two miles. Exhausted from his late night romp, Travis struggled to keep up with his father, though he could never show the old man any weakness without getting a lecture.

After a hard run, they pumped iron on the bench press, the squat bar and they deadlifted weights until Travis' arms turned to jelly. He groaned and flopped onto a bench to have a drink of water.

"Out drinking last night?" Atticus said gruffly.

"No. Hanging with Caroline."

"Hanging?"

"I already told you, there's nothing going on between the two of us," Travis grumbled.

"Listen, I know you better than you think, boy. You're sweet on her, I can tell."

Travis scowled. He hadn't dragged his ass off Chase's couch to get another lecture from his dad about what was best for him. He could figure that out for himself, thank you very much.

"Glaring at your shoes won't do much for you," Atticus continued unsympathetically, "You know, this Caroline has been snooping around the mayor's office since she's been fired. Mr. Calloway down at City Hall said she came to look up polling records and district boundaries from the last election."

"Maybe she's looking for a job at the newspaper," Travis offered weakly.

He was starting to feel sick to his stomach. His father bringing up Caroline again, and the fact that he saw him in a clandestine meeting with the mayor and Zachariah Owens troubled him deeply. They were up to something, and now he'd found out they had eyes on Caroline all over town. Damn it. He'd warned her to be careful, but she'd still managed to attract attention.

"I don't think so, boy," Atticus grunted, "Either way, you stay away from her. Trouble's brewing and I don't want you to lose your career for associating with the wrong folks. I'm sure you don't want to disappoint your mother."

Disappoint you, you mean, Travis thought. He rose, his face twisted in a scowl.

"I appreciate the sentiment, father, but I can take care of myself. I'm a grown man. Even if I've stuck around to take care of ma, that doesn't mean I can stand on my two feet without you."

Before his father could say another word, Travis grabbed his gym bag and stormed off.

11

DADDY GAVE ME A WARNING

CAROLINE CAME HOME in the morning looking more worn out than before. Caleb watched his sister sneak into the house. She thought she could get past him, but he could always hear her footsteps and sense when she was the front door.

They weren't so close anymore now that she always seemed to be chasing after some neighborhood redneck. Or more likely, Caleb realized, they were the ones chasing after her. These white boys like to have their social status and their vanilla neighborhoods but they'd all get tempted by a little chocolate.

They all wanted a taste of life on the other side of the tracks and for some reason, they thought they could find it here, with his sister. Caleb was friendly with Chase Owens. Chase was a decent enough guy and his work on an integrated union made him valuable. Bud wasn't so bad either. He was dumb as rocks but had a protective streak that Caleb liked about him.

It was Travis that Caleb didn't like so much. Travis was too cookie-cutter. He'd do whatever his father told him and he'd justify it later on. Caleb didn't think Travis was on his sister's side. He was one of those guys who would marry a Jackie, but he'd always have a hankering for a Marilyn. And Caroline was his "Marilyn".

"Out late with Travis?" Caleb called to his sister.

"Caleb! You scared me…"

"Sorry. I'm worried about you. I've heard talk that you went down to City Hall?"

Caroline set down her purse and sighed.

"I didn't think anyone knew about that."

"Be careful, Caroline."

"I was going to say the same thing to you, Caleb. What you and Chase are doing at the factory might attract the wrong kind of attention."

"Not half as bad as you starting a journalistic vendetta with our town mayor."

"You've seen Buchanan," Caroline protested, "He flies a Confederate flag outside his house. He believes in separating the races. Just when this town is finally making progress, he's sending us back to the 1960s. He's a bad person."

"That's exactly why you should stay away from him Caroline."

She rolled her eyes.

"Wow, if only Malcolm X had that sage wisdom."

"You're not Malcolm X! *You* went to university. *You* always walked on the right side of the law. Caroline, I love you, but you don't understand the type of people you're messing with."

"I understand that the only people backing me up right now are three white boys!"

"Yeah, real smart Caroline. Travis Montgomery is on your side…"

"He is! He's more on my side than you'll ever be. So leave me alone, Caleb. Just drop it!"

Caroline stormed off and Caleb didn't bother chasing after her or even responding with another snide remark. He'd just about had it with Caroline. She had a problem with Buchanan? Fine. She wanted to risk her life? Fine. But he couldn't have his mother and father left without a daughter.

Caleb got an idea. Maybe it was stupid, he thought, but then he changed his mind. He just needed time to plan and since he had the day off, he would do just that.

"I'm headed out!" Caleb called.

His parents were already out at work on Mr. Brown's farm. He'd given them some land to tend and they spent most of their time there. It didn't hurt that Mrs. Brown made mean chitlins and served it up with moonshine. Caroline didn't respond to her brother's call, so Caleb set out alone.

After a long day, Caleb was ready. Of course, he'd done other things but plot. He picked up some matches at the general store, paid the light bill, picked up groceries for his parents, bought gasoline, went over to drop off some chicken for Earl Samuel. Now visiting Mr. Samuel always took longer than usual. The disabled Vietnam veteran was lonesome while his family worked so he talked Caleb's ear off about HAM radios, the Soviets and even asked him to take a look at the bunion on his toe. By the time Caleb pried himself free, sunset crept over the horizon.

Caleb went home for supper. Caroline cooked pork and greens with yams on the side. The Coulson parents sensed tension between their kids but Caleb and Caroline often had little spats that amounted to nothing. Caleb washed up the dishes alone and changed his clothes, dressing in all black with a backpack over his shoulder. He pushed the front door open to leave only to find Caroline waiting right there for him on the porch.

"Just where do you think you're going?"

"Out."

"Dressed like a thief?"

"Yeah, I'm a thief, Caroline," Caleb snorted.

"Tell me where you're going then?"

"I'm going to take care of this Buchanan problem."

"What do you mean? Please tell me you aren't going to kill him."

"Not kill him. Send a message."

"Caleb..."

Caroline grabbed on her brother's arm, pleading with him to reconsider. Caleb shook her off and disappeared into the night. Caroline shuddered as she stood alone on the porch. Caleb could take care of himself, she knew that, but it was just as well if she waited awake for him to come home.

Caleb took the short cut through the patch of woods that put him behind the Buchanan house. Even if it was customary to take your flag in at night, the confederate flag still hung proudly outside the house.

Caleb could see it from behind the house and he could see that the streets were empty too. No lights were on inside. Either nobody was home or everyone was asleep.

Caleb's heart raced as he crossed the lawn to the front of the house. He froze when he heard the neighbor's dog bark. An old woman came outside and shushed the dog, but she didn't notice Caleb standing close to Buchanan's front porch.

He took the gasoline out of the bag. He'd filled a small carton with just enough to soak the flag. The stink covered his clothes and saturated the air with its heavy chemical smell. He pulled the flag down onto the lawn. This should send the exact message he hoped.

Caleb's hands shook so badly he fumbled with the box of matches and finally got one lit. He dropped it onto the Confederate flag and watched as the flames climbed higher and higher toward the sky, subsuming the flag. Caleb shoved the matches back into his bag and ran back towards the shortcut and toward the woods.

He threw the matches and gas into the creek that flowed through the woods and kept running until he came to the clearing just across from his house. He took off his shirt, then his pants. He'd worn clothes underneath that wouldn't smell like gas. He'd get these tomorrow and burn those too.

Caleb ran across the street and when he got to the front gate, he stopped to catch his breath. It was so quiet that Caleb couldn't even hear the cicadas. He could only hear his heart thudding in his ribcage and his labored, heavy breathing.

Caleb straightened his back and inhaled sharply. He got the terrifying sense that he was being watched. Maybe Caroline was up waiting for him still.

"Caroline?"

No answer. The porch light was off which meant she'd given up and turned in for the night.

"Caroline?"

Caleb heard footsteps but before he could react, a large man knocked him off his feet with a punch to the face. He choked and another man kicked him. There were three of them and as they attacked, Caleb screamed.

He heard his ribs snap and one of the men jumped onto his leg. Standing a few feet off from them, Caleb swore he saw a man in a white hood. He screamed. Another rib cracked and a boot soared toward his face.

"HELP! SOMEBODY!"

One of the men removed their balaclava. Zach Owens. Caleb's eyes widened and he screamed one last time before Zach Owens boot landed a final blow against his head. Caleb lay limp on the sidewalk outside his front porch, blood trickling out of his ear.

12

BUD'S GOT YOU

WHEN CAROLINE FOUND her brother's mangled body lying on the sidewalk the next morning she screamed so loud that she woke everyone on their side of town. She rushed to his body, unsure if he was warm or cold. If he were dead, shouldn't he be stiff by now.

"CALEB! CALEB WAKE UP!" She screamed.

Caroline let out another howl, so piercing that it rattled her ribs and her heart twisted into explosive pain. The light-skinned Mayfair teens ran out of their house. When they saw what was happening, Ezra ran inside to get the cops and his sister Bianca ran to Caroline's side in an attempt to stop her hysterics.

"HE'S DEAD!" Caroline screamed, "MY BROTHER IS DEAD."

"CALEB! NOO!"

By then, Pastor Fielding ran out of his house, dressed in his black clothes, with his baby Colby on his hip. The Pastor covered Colby's eyes and ran inside the Coulson house to get

Caroline's parents. Ezra couldn't get a hold of the police. The phone kept ringing and ringing, but no one answered.

Once Pastor Fielding explained to the Coulson what happened, they ran outside and Pastor Fielding took the phone to call for an ambulance. By the time the ambulance got there, Caroline's hysterics worsened and as the paramedics lifted her brother's body off the ground and tried to take him away from her, Caroline's screams grew deafening.

"DADDY NO! DADDY YOU CAN'T LET THEM TAKE HIM!" She screamed as her father, Kingsley Coulson wrapped his arms around his daughter as she kicked and screamed.

Caroline's mother, Nikita, rode in the back of the ambulance as Kingsley held his daughter back. Kingsley got his daughter into bed and she lay there, clutching her pillow and weeping for over an hour before she passed out from the exhaustion of it all. Kingsley Coulson didn't know what was best for Caroline.

Since she'd lost her job, the only thing that seemed to make her happy was hanging around Bud Landry. She thought it was a secret, but Kingsley noticed her daughter treating that oafish gentle giant how to read nearly every morning on the back porch. Kingsley never brought it up, but he'd noticed.

Kingsley called Bud and asked him to come over. He'd know what to do most likely. Afterwards, Kingsley called the police again, but the officer who answered gave him the runaround. Kingsley's heart fell to the pit of his stomach.

He'd lived through times when a black man could show up dead one day and the cops would do nothing. He'd believed those days were over. After all, his kids had white friends and the town was more liberal than ever. Sure, there were separate parts of town but it was nothing like the way it used to be. America had changed, hadn't it?

Kingsley sank into the sofa and bent his head to his knees. He prayed for his daughter and his son until Bud Landry knocked on his front door twenty minutes later. Kingsley shook Bud's hand and invited him in.

The phone rang.

"Sorry Mr. Landry, hope you don't mind I get that. Caroline's upstairs sleeping."

"Yes, sir. And I'm sorry for… for your loss, I guess."

Bud walked upstairs slowly. He wasn't too good at things like this. He'd lost someone when he was young, but by now that was so long ago. Most siblings didn't have the bond that Caroline and Caleb had.

If Caleb was going to die… Caroline would never be the same.

Bud knocked on her door.

"Caroline? You awake?"

"Bud?"

"It's me. Your daddy called."

"I'm a mess."

"No, you're *my* mess. Can I come in?"

"Yeah…"

Bud pushed the door open. It was dark, but he could smell tears and feel the weight of Caroline's pain.

"He was beat up," she blubbered, "He was beat up because of me!"

Bud pulled her close and hugged her close to his chest as she sobbed.

"It weren't because of you, Caroline… Don't you dare blame yourself."

"Travis warned me and I didn't listen…"

She cried and Bud stroked her hair. His touch always had that soothing effect on her and even if her heart still twisted in a million pieces, Caroline felt somehow safer with him. Bud only pulled away with her when they heard her father's footsteps creaking on the stairs.

Kingsley thrust the door open and said, "Caroline, Bud, you two come with me. Caleb's alive. He's in bad condition, but he's alive at the hospital. I think we oughta go down and see him."

Bud and Caroline piled into the back of her father's 2003 Nissan sedan. When they arrived at the hospital, Caroline and Bud raced ahead. Her mother sat in the waiting room, sniffling into a kerchief.

"We couldn't find a doctor that would treat him for over half an hour. But he just got out of surgery."

"Did you try calling the police again?" Caroline asked.

Her mother shook her head.

"I know what's going on. It's what's been going on for the longest time. I'm sorry you kids had to grow up in a world where something like this can happen to a black man and there would be no justice."

Her mother broke out into sniffles again. Caroline sat next to her and Bud rested his hand against Caroline's shoulder. The second Bud touched her, she breathed a sigh of relief. There was something comforting about his presence, something *understanding*. Even if everyone else thought Bud was slow, there was no one who cared more for people. He couldn't intellectualize his way into hatred, so he felt only love for the people around him. He saw their pain and he had that comforting, human touch that could almost make that pain vanish.

"When the nurse comes out, we can go see him," Nikita Coulson announced.

Her husband appeared and sat next to her. Bud offered to get water for the family and he walked toward the vending machine to get a bottle for everybody. Once he did, he sat next to Caroline and took his hand in hers.

"I'll call the boys in a bit. You just think about Caleb. And pray."

Caroline nodded and leaned her head on Bud's shoulder. For once, she didn't care what other people thought about her and him, or any of the boys. She was just glad to have him close and wracked with guilt over what happened to Caleb. They'd fought. Then he'd gone out and done something crazy stupid to prove he cared about her.

Caroline whispered in Bud's ear, "I can't stop thinking that it's all my fault."

"Shhh," he whispered, "Bud's got you…"

When Caroline went into the room to see Caleb, she winced at his face, bruised and bandaged. A giant cut slashed across his eye and crude stitches pushed the open flesh together. The attackers broke his ribs, the nurse said, and his legs. Caroline wept silently as she held her sleeping brother's hand. Now he had no job either, and there would be medical bills to pay.

Caroline kissed her brother's forehead, just barely.

"I promise I'll fix this, Caleb. I'm sorry," she sniffled.

At least he was alive. And according to the doctors, he'd be fine. After a long visit with Caleb, Caroline gave her parents some time alone with him. By then, Travis, Chase and Bud waited for her outside, standing together, a giant wall of country boy muscle, with grim looks on their faces.

"'We heard Caleb was attacked," Travis said, "Do you know who did it?"

"No," Caroline whispered, "I don't…"

Chase growled, "We'll find the sonuvabitch and we'll kill him."

Travis glared at him, "Can you keep your voice down renegade?"

"Sorry..."

"What do the cops say?" Travis asked.

Chase and Bud exchanged glances, wondering to themselves how their buddy could be so naive.

"They won't investigate," Caroline whispered through sniffles.

"Why not?"

"Travis, don't be dense," Chase piped up, "It's obvious there's some kind of cover up going on."

Travis glared again.

"Sorry, I'll keep my voice down."

"I just want to get out of here," Caroline confessed, "I don't see much of a point waiting around. My parents are with Caleb and I don't want to face that right now."

"Where do you want to go?"

"Anywhere."

Chase nudged Travis, "Should we tell her?"

"Sure," he shrugged, "It's up to her, anyway."

"Go on, spill."

"Travis found an address on his dad's desk. It's for a place up in Marathon."

"Marathon? Isn't that fifteen miles away?"

Travis nodded, his jaw doing that thing boys do when they're nervous that highlights the angles in their jawline.

"What do you think is out there?"

"Some kind of private meeting place. Maybe Buchanan's second home," Chase suggested.

"You boys going to check it out?"

"Sure thing."

Bud nodded and wrapped his arm around Caroline.

"We'll come along. It will be good to take Caroline's mind off everything."

"I'll tell my parents we're going out to lunch."

Caroline pushed the door open and said goodbye to her parents, giving Caleb's hand one last squeeze. They'd have answers soon, Caroline was sure of it.

They all piled into Travis' car and drove to the address in Marathon.

16 Melvin Street.

The house sat at the end of a cul-de-sac, and it was small and run down, not the type of place you'd expect mayor Buchanan to have. There was no sign of Sheriff Montgomery's car. Travis parked and sighed.

"Caroline, you come with me. You two stay here."

"Got it," Chase replied.

"Holler if you two need any help."

Caroline followed Travis out of the car and up the driveway.

"You okay?" He asked.

"No. Not at all. Caleb and I fought last night."

"We'll get to the bottom of this, Caroline, you don't have anything to worry about," Travis assured her.

"I wish I could believe you."

"Trust me," he whispered, in that strong, self-assured Travis voice she'd fallen in love with over the years.

Caroline continued guiltily, "It's my fault. You told me to back off, but you know me."

"It's not your fault for believing in something."

Travis knocked on the front door. No answer.

"Let's go around back and see if we can look through the window."

"Is that legal?"

"With my uniform on it is," Travis replied, a half smile tugging at the corners of his lips.

Caroline could sense he was nervous. She slipped her hand in his and Travis squeezed. They tiptoed around marigolds and chrysanthemums planted behind the house. Caroline noticed that the flowers were the only thing that made the house look lived in. Otherwise, the entire place was run down and covered with dead vines that grew over the steps and pushed up through the concrete.

"Look, there's a window," she whispered.

Travis nodded and approached.

"C'mon…"

Caroline joined him and got right up on her tiptoes so she could see what was happening inside. At first, it was too dark to see anything. Then her eyes adjusted to the light and Caroline gasped. Travis clasped his hands over her mouth. His jaw dropped.

"No…"

Sheriff Montgomery rose from the couch, naked. There was someone else beneath him. Caroline squinted, struggling to see who it was. The woman sat up and it was her turn to gasp. Clara Mayfair. She was the mother of the light-skinned teens that lived across the street. As she covered her smallish breasts with a t-shirt, a sickening feeling settled in Caroline's stomach.

Travis hissed, "Duck!"

His father was coming towards the window so the two of them crouched down low against the siding of the house.

"Atticus," Caroline breathed.

Travis' cheeks reddened.

"He's fooling around… That two-timing bastard!"

"Calm down, we need to get out of here before he notices."

"You're right…"

Travis turned around and slowly raised his head to the window. His father had walked away and they remained undetected.

Staying low to the ground, the two of them hustled off towards Travis' car.

"Don't have time to talk, let's get out of here," Travis announced, starting the car with urgent, trembling hands.

They drove back towards Old Town and Travis pulled over outside his house and shut off the car.

"You two gonna tell us what you saw? It's been a quiet twenty minutes," Chase grumbled.

"My father… is two-timing my ma. You happy."

Chase grinned.

"Damn right, I'm happy. We could use this as leverage to get him to talk and give us the proof about Buchanan."

Bud stayed quiet, but Caroline thought Chase had a good point. She didn't love the idea of blackmailing Atticus Montgomery, but didn't the ends justify the means?

"No. We can't use this," Travis said, "We have to find something else."

"Why the hell not?" Chase retorted.

"This would *ruin* my mother and destroy my family if word about this got out. We can't use it."

"But Travis…"

"I SAID NO."

"You don't make the decisions around here," Chase retorted.

Travis sighed and gripped the steering wheel tightly, responding to Chase in a suspiciously calm voice, "You're right. I'm asking you as my friend to keep this quiet."

"Fine. But we'd better find something else soon."

"You think my father had something to do with —"

An awkward silence descended over the car. Bud interjected, "We can't say anything for sure without evidence. So we'd better get to finding it."

"Thanks," Travis replied, "I know I'm asking for a lot."

"We'd do anything for you, Travis," Caroline said, kissing Travis on the cheek.

He let them out of the car. Bud walked Caroline back to the hospital. Chase returned home. Travis sat in the car and considered what could be done about his father's affair.

At the hospital, Bud waited outside with Caroline's parents as she went in to see Caleb again. By the time she made it back, the sun was about to set and a dusky orange light filtered through the hospital window casting light on Caleb's injured face. She sighed and pulled the blinds shut, approaching Caleb's bed.

"Caleb? Are you awake?" She whispered.

Caleb grunted hoarsely, "Care…"

She squeezed his hand, "Caleb, it's me… I'm sorry. I'm so sorry…"

Caroline broke down in tears again. Her brother squeezed her hand.

"Hey, don't cry. I made it."

"Who did this to you?" Caroline wept, "Please tell me you remember…"

"No. I don't."

"I'm getting scared."

"No, you're getting close. I wasn't sure if I believed you, but something is going on in this town. It's up to you to uncover it."

Caleb's words frightened Caroline. The fact that he lay there, injured because of her, frightened her even more. If Buchanan and whoever worked for him could come after Caleb, then they could come after her parents. They could go after whoever they wanted. She wasn't safe — that meant Bud, Chase and Travis weren't safe either.

Caroline understood why Travis wanted his secrets kept. News of his father's affair could destroy his family. Caroline's family had already been fractured. And what about all the other families that were now in danger because of what she knew?

Caroline knew that she could only confide in one person about Sheriff Montgomery's affair. Since Travis has expressly forbidden her from using what she needed, Caroline had to find a workaround. She knew that he would probably oppose what she was doing on moral grounds, but the next day Caroline called Chase to confess her intentions.

If it all went wrong, at least Chase knew where she was, and at least Chase knew that sometimes you had to play dirty in order to win.

Chase reacted calmly, agreeing that Caroline was making the right choice, and when he hung up the phone, Caroline left her parents house in search of the sheriff. As Caroline approached the police station, the most natural place to begin her search, she noticed Travis' car parked out front. Uh oh. Not good. She clenched her fists and with fierce determination, she powered ahead past his car.

That's when Bud, Chase and Travis got out and formed a barricade around Caroline on the sidewalk.

"What do you three think you're doing?"

"We're trying to help, Care," Travis said gently.

"Good. Follow me inside then and we'll approach Atticus together."

Travis scowled and folded his arms.

"That's not what we mean."

"Thanks for snitching, Chase. I can see what a good friend

you are," Caroline snapped, her brown-eyes narrowing into slits.

Even if she was furious with them, all three men couldn't help but think that she'd never been more beautiful.

"Care, don't be mad. It's just... cool off a little bit. Think things through."

"I've thought things through. And I've come to an important realization. None of you have my back."

"Caroline, that ain't true," Bud said, attempting to break rank and put his arm around her.

Travis held him back.

"If we didn't have your back, we wouldn't be here right now."

"Are you going to physically stop me from talking to the sheriff?"

Caroline waited for a response. Travis seethed but made no moves to stop her. Bud and Chase looked toward Travis for guidance but he didn't say a word. Caroline couldn't make eye contact with him. She felt too guilty about betraying him, about doing what she had always done — put politics and her interests first.

If she didn't put her interests first, who else would in this town? These boys loved her and they supported her in so many ways. One thing they couldn't understand was the color divide in town and how that made Caroline scared that they would turn on her, scared that at the end of the day, she would be the last one fighting this battle because she was the only one who had a real stake in it.

She marched into the police station alone, ready to face whatever hell she'd just brought upon herself. Caroline asked to see the sheriff and a receptionist with a mean stare and thin lips invited her to have a seat and wait because the sheriff was in a meeting.

Caroline waited for fifteen and then twenty minutes. She stared out the window and saw the boys waiting there, leaned up against Travis' car and engaged in a heated discussion. Travis stormed off toward the donut shop. Chase and Bud leaned in closer and spoke for a few more minutes before Bud walked toward the train tracks and Chase disappeared in the direction towards the factory.

The voices in the sheriff's office grew louder and Caroline heard another familiar voice that caused her to rise from her seat and tiptoe towards the door. The receptionist was engrossed in a game of spider solitaire that Caroline could see in the reflection of her glasses. She didn't notice Caroline get up or press an ear to the sheriff's door.

When she heard the voice more clearly, Caroline gasped to herself and knew what she had to do. Staring at the receptionist, she reached for the door handle and pushed the door open to Atticus Montgomery's office. Atticus stood next to the door while Tommy Lee Buchanan sat on his desk, dressed in a white linen suit.

He smiled when he saw Caroline.

"Speak of the devil and *she* shall appear," Tommy Lee stated, bowing his head mockingly.

"Mayor Buchanan, Sheriff," Caroline greeted them stiffly.

"What are you doing here, Caroline?" Atticus Montgomery growled.

"I came to talk to you. To both of you."

"Ah, so you're looking to write another unfounded smear piece?" Mayor Buchanan asked.

"No. I'm here to get you to do the right thing. I know something that you might not be aware of. I think when you hear it… you'll change your tune."

"Are you aware that *blackmail* and *extortion* are illegal and you're in a police station?" Tommy Lee asked again.

Caroline glared at Atticus and said sharply, "If the sheriff arrests me, he'll have to answer to his son and I don't think he wants to make their relationship any more tense than it needs to be."

Atticus averted his gaze. Caroline's heart raced. Finally, she was getting the upper hand around here and before long, she'd have what she wanted.

"Speak then, child. State your demands," Tommy Lee replied, a cocksure grin on his face.

He won't be smiling like that for long, Caroline thought to herself.

She folded her arms and paced back and forth across the office.

"I know you paid off officials at the polling station to rig the election. I know that from the very start, you've been lying to try to send this town back to the dark ages. You bought the election with money from the Buchanan estate, $4.7 million dollars to be precise. That's the exact amount that was listed at a 'charitable donation' to the departments of the four officials you would have had to pay off. I might not have all the proof yet, but I've done my research and now, you two are going to give me the evidence."

"That's a mighty fine story, Caroline," Atticus smirked.

"Isn't it? I know you were paid off, Atticus. The question is, why? That was the missing piece for me, the reason I believed you could never be involved in something like this. There was no why. And then yesterday, I saw where it is you spend your afternoons when you're not with Mrs. Montgomery."

Atticus blanched.

Tommy Lee rose and commanded, "Atticus, sit down."

"Tommy…"

"I said, sit down."

He rose and walked toward Caroline. Every instinct in her body screamed at her to sit down and to put more distance between herself and Mayor Buchanan. This man had ordered her brother to be beat to a pulp. He'd ruined her life already by getting her fired over the article. He was a liar, a violent criminal and common sense told Caroline to just back down.

The thing about revolutionary people, people who are determined to make a change, is that even when their bodies shake with fear, they're committed to an ideal bigger than themselves. That greater purpose keeps them strong when all control has left them.

Caroline summoned the strength of her ancestors and she got right up in Mayor Buchanan's face and hissed, "Nothing you say or do can scare me."

"I don't have to scare you! I just have to keep you quiet. I think you'll be kept quiet when I tell you what I know about you, Ms Coulson. This is something that not even Atticus knows…"

"I have nothing to hide."

"You might not. But see when you, Bud Landry, Chase Owens and Travis Montgomery get together…"

"What are you implying? Yes, I spend time with friends from high school. We grew up in the same town and Atticus knows that."

Atticus nodded. Tommy Lee chuckled.

"What Atticus doesn't know is that you're sleeping with all of these men… *all of them.* And they've been fucking you like the town whore all over town."

"Tommy," Atticus murmured.

Caroline's lower lip trembled. She couldn't cry in front of them. She couldn't break down and betray any of her emotions. How the hell had Tommy Lee Buchanan found out about them?

"You're awfully quiet, Caroline," Tommy said calmly.

"What you're saying is preposterous, Tommy. Caroline and — ...Travis would never..."

"Quiet, Atticus," Tommy hissed, "I am handling things."

"Now, you keep whatever rumor you've concocted about the sheriff and you keep it quiet missy. Because not only will we have you arrested, but we will make sure every person in town knows that you're the town whore. You... Your family... that brother of yours... all of you will regret crossing me."

He sighed, closing his eyes and breathing long and slow.

"Now... Nod if you understand," he replied, his eyes snapping open, cold and dark, the complete opposite of the man who played the role of beloved town mayor. Caroline saw in his eyes then what he was capable of.

She nodded.

"Say hello to your brother, Caroline. And tell him he ought to be careful. Now run along, doll."

Caroline turned and stormed out of the office, walking as quickly as possible out the door. She gasped when she finally reached outdoors and collapsed to her knees, clutching her chest. Caroline shuddered as tears streamed down her face. Travis and the boys were all gone. Caroline rose once her knees stopped shaking and she ran home.

When Caroline got inside, she read a note from her parents on the kitchen table. They were at the hospital with Caleb. Good. He shouldn't be alone right now. Caroline slept on the couch in the living room until a knock at the door awakened her. She woke with a start, her heart racing.

"Who is it?!"

"It's Mr. Hooper from the factory. I heard about your brother and we spoke to accounting to release his pay early afore the medical bills get too serious."

Caroline threw on a sweater and went to the door.

"Thanks, Mr. Hooper."

"How's Caleb?"

"Not doing too well."

"Shame what this town's coming to, isn't it?"

"Yeah. Have a nice day now."

Caroline waved goodbye. What this town was "coming to" was what it had always been for her family. This was nothing different from what life had been like in the 30s, 40s, 50s, 60s and so on.

Caroline sat on the couch with her brother's unopened check, her knees curled up as she contemplated what happened earlier with the mayor. She couldn't back down now, but she'd have to be careful. Without the boys to help, that would make it harder to.

Maybe I shouldn't have trusted them. Caleb always warned me about folks from their side of the train tracks, she thought.

Caroline had never seen the truth more clearly than she had that day. If she couldn't trust the boys to help her, who could she trust?

13

THIS IS HOW COWARDS BEHAVE

"CARRRROOOOLINNEEEEEE."

PITPITPITPITPIT.

Gravel peppered her window pane and Caroline sat up straight in bed. What time was it? Before wiping the sleep from her eyes, Caroline peered out the window and flung it open just as Bud launched another fistful of gravel.

"AHHHHHH!"

"Oh SHIT! Care, I'm so sorry!"

"WHAT THE HELL BUD?!"

"You're late."

"I'm not!"

"It's 8:30. Yes you are."

"Shit! I didn't think you were coming."

"I'm here. Unless you're still too pissed at me."

Caroline scowled and then relaxed her shoulders. Bud was the *least* of her problems. She wasn't the one he was really mad at.

"I'm coming downstairs. But you're still on probation."

Caroline's parents already left for work that morning so thankfully, Bud's crooning didn't wake anyone. She met Bud out on the front porch.

"Did you bring coffee?"

"Yes ma'am. A donut from *Krispy Kreme* too."

"Bud, the nearest *Krispy Kreme* is fifteen miles away…"

"I wanted to spoil you. I know you had a tough time yesterday in that office."

"How did you know that?" Caroline asked through a mouthful of glazed donut.

"'Cause Travis' dad pistol-whipped him last night and threw him out."

Caroline dropped the donut. Bud caught it before it hit the ground, anticipating her intense reaction.

"Is he okay?"

"He's got a black eye but he's fine."

"This is my fault."

Caroline's stomach turned. Someone else was attacked now because of her. Why did this keep happening?

"Here. Eat your donut," Bud replied.

Caroline took the donut from him and tried to stop herself from crying. It was her fault Travis was hurt. She just *had* to go in there guns blazing, didn't she…

"You don't worry about Travis. He's a big boy, he can take care of himself. I'm worried about you."

"Yeah, well you're the only one."

"That ain't true. Travis is messed up over his daddy but that don't — *doesn't* mean he stopped caring about you."

"Whatever. We should get to our lesson."

"Don't think about the lesson today," Bud said, "I learned something that I wanted to talk to you about. But you have to promise you won't talk to the guys about it…"

"Okay. What?"

"I found proof that Zach Owens is the one who told Buchanan."

"What? How?"

"Yesterday, after Travis got hit, I went back to the barn with my torch. I saw bootprints in the mud by the window. I knew I recognized the brand but I couldn't remember when until I stopped by Chase's place this morning."

"You saw Chase?"

"No. I didn't. Zach Owens was waiting outside and he wouldn't let me in. He was acting all shifty and when I looked down at his shoes, I realized he was the peeping Tom."

"What can we do about it? There's no way Buchanan is going to let us threaten Zach."

"I ain't scared of Buchanan. I ain't scared of Zach Owens either. I don't want to tell Chase 'cause you know how hot-headed he can get."

"He'd kill him if he found out," Caroline agreed, shuddering at the thought.

Chase was fiercely defensive, hot-tempered and often got himself into situations he would come to regret. Bud made a good point about not telling him.

"So your plan is to shake Zach down for information?"

"Something like that."

"I'm not letting you go alone."

"Suit yourself. It's my day off but Chase is down at the factory and Mrs. Owens is at work. Zach should be home alone."

"Okay. Let's go."

Bud and Caroline walked across the train tracks to the Owens house. Zach sat on the porch sharpening his pen knife.

"Hey Zachariah," Bud said, puffing up his chest with his hands stuck in his pockets, "Gotta minute?"

"What do you two want?"

"We want to talk. Inside."

"Yeah, I'm not going inside."

Bud grinned, "Sure about that buddy? 'Cause I don't mind shoving my fist up your ass right here for Mrs. Callaway to see."

Zach looked up from his pen knife and set it on the porch.

"I have nothing to say to you two."

"Let me make this real simple for you, Zach. You get your ass inside, or I'll give you a nice big cut to match the one Atticus gave Travis."

Zach rose to his feet and scowled.

"I don't take kindly to being threatened, Landry."

"Move along. I don't have time for this," Bud snarled.

For the first time, Caroline noticed how mean and scary Bud could look once he set his mind to it. Typically, he was a gentle giant. Woe betide the man who gets between a redneck and his girl.

Bud approached and Zach backed up towards the door, opening it and letting Bud and Caroline in. Zach kept distance between them as soon as they entered. He went to the kitchen and asked, "Can I offer y'all some sweet tea?"

Caroline sat, but Bud didn't. He rounded the counters into the kitchen and stood face to face with Zachariah Owens.

"No thank you. I'm here to talk about something serious."

"Get out of my face, man."

Bud grabbed Zach's hand, pulling the fingers back. Zach yelped.

"What the hell man!? Let go of me! What the hell did you do that for?"

Bud kept pulling them back as Zach screamed. He'd been caught off guard. His gun wasn't downstairs and now Bud had the coward trapped in the kitchen.

"We know that you're working for Buchanan and we want answers. You're going to tell us everything you know… *now*."

"Alright! Alright!" Zach squealed.

Bud kicked him in the chest anyway. Zach yelled and collapsed on the ground. Bud threw in one more kick in the shins.

"That's for Caleb Coulson. Now *talk*!"

"Alright, alright! But if I talk, I need you two to do me a favor… *please*…"

"We'll see about that," Bud growled.

Caroline tucked the slip of paper into her pocket. 4-3-5-1-6.

She didn't have to write the numbers down to remember them. She'd never forget until she had her hands on the documents. She walked briskly alongside Bud, struggling to keep up with the giant man's stride as they walked down to the factory.

Zach Owens had given them what they needed and after breaking two of his fingers, Bud sat him down with ice and apologized for having too rough him up like that. Caroline was surprised Zach didn't shoot him right then and there. The thing about Bud was most people knew if they ever got on his bad side, it was their fault.

Bud might have been a gentle giant but he was big enough to but the fear of God in damn near anyone who wasn't carrying a weapon. He had a large, intimidating body, and after howling like an injured fox, Zach had sulked and whimpered the entire time, uttering weak and empty threats under his breath about what Buchanan would do to them or what he would do.

At the police station, Bud went inside to get Travis, who sat at his desk filling out paperwork with his black and blue eye that was nearly sealed shut.

"Travis, c'mon we gotta go."

"I'm at work."

"It's urgent. Caroline's waiting outside."

Travis followed him after hearing that. He knew Caroline was pissed and right now, he was ready to admit she'd been right. Buchanan had something to hide if he'd been sitting on this information, and after his incident with his father, Travis realized that Atticus was even worse than Travis realized. Not only was his father an unfaithful man but he'd accepted money as part of whatever illegal deal he'd made with Buchanan.

I should have listened to Caroline earlier, Travis thought to himself. When he saw her standing there outside, arms folded as her eyes darted around nervously, he wrapped his arms around her and whispered the only two words she needed from him, "I'm sorry..."

Caroline hugged him back and as Travis pulled away, Bud grinned and announced, "Shucks, you two are making me want to get in that group hug."

A pang of guilt surged through Caroline as she surveyed Travis' black eye. His eye was nearly swollen shut.

"Maybe not the best place for that," Caroline said, gesturing toward the police station.

"You're right. Let's get Chase..."

They waited for Chase to get off work. By the time he was off, he knew something was going on since he'd spotted Travis' cop car outside.

"What are you three waiting 'round here for?" Chase asked.

"We're going to break into Buchanan's office tonight and we need your help."

"Uh huh? What's all this about? I'm starving and my neck hurts like you wouldn't believe," Chase grumbled.

He'd been trying to quit cigarettes again to focus on organizing the union and to save up his money in case things all went south. After a hard day at work, Chase found himself itching for one. He rubbed his neck and tilted it to the side.

Chase always looked so tired after a factory shift. Today, he'd been in the sun a lot of the day and a large sunburn spread across the back of his neck. Caroline scowled when she took notice of it.

"Chase, is that a burn? Why didn't you wear sunscreen?"

He rolled his eyes.

"Jeez, am I really going to get a lecture from you about sunscreen?"

"Yes, you are! It's dangerous. Your neck is all burned and—"

"Well, I am a redneck," Chase teased.

"Not funny. Wear sunscreen next time."

"Alright, alright. Now how about you three find a way to get some dinner in me before I lose it."

"I've got an old hamburger in the back seat," Travis offered.

Caroline wrinkled her nose.

"Ew!"

"No thanks. I'll stop off at home," Chase muttered.

Bud scratched his head, "That might not be such a good idea."

"Why not?"

"Trust me."

"Whatever, Bud. A man needs his grub. So grub me!"

The four of them made their way to the 24-hour diner in town. A swinging light outside surrounded by moths illuminated the sign to *Frank & Mary's Diner.* The short-order cook, a man with one arm who whistled old war tunes to himself made a mess of scrambled eggs and bacon for Chase. Bud couldn't help seeing Chase's food and wanting some of his own.

Travis drank black coffee and Caroline sipped on an extra-large glass of orange juice, squeezed fresh.

"Now talk," Chase said, "What's this about breaking into the mayor's office. What made you change your mind, Trav?"

Chase avoided eye contact with Caroline. He still felt guilty over ratting her out. Travis' black-eye attracted stares from their waitress, drawing more attention to the elephant in the room that Caroline had yet to properly speak to him about — and apologize for.

Look at all of them now. How could she have ever doubted that Travis was on her side? He was here now, wasn't he? And with that huge bruise on his face…

Caroline reached for Travis' leg under the table and gave him a squeeze. He looked over at her, raising his eyebrow and then putting his coffee to his lips.

"I'm sorry," Caroline mouthed.

Travis waved her off and now that Chase had scrambled eggs, he was ready to plan.

"We know the pass code to Buchanan's safe. We need you and Bud to stand guard. I'll go in with Caroline to get the safe."

"What about security cameras?" Chase asked through a mouthful of toast.

"I was hoping you could help with that."

"Hm. I don't know what kind of system they're on, but I can cut the power to the whole building."

"That should work. It's a regular combination safe."

"How did you three get the combination?" Chase asked suspiciously.

Bud still worried about Chase learning what his brother had been a part of. If Chase knew, there was no telling how he'd react.

"Uh, I found it," Caroline chimed in.

"How?"

"Old-fashioned detective work."

Chase didn't buy their neatly packaged explanation, but he didn't have much energy to stand, much less argue.

"So when are we going to pull off this grand heist?" Chase asked.

"Neither of us have the day off until Saturday," Bud answered.

"I have every day off," Caroline chimed in.

"I work on Saturday, but it's fine. We can do this on my shift," Travis added.

"You want to break in somewhere while you're on duty?"

Travis sighed.

"I've been maybe thinking about quitting the force," he confessed.

Bud, Chase and Caroline exchanged glances, hoping that someone else would say something. Caroline spoke up first.

"You don't have to leave the force."

"I do. Not now, but soon," Travis admitted to them what he'd been unable to admit to himself for too long.

He'd done police work because of his father and he was starting to get the strong sense that maybe he belonged somewhere else.

"What are you going to do?"

"I dunno. Find some way to support my ma until she divorces my daddy's sorry ass."

Caroline slunk back. She'd known the Montgomery's for a long time and she had the feeling that Mrs. Montgomery wouldn't leave her husband over stepping out. She was an old-fashioned woman — the kind that would rather bite her tongue than put herself first.

"Okay. We support you no matter what," Caroline replied.

Bud and Chase nodded. They must have said the right thing because Travis cracked a smile for the first time that night and winced when it tugged at the sensitive skin around his eye.

"We have a plan then? Saturday night?"

"Sure. But what are we going to do afterwards?" Chase asked.

The waitress returned and offered them more coffee. They all accepted. Caroline put two sugars and so much cream in hers that the coffee turned light brown. The rest of the boys enjoyed black coffee.

"After we expose Buchanan, you mean?" Caroline replied once the waitress was out of earshot.

"Sure. I mean, you must have *some* kind of plan."

"We'll need to have an election and get a new mayor."

"Do you have a candidate in mind?"

"I don't know... But it will be our chance to find someone who actually gives a shit about this town."

"Like you," Bud suggested.

Caroline laughed.

"No way. Do you think the residents in town would elect a black woman as mayor?"

"We had Barack Obama."

"Yeah, for all of five minutes. No. It wouldn't work. I couldn't be mayor anyway..."

Caroline lost her train of thought as she remembered Mayor Buchanan's threat to her. If her secret got out, she'd barely be employable.

Travis paid for dinner and they agreed to meet Saturday night at a new location. The Landry barn wasn't safe anymore.

14

BREAKING & ENTERING

CAROLINE WORRIED Travis was only here to get back at his father, but she kept those thoughts from him when they met at the town well on Saturday night. Travis wisely guessed they'd be safer on Caroline's side of town. Travis should have been on-duty, but his coworker Justin wanted to trade shifts so he could go to his daughter's dance recital the next week.

Travis wore his uniform and Caroline thought the blue was nice against his skin. Even when he was doing something totally criminal, Travis never lost his cool. They walked over, Bud in line with Chase and Travis hanging back with Caroline.

"You okay?" Travis asked.

"Of course, why wouldn't I be?"

"Because... this is a huge deal. You're going to get the proof you needed. A judge will see that thing, he'll be forced to act, especially with the public pressuring him."

"Yeah. It's a big deal."

"You worry we're going too far?"

"I don't want anyone else to get hurt," Caroline replied, "I can't stop thinking about Caleb... or you..."

"Don't worry about me," Travis said, "My dad got a good one in and I hope he enjoyed it 'cause the next time we meet like that, he won't get away scot-free."

Caroline hugged her arms close to her body.

"I ruined your relationship with Atticus."

"No. You didn't ruin it. He did cheating with that Mayfair woman who's half his age, I might add."

"We only found out because of me."

"That's what I love about you, Caroline. You bring out the truth, no matter how ugly it looks in the light."

"I thought that made me a stubborn bitch who doesn't know when to let go."

"No. I like my women strong. So do Bud and Chase."

"Did I hear my name back there?" Chase asked. He'd been cheerful since the night started. It didn't hurt that Bud still hadn't told him what happened with Zach. Chase's brother hadn't been home for a couple days and Chase figured he was with a girlfriend.

"Yup," Travis replied proudly.

"I heard mine too. What are you two talking about?"

Chase and Bud confidently walked backwards in line as they questioned Travis and Caroline about their clandestine conversation.

"Why we love Caroline."

"Oh that. That's easy!" Chase laughed.

"What? You guys are telling me that you *love* me and this is how you decide to do it?"

Bud laughed, "Ain't it obvious, Coulson?"

Heat rushed to Caroline's cheeks. Bud and Chase turned around so they could see where they were headed properly.

"Well… I don't know! I mean, I never thought about it…"

"Why not?"

"Well… It's easy for you three but I don't know if I'm allowed to be *in love* with three guys at once."

"Why not, Care?" Chase asked.

"I… It's just… Wrong!"

"Don't feel wrong to me," Bud shrugged.

"Listen," Travis chimed in, "You love your mom, your dad, your brother. Those are three people. What makes the three of us any different?"

"Just be glad we aren't making you choose," Chase replied.

The three men laughed and Caroline only felt more embarrassed. Had they planned to put her on the spot like this? They got to Buchanan's office without detection. In Old Town, there wasn't a soul up at at 'em at one in the morning except the folks who worked at the diner which was too far off.

"Chase, you get the power. Bud, you keep watch. Caroline and I got this."

"You two be careful," Chase cautioned.

Chase walked to the back of the building. Travis confidently walked to the front door of the mayor's office and pulled a master key off of his belt. He waited until the sound of electricity buzzing through the wires dulled and the tiny lights you could see through the window died.

"Where'd you get that?"

"Everyone on the force has one."

Travis handed Caroline the flashlight and she flicked it on, illuminating the pitch black off.

"Really?"

"It's in case of emergency so we can get into public buildings."

"Won't you get in trouble for using it?"

"Only if we get caught."

Travis winked. Caroline wondered how he could keep his

cool like she. She was freaking out and kept worrying the lights would go on and Buchanan would be waiting to pull one over on them again.

There was no one inside and Travis strode confidently through the office but Caroline couldn't help but stop and stare at what her former work place looked like under cover of darkness. The mayor's office was older than she realized. The carpets were thin and permanently stained by coffee. The ceiling had large brown rings above the desks that housed smokers in the seventies.

Caroline noticed the office smelled musty. When they got to her floor, she glanced at her old office. Loretta's name was on the door. Caroline flushed with embarrassment at those memories which seemed so long ago. It had only been a few weeks, not enough time for her to run out of savings, but enough time that she needed a solution soon.

"C'mon let's go into Buchanan's office"

"Okay."

Travis pushed the door open. Caroline gasped. The place was different from how she remembered. Buchanan had it extensively renovated with new wood panels put in, old furniture of his own including a large ivory elephant tusk on his desk. Those weren't the features that sent a shiver down Caroline's spine.

At their feet lay a large, 100% real, tiger skin rug.

"Is that..."

"Yes," Travis muttered, "It's real. The guys on the force have been talking about it."

"Where's the safe?" Caroline asked, tilting the flashlight around the room.

"Wait, stop there. I think I saw it."

Travis took the flashlight from Caroline and walked across

the room. Caroline winced as she walked across the tiger rug. She whispered a quick apology for desecrating the poor creature's body.

"Remember the number?"

"Yes. 4-3-5-1-6."

"Woah. Good memory."

"I've been thinking about this all day. I mean... I've got to call the newspaper tomorrow. I've got a contact. It's all happening so fast."

Travis stopped before punching in the code and pushed hair out fo Caroline's face, kissing her forehead.

"Don't worry. You've got three guys who love you and want to take care of you. We'll work things out."

"Ok."

"Now what was the code again?"

Travis pulled the manila folder out of his safe and Caroline stuffed it in her purse once they walked back to Travis' car, parked on her side of town.

"I'm not ready to call it a night," Chase replied, "I'm wired. This went well."

Too well, Caroline worried. But they had the documents and in the morning, she'd send everything over to the newspaper and this would all be over before she knew it.

"We can't go to the barn anymore."

"I know somewhere we can go," Caroline offered.

"You?"

"Yeah. It's on this side of town, if you go down to the pond, there's a clearing with a small cabin on it. The owner died five years ago. But it's not furnished or anything, just an empty house."

"It's probably be a little dusty don't you think?" Travis

protested, dusting off his uniform as if he could clean it in anticipation.

"A little, but don't you think it's worth it?"

"Fine. Why the hell not. We deserve a little celebration."

Caroline borrowed the broom from her family's porch and a few blankets from indoors. Her parents slept too soundly to hear her coming in and out. Caleb wouldn't have missed it, but he was still in the hospital. A flutter of sadness surged through Caroline's heart at the thought of how much her brother had been through.

They drove Travis' car down to the pond and walked through the woods a bit to the clearing with the Cabin. Travis was right, the cabin was dusty but they'd made do with an old barn before so the cabin was hardly intimidating.

"This is a sweet spot. How come we never heard of it?"

Caroline bit her tongue. The boys didn't deserve what she was about to say. It wasn't their fault the town was the way it was. And they were working to change it. But if something was on the "black side" of town, most folks didn't bother with it. The boys were different in so many ways but in just a few, they were products of their environment.

Bud rolled out sleeping bags and blankets on the ground as if he'd been *planning* for this. Maybe they all had been the entire time. Travis kept the manila folder in the glove compartment of his locked car so the four of them could just lie in that cabin until morning.

Of course, lying there would have never really happened anyway. It didn't take long before Bud started kissing Caroline. He had the most energy out of anybody and he wasn't afraid to push Caroline down onto the wood floor and climb between her legs while Travis and Chase lay half asleep on the floor.

Bud's breathing always got real heavy when he was on top

of me and he was an aggressive, forceful kisser, so it was hard not to hear what was going on when he got started. Caroline didn't care. She tilted her head back as his thick hands clasped her neck and he sucked on her lips.

"I need you... *now*."

Caroline reached for her pants and shuffled them off.

"You two are really doing this, aren't you?" Chase grumbled.

"No one's stopping you from joining in..."

Chase didn't need much convincing. Once Caroline removed her pants, Bud pulled her panties to the side and stuck his finger between her lips. The honeysuckle sweet smell of Caroline's pussy getting soaked between her warm thighs as Bud kissed her, wafted through the room. Bud pulled his fingers out of her slit and licked her juices off.

"She's ready..."

He ripped Caroline's panties away and before she could protest the loss of lingerie, his thick cock head pried her lips apart and he slid his full length inside her as she moaned with delight. It had been *way* too long since she'd last had Bud inside her. He didn't give her time to adjust before thrusting away at her tightness, grunting as he plunged inside her.

Every stroke was sheer pleasure and Caroline's mind melted away as Bud's extra large dick spread her open and touched the deepest parts of her wetness. Caroline ran her nails down Bud's back and cried out as she climaxed long and hard around his cock. Bud pumped into her harder until Caroline and two more climaxes and he groaned, releasing between her legs.

He pulled his cock out as his seed spurted down her leg. Before she could get used to the empty space between her thighs, Chase spread her legs and pushed them back further, pressing his entire fat cock inside her and pushing some of Bud's seed to the side as he buried his length inside her.

Even slippery wet, Caroline was still magnificently tight and her pussy gripped Chase's large cock like a vice as he thrusted deep between her legs. With her legs so far back, Caroline could feel the tip of Chase's hardness pressing into her deeper. She lost herself to the pleasure of having three men at once as he pummeled her wetness even harder. Caroline moaned and climaxed, her pussy tightening around Chase's cock and pushing him to the edge.

Chase groaned and pulled out of Caroline's tightness, squirting all over her back. Travis couldn't contain himself. By the time Chase rolled off of Caroline, Travis pushed her onto her stomach and spread her legs wide, prepared to enter her. By then, Caroline's hair stuck to the back of her neck and she could hardly get a deep breath in from her heart's euphoric fluttering in the rib cage.

Caroline had never experienced Travis' arousal so heightened. She arched her back and Travis landed an open palmed smack on her ass. Caroline squealed as her ass cheeks jiggled and the tingling from his smack spread throughout her ass right to the sopping slit between her legs.

Travis was rough today… and he needed her more than he'd been willing to admit. Now that she lay there, splayed before him and ready for him to plunge inside her, Travis couldn't help himself. He spread her ass cheeks wide and before thrusting his cock inside her, Travis bent his head between her legs and began to lick at Caroline's wetness.

He licked the juices off of her thighs and sucked on her outer lips until she squirmed and squealed in his arms. Right before she climaxed, Travis thrust his big cock between Caroline's juicy legs. Caroline moaned and clawed at the blankets as Travis' length pushed deep inside her.

Bud rested his hand on her back and she arched so Travis could better access her tightness. Chase kissed her on the lips as Bud stroked her back and Travis pounded her tight little pussy. The walls of the barn shook as Caroline screamed louder and louder...

"Oh Travis..." she moaned as his cock thrust into her...

"Yes, Bud... Ohhhh YES..." she moaned as Bud gripped her ass cheeks and spread her cheeks apart for Travis to pound her deeper.

Caroline moaned, "Yes, Chase..." when he stuck his tongue in her mouth and kissed her deeply as she accepted Travis' cock from behind. Caroline moaned as she climaxed all over Travis' cock again and again. Her three men kept her satisfied all night long.

Travis climaxed and rolled over onto his back next to her. They all lay together and as Caroline gasped for breath, her lids fluttered open and she realized sunrise had already come and they hadn't had a wink of sleep. She laughed. She couldn't help it. Talk about stress relief. No matter what happened in the outside world, the four of them could create their own happiness, their own pleasure that could overcome any pain life had to offer.

15

ANOTHER MAN'S WIFE IN MOTEL 6

ZACHARIAH OWENS PACED BACK and forth across the motel room. He'd been waiting for that fuck-head to call for the past hour and a half. He hadn't been able to sleep. Their plan had worked perfectly, but Zach didn't have all day. He'd have to crash soon and then there was —

"You okay, sweetheart?" Dixie Collins asked.

Zach couldn't stand looking at her after they made it. Her husband Tex was on the force with him and if he looked at her too long, that tug of guilt could drag him along for a while. What was the point in it? Guilt? For sleeping with another man's wife... At least he wasn't like Atticus. That bastard could betray his entire family... his entire race...

"I'm just wondering what type of fuck-head would ever sleep with a girl from the wrong side of the tracks when Old Town makes beauties like you."

Flattery always worked on Dixie. Zach climbed into bed beside her and closed his eyes as he kissed her. He propped his head up on one of these fancy *Motel 6* pillows that weren't a million years old. Ten miles outta town to avoid being seen and it was like crossing into the promised land. Dixie giggled and ran her hands down his bare chest, pausing to suck on his nipple. Zach slapped her face.

"I done told you not to do that."

"Sorry," Dixie grumbled, pouting and pulling away, "You usually like it. I know you're in a bad mood."

"I'm waiting to hear from somebody."

"Who? We finally get the weekend alone and you're thinking about some other girl, aren't you?"

Dixie prattled on for a few more minutes. Zachariah wasn't listening. In a few months, he could cash his check from the Coulson incident and he'd get a brand new Dodge Charger. When he did, Zach knew he'd be done with Dixie Collins and sad, desperate housewives like her.

"I'm not thinking about another girl."

"Good. 'Cause I ain't thinking about another man."

Zach snickered, "Yeah right. What about Tex?"

"I don't love my husband anymore," she purred, "It's all you, Zach."

He pushed her off of him.

"Enough. I don't have time for you getting on like a whore. We did it once, just be grateful."

He stormed out of bed into the shower. As he stepped under the water, Dixie shrilled, "Zach! The phone's ringing!"

Not bothering to wrap a towel around his torso, Zach raced out and snatched the phone from Dixie's hand.

"My boy, I apologize for the late call."

"It's no problem, sir," Zach uttered politely, "I've been waiting to tell you that the plan worked. I switched the file like you asked and I don't think they suspected."

"Good! How's the finger?"

"Not so good. But I've got someone who's helping me out."

He flashed Dixie a wink and she smiled like a kid on Christmas.

"Good. Thank you, Zachariah. I'll be in touch."

"Anything you need, sir."

"Wait for my call."

Zachariah hung up. His head still throbbed where that big lug hit him and listening to phone calls sent a surge of pain through him.

"Was that the mayor on the phone?" Dixie asked.

"Dixie, how about you mind your business."

"Fine?" Dixie shrugged, "I brought glass."

"I'm a fuckin' cop, Dixie. Don't bring that shit around me."

Dixie shrugged. "Suit yourself. I don't know why you're acting all high and mighty though."

She packed herself a needle as Zach sat on the foot of the bed, brooding. That wasn't what he expected from that fuckhead Buchanan. He barely congratulated Zach on the effort and didn't seem to give a shit that Bud had fucked Zach's head and ribs to the point where they still ached. But there was no point going to the hospital now and if Bud hadn't told already, soon Chase would find out what he'd done and that filthy communist race traitor wouldn't understand why Zach had done what he had to.

"Dixie? I think I've changed my mind. C'mon."

Dixie smiled and pulled Zach's sleeve up to get the needle in him. His arm had three pock marks in it. Dixie found a nice spot and Zach winced as he felt the first pinch. And then he didn't feel much of anything — not his ribs, not his head, not Dixie's mouth traveling down his chest all the way down down down.

Zach woke up a few hours later, still groggy. His cellphone

rang and he didn't think to check who was calling before he picked up. It was Chase.

"Zach, where the hell are you? Ma's worried sick."

"Uh… I dunno…"

"You ain't on duty so don't lie to me. She's making meatloaf tonight so get your ass over here."

"Okay. Okay…"

"What the fuck's wrong with you?"

Zach sighed with relief. From his brother's tone, he could tell Bud hadn't spoken to him yet. If his head wasn't so clouded, Zach would have been more worried about what Bud had planned. At least this meant Landry and that Caroline girl hadn't figured out what was *actually* inside the manila folder they'd pilfered. Could they really be so foolish as to think Zach would give up the documents and information?

That was all safe. And when Caroline was taken care of, Buchanan had big plans for Zachariah. Old Town would be restored to the old ways and his ma would never have to work again. And as for that ungrateful commie bastard brother of his…

Chase would complain at first but when he didn't have to compete with these blacks for a job, all his problems would go away. If he weren't so sentimental, he'd see that instead of blaming the boss for not paying enough or not letting them unionize.

Zach got out of bed, hoping he could sneak out before Dixie woke up. She'd fallen asleep halfway through blowing him and she didn't even wake up when he'd slapped her again. He shook his head with disgust but before Zachariah could get to the door, Dixie woke up and stared at him with pleading, cornflower blue eyes.

"Where you headed?"

"Home."

"Don't you want to stay here with me, take another hit?"

"Clean yourself up, Dixie."

"Zach, wait..."

"Are you still attracted to me?"

"Desperation isn't sexy, Dixie. Now put your clothes on and go home to your husband."

She pouted but didn't argue with him. Zach didn't give her time. He escaped Motel 6, driving home in his police issue vehicle. Chase waited outside on the front steps, shucking corn with headphones on. He pulled the headphones out when he saw his brother.

"Woah, who gave you that?"

Great, Bud hadn't actually snitched. Zach grinned.

"Some asshole."

"You look awful. Where the hell were you last night?"

"Need help shucking the corn?" Zach asked. From the time they were kids, it was Zach's least favorite job.

"Sure."

Zachariah sat down next to Chase, avoiding eye contact with him and rolling down his sleeves so Chase couldn't see his arm.

"The way this town's going," Zach mumbled, "It's so fucked."

"What makes you say that?"

Zach snorted, "You commie bastard, you wouldn't understand."

Chase snickered, "Don't start. You think wanting better pay makes me a communist now? It doesn't make sense."

"Whatever. I know you're only doing this to impress your welfare queen."

Chase scowled, "Leave Caroline out of our disagreements."

"Whatever," Zach grumbled.

His head still hurt too much for him to pick a fight with his older brother.

"It's time for Old Town to get rid of some of these traditions anyway. Why hang onto the past when there's a whole wide future out there."

"You're an idealistic fool, you know."

"And you're a pessimist who watches too much *Fox News*."

"Fox News? That network has been bought by the libtards for years," Zach grumbled.

Chase tilted his head to the side, beginning to regret opening this line of conversation with his brother.

"You know what, I think I'll go help ma peel the potatoes," Chase said, getting up and wiping the silk from the corn off on his jeans.

Zach rose and shook his head.

"No, I'll get the potatoes. We can peel 'em out here if we use the basin."

"Fine."

Chase got a basin, filling it from the hose, and Zach walked 'round back to get some potatoes from their root cellar. The boys took out their pocket knives and got to peeling potatoes. After a painfully long silence, Zach interjected again, "Progress shouldn't be rushed, Chase. Remember that. There's a big storm front blowin' across the prairie and none of them are ready for it."

"No politics, brother."

"Fine. Fine."

Zach stared out ahead as he peeled potatoes. Chase scanned his brother's face for what was wrong with him. Zach seemed different — a mixture of exhausted and *different*. When they were done with the potatoes, Zach took the handles of the basin.

"I'd better go see ma."

"You do that," Chase replied.

Zach entered the house and his mother fussed and tutted over him like she always had, as if he were still her baby. Chase noticed something shiny on the step and leaned down to find that his brother Zach had dropped his phone. When he picked it up, the screen flashed on.

4 missed called, Buchanan's Office.

Before Chase could call his brother over, the phone vibrated in his hand. Chase answered it and started walking down the street out of view of the house. As brothers, Zach and Chase had always sounded alike. Chase waited for the man on the other end of the line to speak.

"Owens, that you boy?"

"Yes."

"Good. I wanted to apologize for how I acted when you called about replacing the file. I was occupied. I need something else from you now."

"Sure. Anything."

"Montgomery wants something else done. He wants an alibi for the fifteenth. Think you can arrange something?"

"No problem."

"Hmph. Good to see you less testy than when we last spoke. Go ahead and cash that check now for the Coulson job. You have the all clear."

Chase hung up. His hands trembled. He could go inside and beat his brother to a pulp right now, but there were more urgent matters to attend to. Chase threw the phone across the street into the neighbor's bushes and he forgot all about meatloaf and dinner with his ma. Caroline was in trouble.

Travis had sent her home with the file since he couldn't exactly bring it to work our around the house. Bud was the wrong choice for the file too, so Caroline kept it, and she hadn't opened it 'cause she had a meeting with her contact at the newspaper in the evening when she planned to hand it over. Chase checked his watch. The meeting was in an hour.

He started to run all the way across town, across the train tracks until he got to the Coulson house where he pounded on the front door like a maniac.

"CAROLINE! CAROLINE OPEN THE DOOR IT'S URGENT!"

"CARE! ARE YOU IN THERE?!"

Caroline opened the door, a bewildered expression on her face.

"Chase, are you okay? We're eating dinner."

"Get the folder. Now."

Chase stepped inside and took off his hat. The three other members of the Coulson family stared back at him. Caleb averted his gaze quickly. With flushed cheeks, Chase bowed awkwardly.

"Good evening Mr. & Mrs. Coulson. Caleb."

Caroline's footsteps pounded upstairs and she returned downstairs holding the manila folder.

"What's going on?"

"We'll talk."

"Goodnight everyone."

Caroline left her house before anyone in her family could protest, offering a hasty goodbye and shrugging of her shoulders. Once they were outside, she asked Chase what was wrong.

"What's going on?"

"The folder's a fake."

"What?"

"Open it up. What's inside…"

Caroline opened the folder and gasped. Pictures. Tons and tons of pictures. Of the four of them. Their relationship had been documented in *every* compromising position. Even their last night together had been documented. Pages and pages of doctored text messages and emails made Caroline dizzy. Caroline's leaked emails "proved" she was a prostitute. She'd been so careless that she'd been about to blow up a "fake news" style story about herself.

Caroline dropped the folder.

"I'm going to be sick."

Chase picked the file up and wrapped Caroline in a hug, kissing her forehead.

"Don't worry, sweetheart. Bud, Travis and I will take care of this."

"What do you mean?"

"Don't you worry about that. Just know, ain't anybody gonna come between this redneck and his girl."

Chase kissed her and tucked the folder under his arm.

"Stay safe, Caroline. We'll come back tomorrow."

Chase didn't tell her what he'd overheard. He didn't want her to worry and by the fifteenth, this would all be taken care of anyway.

Caroline kissed him again and Chase pushed her long hair out of her face.

"I love you. We all love you. Don't forget that."

"See you tomorrow then."

"Tomorrow. I promise."

16

HEAVY RAIN, SOUTHERN SUMMER

"We'll wait outside his house 'round midnight. That's when he normally comes home from the bar," Travis laid out his plan for the third time. Bud wasn't getting it.

"And when he goes inside, we get him."

"No. We have to get him *before* he goes inside."

"Uh huh. And then what?"

"We have to kill him," Chase said.

"Are you crazy? We can't *assassinate* the mayor of our town," Travis hissed.

"It ain't assassinating. It's murder," Chase offered up in weak defense.

"How do you spell assassinate?" Bud asked.

"It's not time for a spelling lesson," Travis snapped, "I don't see why we have to kill anyone. We just need to get the truth out of Buchanan and shake him up a bit, threaten him and make him expose the truth himself."

"How are we going to scare the most powerful guy in town?" Chase snapped.

"Break his shoulder," Bud offered.

Chase snorted, "Great. Then he'll get us all killed. Caleb burned his precious flag and look what happened to him."

"We get him inside, then."

"Jesus H Christ, Bud!" Travis and Chase snapped at once.

"No, you don't understand. We tie up his wife and kids. We get him inside. *Then* we threaten him."

Travis and Chase stared at Bud dumbfounded.

"You think we should threaten a woman and child just to get to Buchanan?"

Bud scowled and seemed to be lost in thought. Travis and Chase waited patiently. Bud wasn't exactly an "ideas guy" but they were running short of ideas.

"What if we pretend."

"How are we going to pretend to hurt his wife and child?"

Bud smirked.

"I think it's time you boys leave the planning to me. I have the perfect idea to take down our dear mayor."

Buchanan came home just before midnight like the four predicted. A crack of thunder in the distance indicated a storm brewing. They'd come on foot, dressed in all black and armed. Country boys don't have much trouble coming across weapons, so each had a handgun and a hunting knife. Chase wasn't convinced the plan would work, but Travis had insisted and they had no better options.

Travis had it on good authority that Mr. and Mrs. Buchanan slept in separate bedrooms and that's what their plan revolved around. Mr. Buchanan slept downstairs in his study, while Mrs. Buchanan and her daughter slept upstairs in separate bedrooms.

With Travis' master key, they'd enter the house and trap her upstairs with Buchanan's daughter. Downstairs, Travis and Chase would threaten to hurt his daughters — without touching a hair on their heads — and figure out what Buchanan had done to rig the election.

No plan was perfect and this one certainly had its flaws. The good thing was after they did this, Caroline would be safe across town she wouldn't have to worry any longer. All three men were united in their goal of keeping Caroline Coulson completely safe.

By the time they entered the house, rain poured and the men couldn't hear their own footsteps. Bud made it upstairs without waking anyone. He didn't like the idea of scaring an innocent woman and child, but for Caroline, he found himself capable of far more than he'd ever imagined. That woman had opened his eyes in more ways than one. She'd taught him better than any school teacher and she'd loved him better than any girlfriend. She was a special type of Southern woman that you only get one chance with. Bud refused to screw this up.

He'd seen first hand what Caroline talked about was true. He always knew being a racist was no good. He mightn't have been able to read the Bible, but he'd listened real good in church when they'd gone as kids. Jesus talked about love for your neighbor. Caroline had been his neighbor, even living on the "wrong side of the tracks", he'd never found her so different. She wanted the same things he did — love, family, freedom.

Bud woke Buchanan's wife and daughter and with his meanest country boy look, he tied them up and threatened them to keep it down. Despite his threats, Lacey Buchanan let out a blood-curdling scream, loud enough to awake her father downstairs, who woke to find himself face to face with the barrel of Chase Owens' gun.

Tommy Lee Buchanan sat up with a start, his face blanched. Lightning cracked the sky open and purple hellish light flashed across Chase's face, exposing his rage to Tommy Lee Buchanan. Just look at what he'd gotten himself into. Before Tommy Lee could reach for his gun, he heard a familiar voice, "Not so fast…"

Sheriff Montgomery's boy stood over his bed, pointing Tommy Lee's own shotgun at his head. The boy thought he knew his father so well, but he didn't…

Tommy Lee Buchanan realized he'd been had. He raised his hands above his head.

"Alrighty boys, there's no need for weapons. Let's have a polite conversation."

"Move one more muscle and I'll scream to my man upstairs. He'll paint the walls with Lacey's brains," Travis threatened.

He wasn't sure if Buchanan was buying this. Travis had stolen the creepy line from a movie anyway. He didn't need to *do* anything, Buchanan only had to believe he would. Bad men always believe everyone is capable of the same evil that they are.

"Fine. Fine. But lower your weapon. I don't like the idea of being shot at with my own gun."

Travis lowered his weapon, but Chase remained alert. If there was anyone capable of pulling the trigger, it was Chase. Buchanan had poisoned his brother's mind, injured Caleb, one of his closest friends down at the factory, and he'd actually rigged the election. Buchanan wanted the town back in the dark ages, but Chase wanted the opposite. He was willing to do anything to end the segregated, messed up way they lived. Too many people got hurt who didn't deserve it while Buchanan lived a fat cat's life.

Travis unclenched his jaw, needing to appear calm and in control.

"We know you had Zachariah Owens remove the file from your office detailing how you rigged the mayor's elections."

"Yes. I had Zachariah switch the file... But oh, what the hell."

Buchanan swung his legs out of bed. Chase cocked the gun. Tommy Lee raised an eyebrow.

"Do I look stupid to you boy? I'm not going to try any funny business. I'm going to put an end to this. I was promised an *easy* win and that this town was going to be a piece of cake. I was promised people here believed in *traditional values* that we can be separate but equal. I see that they want none of the separate. I've had more trouble in this town 'cause I'm of the opinion you've all come too close to the wrong side of the tracks. You see these people as your neighbors... I don't know what's come of Old Town, but it's not the place I thought it was."

"Done with the speech old man?" Chase growled.

He was having a harder time than Travis appearing cool, collected and patient. He hated every Buchanan stood for.

"Where's the correct file?"

"I'm warning you Montgomery, you're not going to like what's in there."

"Why don't you let me be the judge of that?"

"I know what stock you come from Montgomery. You might be dabbling with the darker arts right now, but you'll come around and marry a good girl with blonde hair and nice pale skin. You don't want to be doing this."

"You don't know what I want. You might know my father, but you don't know me."

"All us Southern men are the same! Of course I know you. Think I haven't been tempted by one of these jezebels before?"

"Quit talking," Travis grumbled, finally matching Chase's level of frustration, "Tell us where the file is."

"It's at my desk," he gestured across the room. A manila folder sat on his desk. Travis raised his gun again and nodded at Chase, so he could get the file. Travis kept his eye on Buchanan and his finger hovering over the trigger.

Buchanan talked as Chase opened up the manila folder.

"I might as well tell you then, since you'll find out anyway. I know Miss Coulson thinks I've been the one behind the scenes. She thinks I rigged the election and that's all well and good. But have you wondered why nothing's happened to her? She's lost her job sure, but she's come after the mayor and *nothing* has happened."

"You assaulted her brother."

"Yes, her brother, but never her. Young Travis, this town is kept afloat by more than a mayor. There's a group of men, in this town, a circle of good white men, and they make sure that Old Town is maintained the way our proud ancestors once had it — with every color in their place."

Buchanan's voice grew breathy, as if he were whispering a poem into a lover's ear.

"I'm not the leader of this klan. I'm simply their choice. The person who's been pulling all the strings is —

"Travis, get over here," Chase interrupted gruffly.

Buchanan smiled.

"I can't take my gun off him."

"Trust me, I won't be going anywhere," Buchanan chuckled to himself.

Chase handed Travis three letters from the manila folder. Buchanan laughed as the storm roared outside with even greater intensity.

Lottie Calloway,

The knights have come together and decided that Tommy Lee Buchanan represents our best hope for Old Town. There's trouble at the factory and talk of 4 more intermarriages from Pastor Tucker at the church, who is on our side.

The knights require the election to be fixed at 65% in favor of Buchanan and 14% in favor of our current mayor. The rest of the percentages adjust as you see fit. The communist liberal takeover which has led to the insertion of a progressive mayor must be stopped.

Lottie, we also require the removal of the nixxer girl from mayor offices, but do so without any use of violence at this point. I'll send another message to your husband when we need his services.

Remember, our race is our nation.

Atticus Montgomery
Imperial Wizard

Mr. Buchanan,

It gives me no pleasure to approach you again under these circumstances.

Nixxer girl Coulson continues to stick her nose where it doesn't belong. Our page, Z.O. on the force has followed her for weeks. We have people who will prevent her from getting a job in this town.

She is becoming a liability. Have Z.O. and three other men attack the nixxer boy, Caleb Coulson this week. You do not have to worry about an investigation but make sure the order comes from you.

Klannish loyalty is a sacred principle which you are sworn to uphold. Do not let the nixxer girl Coulson's persistence give pause. We are doing the right thing to preserve our race, which is our nation.

Atticus Montgomery
Imperial Wizard

Mr. Buchanan,

We must give new evidence to the contrary of you rigging the mayor elections. Caleb Coulson's life is not guaranteed. A nurse in the hospital is a member of our proud organization. She will do what is required to preserve our race and legacy.

Our last Crimson hour, I will personally handle the problem of the nixxer girl.

In the sacred unfailing bond,

Atticus Montgomery
Imperial Wizard

Travis dropped the letters. A lump formed in his stomach as the weight of a family secret he'd never been aware of spilled out of Tommy Lee Buchanan's manila envelope. He recognized his father's tone of voice, and realized that even some of the language he'd used hadn't been unfamiliar.

Yes, Travis had some memories from when he was a child of men gathered around the fire and his father doling out orders using some of these terms. When he was old enough to be in school, these visits stopped and Travis wondered if he'd only imagined all of it. The memories only surfaced as he clutched the damning letters. Travis' throat tightened.

He regretted everything he'd said to Caroline to deny what she'd known to be true.

Then there was the last letter with its cryptic message beginning, "Our last crimson hour..."

Travis squeezed the letter in his fists and roared, "What does this mean? What is he going to do to Caroline?"

Buchanan shook his head, "Maybe you are not worthy of your heritage..."

"ANSWER ME!" Travis roared.

"NO! I've done enough. You see that I'm not the man who's pulling the strings."

"I SAID ANSWER. WHAT DOES IT MEAN?"

"I REFUSE!" Buchanan yelled back.

Chase called out, "BUD! SHOOT THEM."

The women screamed again. Bud fired two shots into the ceiling and stuffed their gags back into their mouths.

"Answer, or you're next," Chase growled.

"Fine! But you're already too late! It's a date and a time. It's tonight. Atticus is headed over to Caroline Coulson's and he'll put an end to her snooping for good."

As the mayor spoke, Chase shoved the papers back into the manila folder and stuck it in his jacket.

"We've got to go, Travis. NOW."

They didn't bother killing Buchanan. By morning, all of this would be over — but only if they got to Caroline's in time.

"BUD! WE'VE GOT TO GO! HURRY!"

All three men left the mayor's house, running through the rain. The Confederate flag that Caleb burned hadn't been replaced. The charred remains lay soaked into the ground, even after all that time. Travis stomped on the flag, crushing it in the mud as he led the three of them all the way to Caroline's, praying that they would make it in time...

17

THE IMPERIAL WIZARD

THEY WERE SOAKED by the time they got to Caroline's door. The door was open and Travis called, "CAROLINE?!"

No answer. Bud and Chase split up downstairs. Travis went upstairs and pushed open the door to Caroline's parents room. They weren't there. He then opened Caroline's door and his father pulled a gun on him. Travis raised his hands over his head and dropped his weapon.

He hadn't come alone...

Bud and Chase materialized behind him and then it was Atticus Montgomery's turn to drop his weapon. Caroline was curled up on the other end of the bed, naked, shaking and in tears. She yanked a blanket over herself.

"What on earth did you do to her?" Travis growled.

"Nothing at all."

"Caroline?" Bud asked.

"No... He didn't... He tried... but you guys came in through the door."

"Caroline, take his gun," Chase commanded.

Keeping the blanket wrapped around her torso, Caroline went for the sheriff's gun and got it out of his holster.

"I can't believe you're my father," Travis breathed.

"You've been corrupted, that's why. You refuse to see what I've always taught you, that you were proud Southern stock, that you are above things like going to college and having a girlfriend. You're meant to be a knight, to defend this great country from immigrants and colored people."

"You're crazy," Travis said, "All my life I knew, but I tried to talk myself out of believing it."

"Crazy? I'm not crazy for being proud of my heritage."

"If you have to hurt people to be proud of your heritage, maybe you're scared there's nothing to be proud of," Travis hissed.

Chase's eyes widened in surprise. He'd been trying to get through to Travis and teach him for so long, but he never realized how much Travis learned — how he cared so much for Caroline that he'd do anything for her — including becoming a better person.

"The white race was born supreme. People like Caroline Coulson tempt good white men away and it's my fault that my own son wasn't brought up in the old way. It was your mother's fault," he sneered.

"Is that why you cheated on her? To protect the proud white race?" Travis shot back.

"I don't need to explain myself to you," Atticus hissed.

"You're right, you don't. But you need to get out of town, or I promise you, I'll kill you right here."

"You would never kill your own father. That's not how I raised you."

Travis lowered his weapon and got right up in Atticus' face. Their sky blue eyes were eerily similar. Another flash of lightning illuminated their gazes. They were both proud, and angry, but Travis was stronger, younger and motivated by a stronger beast than his father. He loved Caroline. He wanted that freedom to love her and to love her hard.

"I will kill you. I want you to get in your car and never come back. And I'll prove that I'll do it right now."

Surprising everyone, Travis shot his father's toe. Caroline screamed. Even Bud and Chase flinched. Atticus howled like an injured wolf.

"YOU SHOT ME! YOU SHOT YOUR OWN FATHER FOR A NIG—"

Travis shot the ceiling and Atticus howled.

"HOBBLE YOUR WAY OUT OF HERE OLD MAN. GET OUT. THIS IS MY MERCY TO YOU," Travis roared.

Chase and Bud had never seen Travis like this and neither had Caroline. She liked this Travis — the one who would defend her from racism and didn't want to sweep it under the rug and pretend it didn't exist.

Atticus limped downstairs screaming his head off, trailing blood behind him. Travis followed him until he was out on the street. He returned upstairs to the woman he loved and the men he considered his brothers.

Bud and Chase helped Caroline dress. She hugged them both and they apologized for leaving her alone.

"It wasn't your fault... Did you get what you were looking for?"

Chase couldn't help but crack a smile. That was Caroline for you, always concerned with the practical details.

"We found what we were looking for," Chase said, "But it's not what we expected."

He pulled the manila folder out of his jacket. Caroline sat on her bed and flicked on her reading lamp. She was focused so hard on the shocking letters that she didn't hear Travis coming back upstairs. She gasped when he appeared in the doorway.

"He'll go out of town for good if he knows what's good for him."

Chase and Bud patted Travis on the back. What could they say to him at a time like this that could possibly make him feel better.

"I'm so sorry, Travis," Caroline whispered.

"You ain't got a damn thing to be sorry about," Travis replied, "We'll expose the truth tomorrow ourselves."

"Before then, I think we ought to send a message," Chase said.

"What kind of message?" Bud asked.

"Caroline? Mind if we take you on one last adventure?"

Caroline shook her head. It was almost sunrise when the storm stopped. By the time the storm stopped, Chase had all his men in place — the mixed group of union members around town with their black, brown, and white faces, spread across Old Town and they plucked every confederate flag off its staff or window, doused it in gasoline and set it on fire.

In the morning, every "old-fashioned" house in Old Town had lost their markers of their heritage. It was over, Caroline thought to herself. It was finally all over and she could be with her men in peace...

18

GUESS WHO'S RUNNING FOR MAYOR?

CAROLINE SLEPT all day and all night after she dropped copies of the documents off for her contact at the newspaper. The letters from Atticus were only a piece of the puzzle. With the help of an expert in klan history, all the names of the townspeople who had been involved in Atticus' chapter of the organization were exposed. All of them.

Old Town was about to change in a big way, and when Caroline woke up to see the paper, she couldn't help but feel like her troubles weren't nearly all over. Her parents were back at home, but getting concerned over all the hubbub over race in town. Caleb was getting better, and his face healed a bit. Caleb refused to leave town, but suggested that his parents go ahead. He'd been saving money and had enough put aside that they could rent a small apartment for a month.

As her parents deliberated, Caroline sat on the front porch reading the paper. Travis had been the first to suggest leaking everything about his father. Luckily, as far as Caroline knew, his father had shot out of town like a bat out of hell. He didn't expect Travis to shoot him. To be fair, no one saw it coming at all. This was *Travis* for heavens' sake. He had that cool, genteel all the time — except when it came to his girl.

Caroline couldn't help but think of Travis as she read the story, which lay out the conspiracy with all its proof in devastating detail.

"Howdy, Caroline," Bud Landry's voice startled Caroline from her paper.

"Hey. What are you doing here so early? Don't you have work."

Bud grinned, "Nope. We're on strike, organized by Chase and your brother."

"Oh. Wow. I guess I missed a lot yesterday."

"Yes ma'am."

"What brings you here so early?"

"I've been practicing. I want to show you something."

Bud pulled a small King James Bible out of his pocket and he flipped the page to Galatians 3:23.

But before faith came, we were kept under the law, shut up unto the faith which should afterwards be revealed.
Wherefore the law was our schoolmaster to bring us unto Christ, that we might be justified by faith.
But after that faith is come, we are no longer under a schoolmaster.
For ye are all the children of God by faith in Christ Jesus.
For as many of you as have been baptized into Christ have put on Christ.
There is neither Jew nor Greek, there is neither bond nor free, there is neither male nor female: for ye are all one in Christ Jesus.
And if ye be Christ's, then are ye Abraham's seed, and heirs according to the promise.

Bud read without stammering over words and without the shaky voice Caroline had been accustomed to.

"Bud... You're reading... Out loud!"

"Yes ma'am," he replied, tipping his hat, "I wanted to make you proud and I've done it. I reckon soon I'll be ready to take the GED. It's all 'cause of you, Caroline."

Bud took her hands and pressed them to his lips.

"C'mon, give Bud a hug."

Caroline rose and wrapped her arms around Bud excitedly. He lifted her off the porch steps and swung her around as she squealed.

"Bud!"

He set her back down and kissed her long, hard and deep. When he pulled away, Bud whispered, "Thank you for always believing in me and doing the right thing. It's why I love you, Caroline. It's why all of us a do."

"Stop, you're making me blush."

"Good. You're a good woman, Caroline. You deserve the world."

Bud went inside and made a pot of coffee for Caroline and himself. Caleb came home in the late afternoon with Chase. The two of them were closer than Caroline had ever seen them. Maybe there would come a time when she could explain her complicated relationship with the boys to her brother, that time hadn't come yet.

Bud, Chase, Caleb, and Caroline sat around with beer and some cornbread that Nikita Coulson made. Travis was supposed to come by later to join them. He'd spent the day consoling his mother, who after reading the newspaper, learned how deep her husband's depravity went. Despite it all, she still missed him, and Travis worried about how poorly she handled the grief of losing him.

He was running late, but Travis arrived on foot and out of uniform. His cheeks were flushed from the walk outside. The nights had only been getting cooler and cooler.

"Good evening, everybody," Travis crooned.

Travis sat with them and got right down to business.

"Tomorrow, there's a meeting with the city council. We're all expected to attend. Buchanan will be there."

"What are we supposed to say?" Caroline asked.

"We use what we have, everything. The letters. My father's involvement. The affair."

"Are you sure?"

"Yes. I'm sure. If they push a resignation, they'll have elections soon enough."

"Elections?" Chase asked eagerly, more excited by the prospect of political excitement than politics itself.

"That's what I've heard."

"Wow, who do you think should run for mayor?"

"Dunno."

"Travis?" Bud asked.

"Yes?"

"Don't you have a shift now?"

"I quit."

Caroline gasped.

"Why?"

"They promoted me to sheriff. With about half the force implicated, they were running out of clean noses. I told them I had no interest in the job and I resigned."

"What are you going to do?"

"Not sure. All I know is tomorrow, we're going to kick ass at city council."

"Caroline and I will work on what to say."

"I can help," Bud said, "I passed my literacy test."

"Sure, why not."

Travis nodded.

"Perfect. I'll go down to the newspaper and make sure the press knows what's going down."

The three busied themselves in writing their statement for the city council. They decided that Caroline should speak on their behalf as the mayor's office employee who first spoke out and faced the worst consequences for doing so. She was ready. This was what she'd been fighting for — a chance to make a real change in their town.

After deciding what they'd say and after Caroline practiced, the four of them went out for the night to celebrate. Tension in Old Town relaxed a bit. Everyone spoke about what happened with the mayor and spread rumors that went beyond what had already been published in the papers.

They drank and their night ended in their old safe house, the Landry farm. It had been a long time since the four lovers had revisited their old stomping ground. Bud cleaned the place up and spruced it up with candles on old emptied barrels of whiskey, and a thick mess of blankets and lanterns. They'd spent so much time twisted into all these compromising positions on the floor of the barn, worrying about what others would think. Caroline had stopped worrying about that. It didn't matter what others thought as long as they did the right thing — as long as they were strong together, nothing could stop them.

On the floor of the barn, Caroline became the center of their world. Travis stripped her clothing off. Chase kissed her with forceful, possessive passion, and Bud began making love to her with fierce determination. By the time the four of them finished making love that night, they were soaked in each others juices and Caroline lay between them and they stroked her hair and all three of them whispered the words every woman craves, "I love you."

More importantly than that, Caroline felt loved and protected by the three men by her side. She might have dismissed them as just being redneck reminders of her small town past, but everything was different now. Caroline didn't only think of herself and her career. She cared for all four of them and the future of Old Town.

Morning came and they parted ways to prepare for the city council meeting. Caroline dressed in a pink skirt suit with a white blouse beneath it, skin colored tights and matching pink kitten heels. She wore her hair in a tight top bun, gelling down her baby hairs with an old toothbrush to complete her look.

She met Travis, Chase, and Bud at Travis' place. Since his father left, Caroline felt way more comfortable hanging around. He wasn't going to be at the city council meeting, but a rumor had been spread around time that Zachariah Owens might show up. They milled into their assigned seats. Travis hovered over Caroline's side, engaging with the press on her behalf and keeping her away from anyone who might be awkward with her presence. Travis sat next to Caroline and elbowed her.

"Are you nervous?"

"Of course. When is Buchanan going to get here?"

"Soon. Don't even look at him. He's not worth it."

Caroline flashed Travis a tight smile. He wished he could put his hand to the small of her back, or give her some small comfort. Caroline still thought their relationship should be a secret, even if what they'd learned about secrets suggested that a big secret would always weasel its way out of hiding.

Before Travis could move forward and touch his hand to Caroline's side, the doors thrust open and the roar of journalists questions heralded Mayor Buchanan's entrance into the room. He looked older than Caroline remembered, and he had the life drained out of his eyes. His wife and kids already left. Buchanan arrived to face the council alone.

Caroline grew less nervous once she'd delivered her opening statements. Travis whispered that he could sense from the council's response that they believed her. Buchanan didn't bother addressing the concerns himself. His lawyer spoke next and as he finished his opening statements, he said something that raised the hair on the back of Caroline's neck.

"Miss Caroline Coulson is perhaps motivated today by her *deviant* actions and sexual indecencies which I'm certain she does not wish the council today to entertain..."

"Objection!"

"Miss Coulson, there can be no objection."

Caroline stood up and clenched her fists. She couldn't allow Buchanan and his cronies to use what little they had against her. So what if this ended her career in Old Town? She couldn't let herself be blackmailed into silence any longer.

She looked over at Travis. He could tell from the look on her face what I was about to do.

"Your honor, I want to discuss this sexual deviance Mr. Bergen has suggested at with full disclosure and honesty, perhaps a level of honesty that our elected representatives should themselves espouse. Mr. Buchanan, Sheriff Montgomery and all their accomplices are in possession of damning evidence against me and three other individuals. This evidence proves that I had a relationship with three men in this town and we engaged in this consensual relationship at the same time."

The judge raised a brow.

"I fail to see the relevance."

"So do I, your honor. However, the individuals who rigged this towns elections, and went on racist crusades against the citizens of this town seem to believe that knowledge of this consensual relationship should give them an unfair advantage in making political decisions."

Caroline smirked at Buchanan and winked. His face was already beet red.

"Noted. Thank you, Miss Coulson, for your honesty," the judge replied.

Caroline sat and exhaled. Bud and Chase stared at her across the room open-mouthed. Travis grinned and rested his hand on her thigh.

"Every journalist in the state caught that," he said, "This is going to be huge..."

"Not if we do a good job here today. It'll be small potatoes if we can get Buchanan to resign."

"Think you can do that?"

"Yes, I think I can."

Caroline fought hard. The judge, the council members and Buchanan's lawyer hadn't expected Caroline to fight that hard. Once they were finished, the judge sent everyone out except the council members to vote. They'd make a decision after deliberation. As Caroline waited in the hallway, Bud brought her a glass of water and Chase rubbed her shoulders.

"That was brave what you did back there," Travis assured her.

Caroline smiled weakly. Even as the men doted attention on her, she could feel curious eyes from Buchanan's team. They'd gossip about her later and this secret would become talk of the town. Caroline wasn't sure if she made the right choice or not. After the decision, then she'd know.

After two hours, Bud left to get some food for all of them. The room outside was crawling with even more press and Bud was the only one large, strong and tough enough to push past all of them. He came back armed with fried chicken and coffee. Caroline could hardly eat. They were only halfway finished eating before the judge called everyone back inside.

Buchanan smirked as he got to his seat. Caroline's heart sank into her chest. He knew something, didn't he?

The judge spoke, "The council has heard the evidence today and we've reached a decision."

Caroline sucked in sharply. Travis' hand death gripped her thigh beneath their table.

I know, Caroline thought to herself, *I know this is downright terrifying.*

"We are recommending that Mayor Tommy Lee Buchanan resign his post as mayor and within three weeks, Old Town will hold another election. None of the individuals involved in the previous election will be involved and the council has come to a conclusion that no one who has worked in politics in this town before will be accepted as a candidate. It is in this town's charter that we stay true to the principles on which Old Town was founded which includes liberty and the right for the common man to self-govern. Miss Coulson, step up to the podium for a private conference with the judge."

Buchanan kept smiling broadly as they led him out, as if he didn't understand what was really happening. Maybe he was just that good at putting on a show. After he left the room, Caroline approached the judge's bench. Travis followed.

"Your honor, permission to speak."

"Young Travis, no need to ask permission. What is it?"

Travis turned bright red. He'd known Judge Jameson for most of his life.

"I would like Mr. Bud Landry and Chase Owens to approach the bench. They were instrumental in this investigation."

The judge raised an eyebrow.

"Fine. Bring them up here."

Travis waved Bud and Chase over.

"Bud? Is that your government name?"

"No ma'am," Bud responded, "I'm William Ulysses Davis Landry, ma'am. Bill Ulysses Davis. It spells Bud."

He smiled and Caroline stifled a giggle. Apparently Bud was taking his new reading skills seriously. The judge responded with a stiff lipped smile — the best you can expect from a judge.

"Well young William, Travis, Chase, I called Miss Coulson up here because we're considering a mayor election in this town and want to recommend that one of you young people take the helm."

"Oh, I couldn't," Caroline replied hurriedly.

"Miss Coulson, are you sure? I hope you don't feel intimidated about the prospect of being a woman in politics because while it's no piece of cake, I have a feeling you can handle your way around the boys."

Caroline felt her cheeks matching the color of her suit.

"Judge Jameson, that's not it. It's just that... this whole situation has inspired me to think bigger than Old Town. I don't want to just be the mayor of this town... I wanted to run for Congress."

Judge Jameson had underestimated this one. She smiled gently.

"Very well, Caroline. My apologies for underestimating your ambitions."

"Mr. Owens? Would you consider a bid?"

"Your honor, with all due respect, I've just started the union down at the factory. I owe it to the guys to serve my time and make sure we get wages up before Christmas."

"Mr. Montgomery? I heard that you quit your job, and Lord knows your mama could use the help of extra income."

"My apologies your honor," Travis offered, "I would be happy to help with any campaign but I'm studying to take the LSAT and GRE."

"College? Good for you, Travis. What about you Young William?"

Bud's mouth dropped open.

"You can't be serious? Me? For mayor?"

Chase shrugged, "Why not?"

"I just learned how to read, for one thing!"

Judge Jameson smiled, "You learned didn't you? What about your GED?"

"I ain't got it yet. Caroline was supposed to help me take the test...But I can't do this! I can't run for mayor?"

"Why not, Bud?" Caroline chimed in, "Everyone in town loves you, black and white. Plus, I think I'll need practice running a campaign before I try to run for Congress."

"Travis! Talk sense into them!" Bud pleaded.

The judge smiled.

"Mr. Landry, there is no rule that the mayor has to be a genius. He's supposed to be a good man, and I can tell by the way your friends here support you that you're a good man. If you did run for mayor, I think you'd do a good job."

"What what I say? I don't know a thing about speeches or politicking!"

"But I do," Chase chimed in.

"So do I," Travis replied.

"Like I said, I could use the practice," Caroline replied.

"Fine. I'll do it. But just so you know, this is crazy. I'll never become the mayor of this town."

"Crazier things have happened," Caroline replied, giving her boys a special look, a glance reserved just for them, that not even Judge Jameson noticed.

EPILOGUE

Night Of The Old Town Mayor's Election

"I would like to thank you gathered here today for electing me the mayor of Old Town. I've grown up my whole life. I've been a redneck through and through. I never knew a world outside of Old Town and tonight, I'm proud to stand before you for what these values represent. The *new* values of Old Town — freedom for our brothers and sisters regardless of their skin tone, freedom from discrimination, an end to symbols of hate and hate speech from our elected officials, and a pledge to destroy the abandoned tracks that separate both sides of this town, black from white. Tonight, we put an end to these barriers. Tonight, we put an end to hatred. Tonight, we become the change. Thank you all for coming."

"CHEERS!"

The crowd rung out, glasses clinked around the room, and Caroline kissed Bud on his cheek.

"Amazing speech!"

"I won. I can't believe I fuckin' won!"

Bud whooped and finished his champagne.

"You'd better go to meet and greets. Travis is giving a statement to *The Standard* right now, but they'll be wanting a quote from you."

"Where's Caleb?"

"Downstairs with the union men giving a statement. Everyone's going to know that Mayor Landry stands with the unions and working class people."

"Excellent."

"You go find Travis. I'll get Chase."

"Alrighty, Caroline."

Bud kissed her on the lips and Caroline scurried off into the crowd to find Chase Owens. Chase had just finished up with reporters when Caroline found her way to him.

"Hey, how's it going?"

"Fine. Wondering how we're going to handle it when I announce I'm running for Congress next week."

"The good thing is we're getting your name out there. And Bud... Well the bastard actually fuckin' did it."

"It's all been a blur."

"It has. Are you ready for the after party?"

Caroline nodded, "Yes. I am."

"Good. We're going to slip out of the party around midnight."

"Meeting at the barn?"

"Yup. It's been renovated and looking mighty fine."

"Perfect. I just need to see Caleb before I go."

Caroline milled around the party, spoke to reporters, shared glasses of champagne and received congratulations from everyone who knew the role she'd played in Bud's campaign.

He'd be a great mayor. Since the win, Caroline knew she'd be in for a wild night. The men were up to something, and they knew that since she'd be running for Congress soon, they'd only get busier and busier, changing the world one step at a time.

Next week, the old train tracks would be pulled up and the school system would be properly integrated, and everything that kept Old Town comfortable for men like Buchanan would melt away. Caroline trusted Bud to do the right thing. His plans for appointed officials included people from both sides of town. Change wouldn't happen overnight. Some families had already moved and others were only planning on it. Old Town's trajectory was set despite the naysayers.

At midnight, Caroline was still invigorated from the party and giddy with success. She hadn't spotted Travis and Bud in a while; she suspected they'd snuck out. Caroline hastened out the door after she said goodbye to her brother and told him not to wait up. Caroline had never walked to the Landry farm so fearlessly. Bud had been working off his nervous energy from the election by putting all his efforts into repairs on the barn.

Caroline could smell the fresh coat of paint and pine wood as she approached the dark field. Caroline pulled the door open and gasped.

"Surprise!" Travis, Bud and Chase announced at once.

Bud turned the lights on.

"It's… It's like a *real* office in here. Like a real house!"

The old wood had been repainted and the roof repaired. Large glass windows existed where none had before. Instead of old blankets on the floor, there was a large, leather pull out couch and desks with expensive equipment, a fancy espresso machine and gorgeous chandeliers.

"What is this for?!"

"It's for you," Bud said, "I thought you'd need somewhere

to run your campaign out of and we'll all want to be comfortable."

"I picked out the chair," Travis bragged, lounging back on the cozy leather couch.

"I got the chandelier," Chase added, "It was at Buchanan's yard sale. I thought it would be fitting."

"It's beautiful," Caroline breathed.

Bud nodded and replied, "I thought you'd like it. I picked the colors just for you."

"It's beautiful. Thank you!"

Caroline ran into Bud's arms and wrapped her arms tightly around him. Travis stood up and wrapped his arms around her. Chase joined from her right. Their different scents and weights pressing around Caroline sent a shudder of warmth through her. This place... all three of them... they were perfect. Nothing could have made them *more* perfect.

"We love you, Caroline," Travis whispered.

"He's right. I love you," Bud affirmed.

"So do I," Chase answered, "I'm so crazy in love with you, that I don't even mind sharing."

Travis smirked, "We share so many things we love, what's one more?"

"We're devoted to you, Care. We're going to see you in Congress. I know it."

Caroline stopped herself from crying. Before anyone could notice, Bud provided a welcomed distraction and kissed her long and hard on the lips. Good. She'd been wrong. There was one way the night had become more perfect — when her three sexy redneck rebels admitted that they loved her.

Most people can only hope for one great love and Caroline had found three. They didn't need to compromise. They co-operated, and loved each other together in all the right ways.

Chase kissed her shoulder, slipping Caroline's dress strap over the bone and running his tongue along her flesh as she shuddered.

Travis lifted her hair and kissed the back of her neck, all the way to the top of her zipper where his hand hovered for a moment as he pressed his weight into her and whispered into her ear, "We're going to fuck you right now, Caroline..."

"Yes..." she whimpered.

"We're going to fuck that tight, perfect little pussy and make you ours."

"Yes..."

"It's official," Bud replied, "You belong to us..."

Chase murmured, "Ours..."

The apex of Caroline's thighs already dripped with anticipation at the thought of accepting all three of them between her legs again. She ached to feel their cocks again. It had been far too long since she'd focused on what was important to her — these men, these crazy bad boys who had gone through hell for their queen. Caroline stuck her ass out and rubbed it against Travis' crotch. He groaned and she could feel his cock stiffen.

Chase pulled a handful of her hair and yanked her neck back. Bud sucked hard on her neck, most of her flesh fitting between his lips where he gripped her hard. She was powerless to wriggle in his grasp. Bud pulled his lips away and returned them to hers, a deep growl purring in his throat as he palmed Caroline's breasts while kissing her.

"I want to stick my cock in her pussy and then fuck her little ass until tomorrow morning."

"I think Caroline is finally ready for us to unleash our wild sides," Travis whispered as he hurriedly pulled his cock out of his pants, his breath hot and urgent on Caroline's neck.

"One day we're going to fuck her and put a baby right

between these milky chocolate thighs," Chase moaned as his tongue flicked over Caroline's nipples.

She exploded with a climax with no cocks inside her. Just hearing the way her men talked about her like they were going to use her pussy and give her the insane, overwhelming, fantastic sex she craved. Her pussy lips were slick and dripped down her thighs, sticking her tights to her curved hips.

Travis hiked her dress up.

"These tights are covering up that tight little pussy."

"Rip them off. It's time to stop teasing," Chase urged.

He had his tongue suckling on one of Caroline's breasts while Bud worked her other tit, massaging it and then sucking on it hard as surges of pleasure rushed down Caroline's spine. She tilted her head back, hair draping down her neck as Travis grabbed her tights and ripped them off her thighs, pulling away the only remnants of her modesty so he could have easy access to her cunt beneath the dress.

Caroline squealed as Travis bent to his knees and spread her legs so that he could kiss her thighs and lap up the juices that spilled down her legs from her gushing cunt. As Travis kneeled between Caroline's knees, Chase moved his lips from her breasts back to her mouth and kissed her long and slow, pausing every few moments to catch his breath.

Bud's rough hands worked their way down Caroline's hips. His grip was tight and his hands still tough and strong as she remembered them. Caroline moaned as Travis' lips parted hers and his tongue drove between her legs. He slipped and slid around her pussy lips, sucking on her outer lips and then thrusting his tongue inside her until she moaned.

Travis licked slowly and softly over Caroline's clit and squeezed her thighs when she finally exploded from the overwhelming pleasure, cumming all over his face and lips. Travis kept eating her pussy until Caroline came three more times. Then he rose to his feet. Bud bent Caroline over her leather chair so her beautiful ass stuck out and he spread her thighs apart.

"Mayor Landry, I think you deserve to go first," Chase joked.

Bud didn't need a second invitation. He disrobed his thick, muscular lumberjack's body, stripping away the suit that was so unnatural to him and he entered his most primal state of mind — arousal. As Caroline's scent rose to his nostrils, Bud was a man possessed. He pulled his monster cock out and thrust it inside her with one swift motion. Caroline cried out as her pussy gushed even more juices than before.

Chase kissed her on the lips and stared into her eyes, taking in her moans of pleasure and enjoying every twisted expression on her face as Bud's monster cock pummeled her from behind. When Bud made her cum over and over again, he moved his hardness straight to her ass.

Caroline was just as scared as the first time. She squeezed Chase and Travis' arms for comfort as Bud began to slide inside her tightly puckered hole, using her juices as lubrication as she moaned and arched her back to take him inside her nice and deep. With his cock buried in her ass, Bud went even wilder then before. He pumped between Caroline's legs and as she trembled and screamed in climax, Bud groaned and emptied his seed deep inside Caroline's perfect ass, as round and juicy as a Georgia peach.

Bud leaned back on the couch, catching his breath as Chase positioned himself behind Caroline and slid his thick veiny cock between her thighs. Caroline could *feel* the difference between Chase and the others. The girth of his cock was just different and with all these bulging veins, he ribbed the inside of her pussy and rubbed against all her sensitive bits extra hard.

Chase was gruff yet loving today, celebrating with masculine vigor as he thrust deep between Caroline's thighs. She gripped the arm of the couch and moaned hard.

"Cum baby," Travis whispered, "Cum for Chase… I like the look in your eye when you cum for him…"

How could Caroline hold back as Travis whispered these nasty little phrases in her ear? She never stood a chance against any of them. Caroline moaned and came again as Chase pounded her. Chase smacked her ass as he pulled out of her and leaned forward so he could whisper into Caroline's ear on his own.

"I'm going to fuck your ass so hard that you'll never forget my cock, even if you run for president…"

Caroline's pussy dripped even more. These three men didn't just support her and make love to her, they'd stay by her side all the way to the top. She gasped for breath, taken by surprise as Chase slid his full length deep inside her tight asshole without much warning. She was wet and dripping and there was plenty of lubrication for him to nestle in there.

As Chase's cock stretched her forbidden hole, Caroline moaned and Chase plunged into her deeper. Chase's cock pleasured her hole in new ways as he moved between her thighs.

"Take my big dick! Take it," he groaned.

Caroline whimpered and thrust her hips back, allowing his cock to slide deeper inside her and deliver even more pleasure than before. As Caroline came again, stimulated to a deep, anal orgasm, Chase pulled his cock out and thrust it back into her pussy where he came long and hard. Caroline moaned and collapsed on her breasts as Chase erupted inside her pussy and his juices gushed down her thighs mixed with Bud's.

Chase removed his cock as Caroline caught her breath. Travis slid behind her and thrust inside her. Caroline cried out… She was in for a long night…

Travis made love to her nice and slowly, in a way that reminded Caroline of just how much the three loved her. As Travis slid between her thighs, Bud pressed his hand to her back. Chase kissed her, and all three cemented their love for her by releasing their deep orgasmic pleasures onto her.

When Travis finished between her thighs, Caroline collapsed back onto her couch. Travis lifted her naked, off her feet and whispered, "We're not finished with you yet… We've got a little surprise."

Bud disappeared for a moment and returned with whipped cream, handcuffs, a tall candle, a fresh nectarine and long brown ropes. Caroline gasped, very much surprised indeed.

THE END.

Flip the page to read a sample of Book #2

Click here to order Book #2

REDNECK REBELLION

FREE Preview Ahead...

smarturl.it/redneckrebellion

REDNECK REBELLION

BOOK TWO

JAMILA JASPER

1

THE THREE MEN

CAROLINE GASPED as rough lips caressed her neck. Bud lay on top of her, his large muscular body firmly planted between her legs. Chase gingerly ran his tongue over her shoulders while Travis massaged her nipples, pinching them between his thumb and forefinger as she moaned. Caroline groaned as Bud's beard tickled the wet spot on her neck.

"We gon' spend the rest of the day testing this damned bed out," he murmured, rubbing his hands over her waist.

Caroline giggled.

"No," she whispered, "We have to... We have to..."

She lost her train of thought as Travis traded his fingers for his tongue. His tongue tickled her sensitive nipples as Bud hiked her thighs up.

"Bud," she whispered, "Not now..."

"Oh yes, Caroline," he whispered, "Welcome to your new home..."

Caroline responded with a loud moan as he slid inside her. Travis and Chase weren't naked yet. They'd taken their shirts off, which gave Caroline quite the view. Chase still had a sunburned neck, despite all her warnings about sunscreen while he repaired the porch. Travis heeded her warnings about sunscreen, but his time in the sun turned his blond hair so light it was nearly silver.

Bud buried himself inside her to the hilt and Caroline squeezed her eyes shut as he ardently thrust into her. She reached over his broad, farm-boy back and duck her nails into the thick muscles. Bud groaned and grunted, rutting between her legs like an animal.

His body warmed hers right up. January in Old Town didn't get freezing cold like towns in the North, but it was cold enough to be uncomfortable without three warm bodies in her bed. Once she got used to the three of them, she couldn't live without them. Better than blankets, that's for sure.

Bud tensed up and let out a half-moan, half-growl as he emptied himself between Caroline's legs. He was big. Enormous. And as he withdrew his staff from her sex, Caroline couldn't help but moan as juices erupted from her thighs and her yearning mounted.

Before the three boys: Travis Montgomery, Chase Owens and Bud Landry, she would have never assumed she was that type of girl. The type of girl to let three firm, well-built rednecks have their way with her. Especially not in a town like this one.

They'd hooked her in. More accurately, she'd hooked them in. And once she'd accustomed to having all three of them, her urges grew to match theirs. They were all three insatiable. Bud liked to have her first thing in the morning. Sweaty and gross and smelling of sleep was how he liked her best. Travis enjoyed her in the shower.

He'd murmur, "Let's get a little dirty before we get clean." Then he'd drop to his knees and spread her lower lips with his tongue before sponging her clean with ferocious vigor. Chase had her after work. He'd get back from the factory smelling like grease and sweat, having had some big argument usually, and he'd pin Caroline against the wall and plead with her to help him work out his pent up tension.

This time, all four of them joined in bed, a rare occurrence these days, but important on such a special occasion. The bed was new. And they'd spent the past few days sleeping on couches on sleeping bags until Bud finished stitching up the mattress.

As Bud rolled away from Caroline's split thighs, Travis hurried out of his pants, crumpling them at the base of the bed as he flipped Caroline onto her stomach and took her from behind. Travis celebrated with slow, deep strokes, whispering into her ear. If it weren't for Chase kissing her on the lips and Bud trailing kisses down her bare, spread legs, she might have forgotten that she and Travis weren't alone in the room.

When he finished inside her, Caroline didn't think she could stand any more of them. But Chase wouldn't let her off that easy. He flipped her onto her side and entered her right where he lay, his trousers only halfway down his thighs. The delicate curve of his hardness hit all the right spots. Bud and Travis sucked on her breasts as Chase moved between her legs. Her hair came unraveled from the tight bun and Travis wrapped some of it around his fingers as he pushed his tongue into her mouth, kissing her deeply.

Chase finished inside her after she came two or three more times. By then, the four of them were a mess. But very satisfied.

"Looks like the bed works fine," Bud said. His broad chest rose and plunged. Caroline predicted they would only have a few minutes before he wanted her again.

"Told you we could make it," Chase answered, drawing Caroline's naked body into his so her butt pressed against his groin.

The boys made the bed custom for their new house. The boys were good with their hands. Chase drew up the plans, Travis bought the supplies and Bud spent all his time out of the office hammering away. Caroline sat up, hair spilling over her breasts as Chase joined her in leaning against the soft velvet headboard.

"Do you think people suspect we aren't really roommates?"

Bud grinned, stroking his chin and running his hand down his flat stomach.

"I'd like anyone with suspicions to come talk to me about it."

Caroline giggled.

"Mayor Landry, we suspect you're living in sin with a woman and two other men," she mocked a potential citizen complaint and Bud chuckled.

Travis didn't find it so funny.

"We have to be careful," he said, "Caroline's right. Especially with the campaign coming up."

Chase folded his arms behind his head and sighed.

"Has anyone checked the mail yet?"

Caroline folded her body up nervously. They'd waited for the past three weeks for the letter. She'd spent ages gathering signatures and convincing residents of both sides of Old Town to sign her petition. They'd get news soon if they'd allow her to run for congress. She'd represent Old Town, Virgil and Moravia in Congress if she won the seat. Before all that, she'd need approval to run.

Bud rolled off the bed and groaned.

"I'll get it," Chase filled in, "I need to take a walk down the street and check on Ma, anyway."

Travis got up and stretched.

"Fine. I'll get supper started. Do we have anymore pork chops?"

Caroline searched the crumpled pile of clothes in the bed for a t-shirt.

"You three spoil me."

Bud grinned, "Ain't that what every Southern man wants? A little lady to spoil. I'm takin' a leak."

He ambled off to their en suite bathroom while Chase and Travis bustled off to busy themselves with various chores. Caroline slipped into one of Travis' white shirts. It smelled like sweat and magnolias. She found her underwear, a tight pair of black cotton panties and then a pair of Bud's sweatpants. She pulled the drawstring tight, so they'd fit around her waist without slipping down.

As she finished dressing, Bud emerged from the bathroom, naked except for a pair of red boxer briefs that hugged his tree trunk thighs. He hung onto the top of the door frame and bit his lower lip as he stared at Caroline.

"Too sore for me to take you again?"

Caroline's cheeks warmed.

"Bud..."

"Just joshing. How'd'you like the house?"

"It's strange. Living in Buchanan's old place. It feels... somehow wrong."

"I know. I know. It ain't exactly what you wanted, living in a plantation house and all that. But I'm the Mayor of this town and you're my girl. It's my job to care for you."

He nodded and gestured to Caroline, beckoning her closer. She obliged, tiptoeing across the large room before wrapping her arms around Bud's thick neck. He gazed down into her eyes, and she noticed a smattering of freckles across his face. Her thighs melted together. Bud was attractive. And up close he smelled like aftershave and hay.

"I love you," he murmured, "We all love you."

"I know," she sighed, "I hope I make it. I don't want you three working your butts off to take care of me while I sit around doing nothing."

Bud flicked the tip of Caroline's nose with his thumb.

"You could always have babies," he said, grinning from ear to ear like this was the most brilliant suggestion in the world. Caroline reached up to peck him on the lips. Crazy Bud.

"Babies? Would the three of you want that? I mean… it's one thing to share me, but what about kids…?"

Bud shrugged.

"I'm a simple guy. Ain't gonna complicate things. If you have a baby… we'll share the responsibility. Like we share you."

Caroline teased the nape of his neck with her fingers. Talking about babies gave her the powerful urge to have Bud again. Between her thighs. Inside her. Touching every inch of her…

Before they could continue their discussion — or escalate it — Chase and Travis bounded upstairs, thrusting the door to the bedroom open. Travis held up an envelope, his cornflower eyes wide with excitement.

"It came," Chase said.

Bud spanked Caroline on the ass, encouraging her to grab the envelope, egging her on like one of his horses. She grabbed the envelope from Chase.

"You didn't open it?"

"We thought you ought to do the honors."

Caroline bit down on her lower lip and ripped the envelope open fiercely. She intended to make a big show of it, slowly opening the envelope and reading each word out loud to her three boys. Once she'd fished the thin sheet of paper out, she couldn't help herself.

Caroline screamed. Loud.

"I'm in! I'm going to run for Congress! Holy shit!"

Bud lifted her off the ground as she screamed. Once he set her down, Travis threw his arms around her waist and kissed her. Chase set his hands on his hips, patiently waiting for Travis to finish.

"Don't forget the little guy once you make it to Washington," he said, a cocksure grin spread across his sunburnt face.

"There's no way I'm getting to Washington without your help," she said, "I've got to run a good campaign. Do you have any idea who I'm running against?"

The boys shrugged.

Chase said, "Dixon's retiring this year so whoever it is will be fresh. Someone young."

"If it was someone in Old Town, we'd know about it right?" Caroline asked, wracking her brain for anyone she knew who might run for Congress.

Their town's election for Mayor had been tough enough on Old Town tensions. Her parents even moved away at her brother Caleb's behest to get away from everything. He was staying up in the house now, alone.

"Maybe it's someone from Virgil?" Travis suggested.

Bud stroked his beard and shrugged.

"Don't matter. We'll make sure you kick anyone's ass."

Caroline's heart fluttered as the reality set in. A part of her didn't think they'd accept her running for Congress. She'd tried, but she didn't expect to make it this far. She was a black candidate, running for Congress in a rural county with three segregated towns. She couldn't win on the black vote alone. She'd have to win over voters from both sides of the tracks. Her head swam with the complexity of what she'd gotten herself into.

"Care?" Chase whispered, holding onto her shoulders and bending at the knees to meet her eye, "You okay?"

"Yeah."

"She's nervous," Bud said, "like a skittish mare."

Caroline rolled her eyes.

"You're comparing me to a horse now?!"

"She has every right to be nervous," Travis pointed out, which didn't help Caroline, but at least softened Bud and Chase. Chase pecked her on the lips.

"We'll stand by you. We promise."

"I know. I guess I never thought I'd make it this far. It's time for me to saddle up."

Chase's facial expression changed, and he glanced at Bud. Caroline noticed an entire conversation exchanged in that glance.

"We have news," Chase blurted out.

Travis nervously chewed on his fingernails. Bud remained calm and nodded slowly, urging Chase to continue.

"What?"

"My brother's back and he's on the force."

Zach Owens. Caroline's skin crawled when she heard the name. She'd gone several weeks without thinking of Zach Owens. She couldn't help thinking of Buchanan. Bud bought the old Mayor's plantation house with his new salary and some of Travis' savings, and they'd spent all their free time fixing the place up.

Caroline couldn't help thinking of Buchanan as she sanded wooden railings in what had been his house.

But Chase's brother had been far from her mind. And his return wasn't good news.

"Do you think he'd run for Congress?" Caroline asked.

2

THE OPPONENT

ZACH OWENS WASN'T RUNNING for Congress. But thinking about her opponent made Caroline realize she had to do this. Buchanan waltzed into the mayor's office and access to that much power nearly got most of them killed. Caroline shuddered at the thought. The very next day, she submitted her ultimate confirmation: she'd run for Congress.

The boys insisted they have a celebratory dinner. Chase couldn't get the afternoon off until Wednesday. Bud cleared off his schedule and Travis had all the time in the world since he quit the police force, a situation he wasn't particularly happy about.

Chase bought the ingredients for their celebratory dinner. Travis got an old family recipe out for pecan pie and Bud grilled the pork ribs out back using a special "meat rub" he'd invented. Caroline tried to help, but the boys would swat her on the bottom of with their spatulas or other implements, so she got stuck hovering around while they prepared dinner.

Travis poured Caroline whiskey and ginger ale and had himself a glass while he waited for the pie to bake.

"So. I'm taking the LSAT again soon."

"You're going to do this?"

"I believe in this justice system, Caroline. It's served us well for many many years."

"It's served some people well," Caroline muttered.

Before their conversation could take a more negative political turn, Travis reached for her fingers, intertwining his hands with hers.

"I need to provide for you, Caroline. I know you're a powerful woman and you can handle business yourself but... the Montgomery family takes care of their own."

His eyes were so blue you could swim in them. You could drown in them. Caroline ran her thumb over Travis' large veiny hands.

"I never thought I'd end up here," Caroline said, sipping on the strong whiskey.

"Neither did I. But we're here. And we're going to get you to Congress. All of us."

"Aren't you worried?"

Travis shook his head.

"If Bud Landry can end up in the Mayor's Office, we can get you to Washington."

"Maybe Old Town isn't ready for a black Congresswoman."

Travis shrugged.

"It doesn't matter if they're ready for the future. It's coming."

Travis got his pie out of the oven. The sticky, sugary smell of pecans filled the room. Chase carried side dishes into their dining room from the kitchen with Caroline's help, and Bud hauled in the meat.

"Good food, good meat, good God, let's eat."

"Was that your idea of grace?!" Caroline squealed at Bud.

He winked and dipped his finger in barbecue sauce before sticking it in Caroline's mouth. She wrapped her lips around his finger, tasting the tang of honey and tomatoes with a healthy dose of mustard and black pepper. Bud pulled his finger out of Caroline's mouth and smirked. She playfully smacked his bicep, and they dug in.

Chase gave a toast. He would have stood right on the table to do it, but Travis talked him into standing on the chair.

"To Caroline, the woman who brought us together and the woman who will take us to Washington. A brilliant woman, well deserving of sitting in the House of Representatives."

"Hear, hear!" Bud responded in a sonorous voice that might make you think he was calling to a crowd.

"Now, Mister Mayor," Caroline whispered, "Can we dig into the pecan pie? Why don't you cut the first slice?"

Bud cut the first slice, and Travis apologized profusely on the off chance he'd messed up his family recipe. There wasn't a chance of him spoiling it. From the first bite, Caroline wanted to devour the entire pie herself.

The boys crowded around the sink and wouldn't let Caroline so much as rinse off a spoon.

"Am I supposed to stand here doing nothing?"

"Get more whiskey in you," Bud growled, "You'll need it."

Caroline's thighs melted together. She knew exactly what it meant when Bud used that tone. He meant business and normally the kind of business that made it difficult to walk the next day. Tonight was about celebration and tomorrow, she'd meet with the paper and the party mentor helping to run her campaign. Caroline appreciated the boys' support, but she knew the chances of her winning this Congressional election were slim to none. In three months as Mayor, Bud made some changes around town, but he was still one of them. He was a Southern man who rode horses and played football.

Caroline was still an outsider. And Old Town was still segregated. And the other towns in the county were even worse. Chase broke away from the boys early and grabbed Caroline by the waist, pressing her against the wall in the hallway to their bedroom, a precursor of what was to come. Their high school portraits hanging on the wall rattled as Chase manhandled Caroline with a necessary kiss.

Caroline raked her fingers through his copper hair.

"What's that for?"

Chase grinned.

"A precursor to bad news. Zach's back in town and living with my ma. It's nice she has someone to take care of her but… he's different. Worse somehow."

"I'll stay out of his way."

"If you want me to run him out of town, say the word. I'll get one of Landry's guns and scare him off."

"No," Caroline whispered, "No guns. No fighting him off. We're doing things the right way now."

Chase buried his nose in Caroline's neck and came up for air, stiff and eager for her.

"Travis rubbing off on you, huh?"

"Maybe," Caroline answered.

"Yeah, well, he used to be a cop. It scrambled his blond brains."

"Chase…"

Chase took her lower lips between his and kissed her again, pinning her hands over her head. The floorboards creaked as Travis wandered down the hall, shirtless, with his jeans unbuckled.

"Heating up dessert?" he teased Chase.

"I'll leave that to you," Chase murmured, breaking eye contact from Caroline and twirling her down the hall into Travis' arms.

Travis dipped her dramatically and pulled her up for a kiss. Caroline's fingers danced over his broad shoulders. Caroline rested her head against Travis' shoulders and he scooped her up and brought her to their custom-made bed — perfect for exactly four.

By the time Caroline lay on her back, Travis pulled her clothes off and Chase crawled in beside them. He patiently kissed Caroline's neck and shoulders as Travis eased his trousers off and thrust his hardness into her. Caroline moaned, digging her fingernails into Travis' back, moaning as he entered her. Travis made love to her tenderly, taking his time thrust deep inside her, eagerly diving into every sensation of making love. Her tightness wrapped around him and Caroline crossed her ankles over his taut buttocks.

Her fingers clutched the back of Travis' head as her skin lit up with pleasure from Chase's tongue sampling every inch of her bare flesh. Travis pressed his forearms into the bed, his bicep tense next to her cheeks as his hips swiveled slowly between her legs.

His cheeks grew pink with each thrust, his skin holding a rainbow's range of shades as he took his pleasure from her sex. A climax surged in Caroline's core and she moaned, tilting her head back and causing her breasts to spill on either side of her chest where Chase eagerly wrapped his lips around her nipple and sucked so hard that she came. Her tight heat wrapping around Travis' invading member pushed him over the edge and he spilled thick spurts of hot cum between Caroline's eager legs. The three rednecks knew how to make her lose control. The moment Travis rolled off her, Chase pulled her on top of him. She raked her fingers through his hairy, masculine chest and kissed him as she lowered herself onto his protruding tumescence.

Chase moaned, as he steadied Caroline's hips, bringing her warmth down over his cock slowly. Once her wetness enveloped his dick, her fingers gripping his masculine chest, and she rode him nice and slow, taking her time to draw her fingers along Chase's muscular chest, sculpted by brutal factory work and daily passionate lovemaking.

Chase groaned as she moved her hips in an unusual swivel shape and he reached for her nipples, pinching them between his fingers as Caroline moaned and rode him faster. Chase's cock hit all her deepest spots at this angle, and when she came, her pussy gushed with her juices and the remnants of Travis's cum between her legs. The heat and wetness proved too much for Chase and he erupted inside her, a thick glob of cum coating the back of her tightness as he shudders and squeezed Caroline's hips desperately. Caroline removed her sticky entrance from Chase's hardness and rolled onto her back.

Travis emerged from their bathroom with a warm washcloth. Chase hiked her legs up and Travis wiped her clean. The warm rag tickled her inner thighs and once her thighs were cleaned, her legs and pussy tingled. Bud's thudding footsteps came down the hall.

"Bud..." she whispered desperately, grabbing one of their pillows and curling up.

There was one more enormous cock to take before the night ended. Bud stood in the doorway grinning at the two men naked in bed with Caroline.

"Y'all tuckered her out."

Travis stole Caroline's protective pillow away, and Chase pushed hair out of her face.

"Our girl can handle it."

Bud whipped his belt off and cracked it like he planned to use it for a spanking. Caroline squealed and Bud tossed the belt aside with a grin.

"Not tonight, buttercup."

He undid his shirt and gestured at Chase and Travis. By now they could communicate their bedroom needs without words. Chase flipped Caroline onto her stomach and held one of her legs down. Travis held down the other leg. They pinned her down good. She felt Bud's knees sink into the bed. Then she felt his tongue. His large, flat tongue felt almost too big to be a human tongue. He licked her until she was soaking and until she'd cum three or four times.

As she recovered from her fourth (or third) orgasm, Bud thrust his cock into her hard and pressed his enormous weight into her. She gasped for air as Bud took her hard from behind, grunting and rutting into her with animal fervor until he spilled his seed inside her and instead of rolling off Caroline, he collapsed.

"Bud!" she squeaked, "You are killing me!"

He pulled his hips off her a bit and flipped her over onto her stomach before kissing her.

"Not yet, little lady. I'm ready for round two."

Bud fucked her three more times. Then Travis had another round and then Chase woke up from a power nap and fucked her twice again. Caroline didn't think she could cum anymore than this. Were other women really satisfied with only one guy? Three insatiable Southern men changed Caroline's sex drive permanently.

Tonight, she slept cradling Bud's giant body, fingers on one hand interlaced with Travis' while Chase spooned her from behind. They slept like puppies after a good feeding.

Their good night's sleep wouldn't last. A crash came downstairs. Then another. Caroline woke with a start.

Bud was already out of bed, and he had his shotgun.

"Bud!"

"Someone's knocking," he said, "Let's find out who it is."

"Don't jump to shooting them!" Caroline protested, searching for a t-shirt to slip over her naked body.

Bud didn't care about greeting anyone at the door stark naked apparently, but the other boys had the decency to slip their pants on while Mayor Landry stalked through the house bare ass cheeks sliding past each other. Caroline wore Bud's oversized shirt as she tiptoed behind him.

Chase grabbed an ax from the top of the stairs and Travis pointed to the kitchen, indicating the pistol he stashed at the bottom of the sink — and left Caroline to discover with a shriek one day. Caroline flicked on the porch light and they all lowered their weapons.

Nothing to worry about. It was only Caleb. He pounded on the door again.

"Caroline, open the damn door!"

Caroline thrust the door open and Caleb's eyes dropped to Bud's... pistol. Bud cleared his throat and stepped behind Caroline so his genitals were no longer in view.

"Y'all need to hurry up the road. We got a problem."

"What? It's three in the fucking morning, Caleb."

"Zach Owens was on patrol. He shot Ezra Mayfair. The Mayfair boy... He's dead."

3

WE MUST COME TOGETHER

CAROLINE FROZE when she heard the words. Zach Owens shot Ezra Mayfair.

"He's dead?"

"You need to come. Now. All of you."

Caleb tipped his hat and muttered, "Mayor Landry."

Bud became conscious of his indecency and turned tail to pull on his clothes. And the other two men set down their weapons. Caroline froze in the doorway. Her brother grabbed her shoulders.

"Caroline," he said, drawing her in with his voice, "You need to watch yourself tonight. People are angry. Furious. And it's a complete mess. This is it. This is the spark that will light this town on fire. Do you understand?"

Caroline didn't. A faint ringing in the back of her ears distracted her and her tongue hung heavy in her mouth. Ezra Mayfair and his sister lived across the street. He was a good boy. He always had a smile that cracked open his cinnamon-colored face and a warm demeanor.

He'd joke with Caleb sometimes about getting out of Old

Town. He'd stop and stand in the middle of the streets to watch the sunsets. He'd seen his last sunset. Had he known it would be the last? Caleb tore up the street, and Caroline flinched when firm hands touched her shoulders. Chase.

"You okay?"

"No."

"We're ready to go up there. Bud's taking the truck."

Mayor Landry bought himself a new truck to go with his new house. Bud hurried past Caroline and Chase to fire up the engines. Chase sat in the backseat with Caroline. Travis sat in the front. Neither Travis nor Bud spoke. Caroline could imagine what Travis was thinking, so she didn't bother saying anything. He believed in the law, and he couldn't understand a world where the people he grew up with might act unjustly.

Chase was different, at least. He didn't see a reason someone ought to shoot a man in cold blood without rights to a trial or a jury of his peers. Caroline laced her hands with his. Chase pressed her hands to his lips, rough stubble prickling her knuckles and warm lips sending a shiver through her arm. Hot tears rose in her lower lids and Caroline pushed them back.

Don't cry. Don't cry yet.

When the Mayor's truck pulled halfway onto the sidewalk, a crowd formed around it. Police officers. Bud got out of the truck and the world disappeared around him. Caroline knew he'd impress as Mayor, and now she watched him in action. Bud Landry towered over all the men. Their uniforms and guns holstered on slender hips didn't carry the same intimidating power when they stood next to gigantic Bud Landry.

"What the hell happened down here?" Bud growled.

"We've got Zach Owens to safety, sir. The medics are over there with the body. They're taking him to the hospital but... he's dead, Mayor."

"How the hell did this happen?"

Caroline's mouth went dry. She felt an arm around her waist. Travis. He never touched her like this in public. And she wasn't sure she wanted him around. Ezra Mayfair could have been anyone she knew. He could have been Caleb. But Zach Owens... Zach Owens could have been Travis, and somehow Caroline felt worse.

"I need to... I need to..."

She pulled away from Travis and propelled by emotion rather than better judgment she ran toward the crowd surrounding the ambulance. She saw all her neighbors huddled together on one side of the ambulance and on the other side, people from the white side of town, the part of town where Caroline now lived. I'm betraying them, she thought. I've been enjoying myself living in an enormous house with three attractive men, and I thought that was improving my circumstances, but what I've really done is I've betrayed them. She burst through the caution tape and ended up on the other side before anyone noticed her. And not knowing what else to do, she flung herself onto Bianca Mayfair, who stared at the white sheet covering her brother's body and gasped when Caroline's weight fell into her.

They only knew each other in passing. But Caroline needed to hold someone. She needed to hold another black woman and mourn. Ezra Mayfair's life ended, but grief wouldn't end there and they both knew it. This sadness would ferment and grow, and it could sour every bit of happiness from their lives if they let it. Bianca emitted a shuddering sob, like she knew everything Caroline was thinking, like she'd had the same thought herself.

"He's gone," Bianca whispered, and the two words split Caroline's heart in two. By the time she pulled away, the light-skinned woman's face turned purple and Caroline held her hand. They heard another sound. Cars. Trucks. And then chaos. Two news vans.

"Go," Caroline whispered to Bianca, "Go to the hospital before they find you."

Bianca nodded. Caleb found his sister and grabbed her by the forearm.

"Travis is looking everywhere for you."

"Okay."

"You need to get out of her, Caroline before it gets crazy."

"Okay."

"Bud's staying behind to talk to the news trucks. Chase and I will walk you home."

"What about Travis?"

Caleb patted Caroline's back and pursed his lips.

"Don't worry about Travis."

The next forty minutes blurred past. Chase sat on the arm of their parlor couch and passed a mug of tea over to Caroline before he took Caleb to the door and they spoke to each other in hushed voices. When Chase shut the door, his boots thudded against the hardwood and he leaned in the parlor's doorway. His eyes met Caroline's and her throat tightened.

"Baby..." Chase said, and the anguish on his face reflected her own. Caroline sobbed. How many years would they have to fight?

"Don't," Caroline whimpered, "I don't have time to be weak right now."

"You ain't weak. You ain't weak for feeling. Goddammit, you don't have to be a soldier all the time."

"Don't I?" Caroline whispered.

Chase stroked her hair. He wasn't as soothing as Bud. He had rough, workman's hands and little delicate about him.

"The cops are protecting their own on this one. But there weren't any reason for it as far as I can tell. Zach... my brother... he shot an innocent man."

Caroline gazed up at him again. His mother was out there. His brother killed someone. But he was here. With her.

"Your mom," Caroline whispered, "I'm so selfish. I didn't even think about her."

"Don't," Chase responded sharply, "Travis will look after my ma. He's... he's talking to my brother."

"Shouldn't you look after them?"

"Caroline. If I have to see my brother tonight, I'll kill him. And I won't do us any good behind bars."

He was earnest about killing his brother. He'd come close, Caroline knew that. And Chase didn't have that ability to stop himself from acting on his impulses. He was brash. And crazy. And Caroline didn't want to love that about him, but she did.

Chase settled next to her on the couch and wrapped Caroline in his arms. He was warm and eventually she cried herself to sleep pressed against his chest. They slept through the night on the couch together. Caroline woke to hushed voices. Travis's slow drawl and Bud's gruff grunts in response. Chase shifted beneath her, rousing Caroline from sleep. He'd lost his shirt in the night and her bare cheek pressed against the hair on his chest. She ran her fingers through it before sitting up and yawning.

For a few moments, before she was properly awake, it was like a normal morning. Then she remembered, and her shoulders slumped.

"G'morning," Travis said, pushing a plate of eggs and toast across the coffee table.

"We made breakfast. I ate already."

"Great."

Caroline stared at the plate. How could she eat at a time like this? Chase didn't have that problem, and he crudely plopped eggs onto toast with his fingers. Bud kept the mood light that morning. Caroline could tell he was trying his hardest not to burden them all but his eyebrows knitted together seriously between his wisecracks and she knew he hadn't forgotten.

They spent a quiet morning together until Caleb dropped by around 11. Chase led him into the living room while Travis studied for the LSAT upstairs and Bud hollered on the phone. Chase cleared his throat and exchanged a knowing glance with Caleb.

"You two are planning something."

"Yes," Caleb said, "A protest. What happened to Ezra Mayfair wasn't right. We can't let Old Town continue like this. Not anymore. Zach can't get away with this. No offense, Chase."

"None taken. I'd be the first man in line to kill that sonofabitch."

Caleb flashed Chase a prohibitive look but dismissed his rough talking as Chase being Chase.

"What do we do, then? Make signs?"

"Yes," Chase replied, "Against my inner desires, we are going to organize the people non-violently to protest the unlawful killing of Ezra Mayfair. No weapons. Nothing but silently showing our disapproval."

Caroline shook her head.

"What? You're not onboard?"

"It doesn't matter how we protest. They'll make us look like the bad guys."

"We have to do the right thing," Chase urged, "We know the cops in this town. I mean..."

He lowered his voice and whispered, "Sherriff Montgomery had KKK affiliations. We had proof."

"I'm running for Congress. Won't this affect my campaign?"

"Look," Caleb said, "You're my sister. I want you safe. I won't begrudge you avoiding the front lines. But there's Bianca Mayfair to worry about. Ezra provided everything for her. And what's going to happen if she doesn't have two pennies to rub together to provide for their family? We need to get justice for them. For her."

Caleb had a point. Caroline remembered holding Bianca, how numb she felt. How they both cried about a shared pain that they didn't realize they had. Only last year, Caroline thought she'd been in the same position with her brother. She would have wanted people to protest. She would have wanted justice for him.

"The story's picking up speed," Chase pointed out, "The goddamned internet finally knows about Old Town."

Caroline wondered if that would become more of a curse than a blessing.

"So. A protest. Where?"

"The park, the mayor's office, maybe the police station."

"You want to protest outside of Bud's office?"

"He'd support us. He does," Chase pointed out, "That might count for something."

"Some folks from out-of-town want to come here and help us organize," Caleb said.

Travis appeared in the doorway.

"A protest?"

Caleb's expression changed. He'd never liked Travis as much as Chase. Caroline couldn't imagine the rage her brother felt for him now. Travis was one of them. Even if he'd taken off his uniform. He thought like a cop.

"Yessir," Chase responded with a grin.

He and Travis disagreed often. He was better at diffusing situations than Caleb. Travis shook his head.

"That ain't the way to get your message heard in this town. You protest, it'll seem like you have a problem with the cops. Is that the message you want to send out here? I mean… Zach Owens doesn't speak for all of us."

Caroline wanted to sink into the couch. She could feel her brother's mood changing. He was too angry to listen to Travis. To hear him. He was like Caroline: grieving. And he had every right to grieve. Chase rose and clapped Travis on the shoulders, perhaps more rough than friendly.

"Travis, buddy? My brother shot an innocent man. Protesting ain't illegal. First Amendment rights protect it. So until we get that boy the justice he deserves, we'll exercise those rights."

Travis shrugged, but his cheeks were pink and Caroline sensed their conversation had not finished.

4

PEACEFUL

TRAVIS DIDN'T APPROVE. Caroline sensed his disapproval. What was wrong with a protest exactly? Chase was right. They had rights, and they had to get justice for Ezra Mayfair.

"When they bring Zach to court, they'll handle him. If you go out there in the streets, it'll be like looking for war."

"It's a peaceful protest," Caroline snapped, "Peaceful."

"Yeah, well. Those things have a way of not staying peaceful," Travis responded.

Caroline glanced over at Chase, who patted her on the thigh.

"Listen, man. How about we discuss this when we've all cooled down? I'm thinking about Caroline."

"So am I," Travis snapped, "And she doesn't need you going off half-cocked ready to cause more trouble in this town than she can handle."

Bud ambled into the room.

"Y'all fighting?"

"No!" the three responded sharply enough for Bud to assume they had more conflict than they let on.

"We're protesting. Landry knows about it. That's all there is to discuss."

"Bud..." Travis reddened and turned to his old friend.

Bud shrugged and responded with a grunt.

"You can't grunt your way out of this, Mayor Landry," Travis insisted.

"They got rights. You got rights. From what I've heard, Zach Owens had no right to fire a weapon on that boy. He wasn't in uniform. The boy wasn't doing anything wrong. He shot him in cold blood."

Caroline bit her lower lip to stop it trembling. How could Travis stand there and not see plain as day what she saw? Ezra could have been her brother.

"It could have been Caleb," Caroline whispered.

Chase kissed her cheek.

"Travis. Maybe you ought to give her space."

"No," Travis insisted, "She's my girl."

"She's our girl," Chase corrected him.

"Exactly, which means she's mine too. And I won't have you two leading her astray when she has bigger things to worry about than Ezra Mayfair."

"Shut up!" Caroline yelled.

All three boys stared at her.

"I'm sick of listening to you all arguing. I'm going for a walk. Don't follow me."

"Caroline..." Chase pleaded.

"Reason with him," she snapped at Chase before storming out of the house.

Caroline didn't want to go back to the crime scene. She needed to get away from the boys and their incessant arguing. She appreciated Chase standing up for her, but he ought to know better than picking a fight with Travis. Bud never involved himself in arguments. He cared too much about being liked, Caroline thought. And Travis...

Caroline's eyes pricked with tears. Her relationship with Travis had always been different. He was more protective. More gentle than both Chase and Bud. And now.

"He doesn't mean it," Caroline whispered, "he's just looking out for me."

After all they'd been through, there was no way Travis sided with Zach Owens. He thought about the world differently. Caroline had always known that. And she'd never let these differences tear them apart. But this was different. Ezra Mayfair didn't live far off. Caroline entered a cafe on Old Town's Main Street. The two blonde girls behind the counter stared at her too long.

"Um... may I have a black tea?"

The one at the cash register left to grab the tea without saying a word. Caroline wondered if she'd imagined their coldness. The girl behind the counter looked like Augusta Abernathy. They might have been related. She handed Caroline the tea and Caroline winced as she grabbed onto the cup. Too hot. She sat at a table outside and sipped the tea, thinking of nothing and everything.

Did this count as grief? She hadn't been close to the Mayfairs. They were neighbors, which meant you had someone to wave to, someone to grab your trash can lid when wind dragged it halfway down the street. A flicker of recognition when you crossed them downtown. And Ezra... well, he'd been a flirt. Too young for Caroline. Way too young. But he was one of those young men who would grow up handsome, with a string of broken hearts left behind when he finally left Old Town.

Caroline's hands shook. He wouldn't grow up, though. He'd

never flirt with another shopkeeper. He'd never smile. Didn't Travis get it? Didn't he get how badly it hurt to know that Zach Owens shot him in cold blood and because this was Old Town, nothing would ever come of it. That was the unspoken truth of the matter. Without marching. Without nationwide attention. With none of that, Ezra Mayfair would fade and they'd forget him. Only the Mayfairs would remember and twenty years from now, Old Town ladies would pull their friends close and whisper, "Remember their son? They shot him all these years ago and things were never the same."

Caroline didn't finish her tea. She left the cup on the table and wandered away from town onto one of the dirt roads leading to Virgil. Trees hung over the road, softening the sounds of the parallel highways to the bigger cities. Caroline kicked a few loose stones.

Caroline lost herself when she heard footsteps in the gravel. She whipped her head around. She couldn't hear anything except her own loud breathing, which she suddenly perceived as far too loud.

"Hello?"

It could happen again. Zach Owens popping out of the trees, armed. Or someone else.

"Hello?"

Caroline folded her arms and yelled, "I know you're following me."

A pair of legs dropped from the tree behind her. And then she saw him... Zach. No. Not Zach.

"Chase! You scared the hell out of me! What are you doing in that damned tree!"

"When I heard you call, I shimmied up there."

"You little monkey," Caroline grumbled, "Why are you following me?"

"I'm looking after you."

He reached into his Carhartt pants for his box of American Spirits and stuck one in his mouth. He struck a match and lit his cigarette. Caroline rolled her eyes.

"I don't need you looking after me."

"I know. That's why I hid."

"I didn't notice you downtown."

"I'm a master of disguise," Chase said, winking.

Caroline walked ahead and Chase half-jogged to catch up to her.

"Don't run off now. Sorry we pissed you off."

"You didn't."

"Travis…"

"He picks the worst times to put his foot down. I mean… I know he isn't like Zach, but he's defending a killer."

"Travis thinks different from you and I. His daddy was the sheriff of this town. That means something to him. This system works for him."

"It works for you. But you get it."

Chase shrugged.

"Fourteen hour shifts rarely give you time to think, but I talk to the guys on my smoke break. Old Town's always had two sides. A white side and a black side. We're closer to becoming one. I know that."

"I thought with Bud becoming mayor, that would end. Everything we went through didn't make a difference."

Caroline wanted to believe in Chase's vision of unity, but one side of Old Town refused that. There were still KKK members active in the town. Caroline stopped worrying about them when Buchanan left. But she'd been foolish to forget. Maybe if she hadn't forgotten, she would have worried more that Zach Owens came back to town. She could have done something. Chase pulled her out of her guilt and self-blame.

"That ain't true, Caroline."

Caroline wanted to believe him, but she couldn't help but think Chase only said this to make her feel better.

"What do you want, Chase? I'm not ready to come back. And I'm not ready to talk to Travis."

"You want the truth?"

"Yes."

"I want to walk with you. I don't want to be alone right now any more than you do. Caroline… I might kill my brother."

"What?! Chase… Don't you think that's extreme."

"Yes. But a life for a life. It's only fair. If he gets out of prison… I'll take his life. And I'll do my time. I'm not like other guys, Caroline. I know that I'm ready to lay my life on the line for what I believe."

Caroline stopped walking. Chase stopped too, and they faced each other. He stomped out his cigarette butt. Caroline squeezed her eyes shut.

"I can't believe I'm saying this but Chase Owens, promise me you won't kill your brother. Because if you leave me to go to prison, I will never forgive you. You aren't any use to anyone in prison."

Caroline waited for him to promise. She heard his boots against the gravel and then felt his hand on her cheek. And when she opened her eyes, Chase closed the distance between them and had both her cheeks in his hands, cupping her gently, like if squeezed too tight she'd fall apart.

"I promise," he murmured, "For you. Only for you."

He kissed her and spread her lips with his tongue instantly. And walked her off the path and against a tree with a large trunk. Caroline kissed him back, heat rising between them with each second that passed. She could taste tobacco on Chase's lips and smell his rough masculine musk. He took her hands and pinned them over her head.

"You make me crazy," he murmured.

Caroline giggled, but Chase ran his tongue along her neck.

"Chase," she whimpered, "What are you doing?"

"We're off the road," he whispered, "I can be quick."

Before Caroline could question him, he unbuckled his belt and hiked her back against the tree. Bark prickled Caroline's back through her shirt, but she didn't fight Chase. She wrapped her legs around his torso as he removed his hardness and stripped her pants down far enough to drive his dick inside her.

"Chase…" she gasped.

"I love you," he murmured, repeating it to her with each thrust. I love you. I love you. Caroline came. Fast. He was big. And urgent. He needed her and Caroline needed him too. She needed his broad, factory-hewn body to press against her and make her forget her hurt. She tangled her fingers in his brown hair, releasing a woody tobacco smell as he plunged into her deep.

"This is crazy," she gasped. Chase thrust between her legs harder and Caroline came again. Anyone could walk by, but by her third climax, she stopped worrying about the fact that they were only 20 feet off the dirt road.

Their bodies intertwined and Chase pressed his forehead to hers as his tongue played with her lips. He groaned as he erupted between her legs and Caroline squeezed her thighs around his torso as he removed his sloppy wet cock from her entrance and set her back on the ground.

"Dress," Chase commanded.

Caroline nodded. He'd fucked the good sense out of her,

because she'd been about to wonder back onto the dirt road with her ass out.

"Anyone could have heard us," She whispered.

"They didn't," Chase promised, "We're alone. Trust me."

His fingers interlocked with hers.

"Home," Caroline whispered, "We'd better go home. And I'd better talk to Travis."

Chase nodded.

"We're protesting. He doesn't have to like it."

"I know. But I want him to support us. This matters. Ezra Mayfair mattered."

"I know that. Let's go home and talk. Travis loves you, Caroline. I don't want to say he loves you more than any of us, but what he feels is real. And Travis comes from an old Southern family. It's hard for him to watch this unfold."

"I know. I get that."

"Come here, little lady. Mind if I have another smoke?"

"You ought to quit," Caroline teased.

"I know. I know. But damn, it's hard not to have a smoke after a damn good fuck."

Caroline's cheeks warmed. Chase's bluntness appealed to her. And she felt safe with him. And after their wilderness romp and his loving touch, she was finally ready to go home.

5

A HORRIBLE INCIDENT

"Come. You have to see this."

Travis grabbed Caroline's arm as she walked through the door. Caroline slipped out of her shoes while Chase banged mud off his boots against the porch. Is this how Travis planned on talking about their disagreement? Bud was already in their TV room and he patted the seat next to him. Caroline sat. Travis jumped over the back of the couch and sat next to them.

Ezra Mayfair's picture flashed across the screen. Caroline's head swam. She wriggled uncomfortably.

"He'll come back on soon," Travis murmured.

It felt good to sit next to him again and remember that Travis loved her. For all his flaws, he cared. He had a strong sense of ethics and he wouldn't betray her. Caroline couldn't take her eyes off Ezra Mayfair's picture. His eyes. Large. Brown. And empty the way photographs usually are. A coiffed blonde reporter pursed her lips and rattled off information about Ezra from a teleprompter that was a sum of his life — but not the life Caroline knew.

"Ezra Mayfair, a young resident of a poor Southern Town was murdered by a police officer while walking home..."

Caroline's ears rang.

"... He attended Robert E. Lee High School in Virgil and lived with his sister. Our investigative reporters turned up some unfortunate evidence about Ezra's past that may have led to his death. John? Can you hear us?"

"What unfortunate evidence?" Caroline spat, her voice shakier than she expected. Bullshit. It was all bullshit. Ezra wasn't a perfect kid. He'd stolen flowers from their garden once when he was a boy, and Nikita Coulson had whooped him and sent him home to get another whooping from his mama. He fought at school sometimes and came home with a busted lip. He might have smoked cigarettes. But he wasn't a monster.

"He didn't deserve this!" Caroline yelled.

Travis grimaced and murmured, "I know. I know, Caroline."

She leaned into Travis.

"He's coming on," Bud grunted, tilting a beer back down his throat, his wide neck bobbing as he swallowed. Caroline couldn't read Bud's reaction. He didn't let much ruffle his feathers.

Chase stalked into the room and leaned over the couch, rubbing Caroline's shoulders briefly. A shiver ran down her spine from their public romp...

"Jesse Clark, Virgil resident and son of the county District Attorney, Jebediah Mason Clark, chose today to announce his run for Congress! Jesse gave his well attended public address outside of the District Attorney's office today. We'll show you some of that speech now..."

Bud's hand ran over her thighs now. He did that when he wanted to calm her. So whatever was coming would be bad. It would have to be to get Bud to react like this.

Jesse Clark appeared on the screen. Caroline didn't know him, but judging by Chase's offended grunt — he did. He was tall, around Bud's height, and lean, with a sharp clean jawline and curly blond hair that fell to his neck and hung around his head like a halo. Aquamarine eyes glinted in the sun, and Caroline thought he looked like a cat. He had a piercing stare, even on camera, and he made eye contact with each camera like he knew which one they'd choose for the evening news.

Like he'd been born for this. Jesse Clark was her opponent. A rich boy from Virgil whose dad raised him in politics. Caroline thought this was what her boys braced her for until Jesse spoke.

"My name is Jesse Clark. Today, I'm announcing my run for Congress..."

A cheer erupted in the crowd. Caroline's stomach flipped.

"... But I have a more important matter to discuss with you today. A matter that affects all the good and honest people in our country. A matter which represents the descent into dishonesty, criminal behavior and anarchy in this country."

He paused, and Caroline sucked in air. Each of the men had a hand on her now. Either they'd heard the speech before, or they knew Jesse Clark well enough to know what he'd say next.

Jesse continued, blue eyes matching the blue of his gingham button-down, tucked into his khakis.

"One of the good, upstanding citizens of Old Town, while performing his duties as a police officer fired at a young man, a criminal, no doubt, who threatened the safety of everybody in Old Town. This young man passed away, and the county currently holds the police officer in custody. I have a few words to say about this event..."

He'd said enough. Caroline felt sick. This was her opponent. And he didn't look like a monster. His polished words flowed smoothly. His face was Hollywood-attractive and when he smiled, even her chest flickered. She swallowed and leaned in, hanging onto his words, knowing each one would cut deep.

"Our county is a traditional county and always has been. We represent the good people of America. The honest, hard-working people who don't commit crimes, who don't do drugs, who don't lie and cheat and steal. Dishonest people, criminals and thugs, threaten our American values and they threaten everything the constitution of this great country stands for. When I win my Congressional seat, I will make sure Old Town and Virgil and every town in our county returns to these values. We need to stop seeing segregation as a bad thing. We need to stop this attack on our police officers. And more importantly, we need to destroy the roots of anarchy and disobedience in this town and return to law and order…"

Bud put the television off. Caroline buried her head in her hands.

"You have to whoop this guy," Travis blurted out, "I swear to God, if I could get in the same room as Jesse Clark, I'd punch his smug fucking face."

"You three know him then?" Caroline murmured.

She could barely hear her own words over her racing heart. Bud's large hand thumped on her back.

"Yeah. We know him. We stuffed his fucking ass into a locker once."

Chase scoffed.

"Bud, that was all you."

"He made fun of me 'cause I couldn't read. Well, who's laughing now!"

Caroline didn't have the heart to tell him that Jesse would probably have the last laugh. He was rich — he had to be, with daddy as the District Attorney. And he already spoke publicly.

He had a foot in the door and Caroline was just… normal. An Old Town girl who wanted change but didn't have the teeth for this.

"I can't do this," Caroline whispered, "I'm going to lose. I can't beat him."

"Stop it," Chase snapped, "He represents a loud and vocal minority, but you represent the future. Change always wins. We can't avoid it."

Travis offered a more realistic perspective.

"We'll have to toughen up if he's who you're running against."

Caroline hadn't thought it possible to come up with a worse person as her opponent than Zach Owens. She wished he'd run for Congress. Not… Jesse Clark.

Bud finished his beer and grunted.

"Fuck Jesse Clark. I swear, I'll throw my entire weight as Mayor behind you, Caroline. I'll do whatever it takes."

"What are we going to do?"

Bud thumped her on the back again.

"We need to sleep on it. And tomorrow, we'll all discuss."

Caroline turned to face Travis. He leaned over and kissed her.

"I'm sorry," he murmured.

That would have to be enough. They'd been through hell together and they had more to go through. Jesse Clark might clean up good, but Caroline could tell he'd play dirty. Bud made supper. They showered and cleaned up nicely before heading to bed for the night together. Caroline curled up in Travis' arms while Bud and Chase passed out. Travis climbed on top of her, his hardness bursting through his flannel pajamas.

He didn't take it out or enter her. He grabbed her face and

kissed her. He felt bad. Caroline kissed him back and his lips trailed down her neck.

"I'm sorry, Care."

"Don't," she whispered, "We're going to disagree sometimes. I get it."

"I love you," he whispered back.

"I love you too."

"I love you with them. I love you without them. I love you. Don't forget that."

"I won't."

Travis shuddered and rolled over, dragging Caroline close to him so she rested her head against his chest. He stroked her hair until he fell asleep. Caroline woke up alone in bed. She checked her phone. Shit. She'd slept in too late. She washed her face and wandered downstairs in one of Bud's giant red button-downs. He stood — naked — in front of the stove, frying eggs in a cast-iron pan.

"How can you cook with your dick so close to the fire," Caroline yawned.

Bud turned around and grinned.

"Sausage and eggs?"

"You're gross," Caroline muttered, "Where are the boys?"

"Travis went out for a run and Chase is with your brother at your family's place."

"Still planning the protest?"

"Yes, ma'am."

Caroline didn't expect Bud to be such a naked-person before they moved in together, but his thick meaty cock and tight athletic ass cheeks made a nice morning view. His butt cheeks looked good enough to eat. But not better than the eggs he fried up.

Bud slid the eggs onto a plate and poured Caroline an overflowing glass of orange juice. They ate in silence together until Bud slid his new phone across the table.

"I've been reading the Times every morning."

"Good. It's good to practice."

"Some words ain't easy."

Caroline nodded and glanced down at the article. It was about Ezra Mayfair. And despite all their digging, no journalist found anything in his past to drag to the surface, so they stuck to publishing unfounded speculations about possibilities.

"He was a good kid," Bud grunted.

Caroline nodded. Was. The 'was' hurt the most. The stopped potential. The future zapped away.

"Any word on Zach?"

"No. I made Chase promise not to go down to county."

"Good. Thanks. He's too… impulsive. We probably ought to stay out of trouble until election day."

"Yes, ma'am. Do we have a strategy yet?"

"If I did, I'd have to change it after what I saw last night."

"I fucking hate Jesse Clark."

Bud didn't hate anyone. Caroline found herself curious about why he hated Jesse so much. Everyone liked Bud, and he liked them back. He was one of the few people she'd ever met who was genuinely easy going.

"Why?"

Bud reached over on Caroline's plate to steal a bite of her eggs — he'd polished his off quickly — and shrugged.

"He ain't right in the head. Senior year, us fellas organized to go on a hunting trip. We took our guns and went out yonder. Jesse had the best guns. A new gun his daddy got him. Fancy ass semi-automatic Winchester shot gun. And he took the fucking gun, and he turned it on Jeremy Watts. And the kid. I mean… the kid fucking pissed himself. You grow up around guns, you never point a shotgun at a fucking human being. It doesn't matter if ain't loaded!"

"He didn't shoot him, right?"

"No. But the damn kid spent the entire day covered in his own piss while we shot the necks off turkeys."

Bud cleared their plates, and Caroline walked over to the sink to wash the dishes. Bud pressed his weight behind her. He was still naked. Very naked.

"What do you think you're doing, little miss?" he whispered.

"I think I'm cleaning up," Caroline teased.

"Daddy needs sex," Bud whispered, "Now turn around, let me hike your little ass on the counter."

"Bud..." Caroline protested. But there was no protesting Bud. Not while she wore his shirt. Not while he ate breakfast across from her with his dick hanging between his thighs.

He flipped her around and hiked her on the counter, running his hands over her thighs and feeling beneath her enormous shirt.

"No panties," Bud whispered, "Exactly the way I like my breakfast."

Click here to continue reading:
smarturl.it/redneckrebellion

! COCKY COWBOY FREE !

Get This Book FREE!

READ FREE HERE : https://dl.bookfunnel.com/qm6r71bgzx

NEW SERIES...

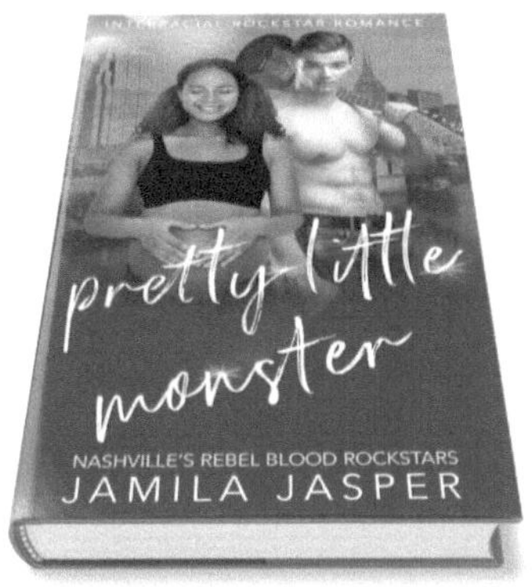

Flip the page to read a small sample...

PROLOGUE

5 years ago

Seb Jefferson
21-years-old

Angie Victor
18-years-old

"PLEASE DON'T HURT ME," she whispers, "I want to have sex with you but...I don't want it to hurt."

"It won't hurt if you do what I say," I snarl.

This girl is pretty. And she's dark. I like them dark. I like them even better when they're pretty. But that don't really matter for my purposes. She nods and then makes sure that I'll hold up my end of the deal.

"You'll leave him alone after this? You won't beat his ass no more or anything?" She says.

"Listen princess, I won you fair and square. Your shit head boyfriend will be fine. Now show me what I paid for."

"Seb Jefferson," she whispers her voice dripping with loathing, "People wouldn't believe what a monster you are."

Her hatred gets me hard. Really hard. But that might be the cocaine. I can hear the twang in her voice too. She probably worked for years to hide it, trying to make something of herself in L.A.

Tonight, that doesn't matter. Tonight, *she's mine.*

I push the pretty dark skinned girl against the wall and she grabs me, pulling me against her. Succumbing to me.

"I love doing this," I whisper, "I love destroying another man's property. Trust me, princess. If you were mine, I wouldn't share you. Not for all the money in the world."

I run my tongue over her neck and she trembles. I want to grab onto her hair and kiss her neck more, but I'm *high* and there's an even better prize waiting for me between her pretty chocolate legs.

She takes her clothes off and I drop to my knees. She's surprised, but she accepts my face between her thighs. She's perfect. They don't make girls like this back in my part of Tennessee.

Or if they do, they keep 'em locked up far away from redneck assholes like me. That's the best part about having money. I can fuck who I want. Eat who I want. White or black. No woman says no to Sebastian Jefferson. Not anymore.

I dip my tongue between her legs and come away with a muscle coated in her clear juices. When I gaze up at her, ready to mock her for her dripping tightness, she closes her eyes. I lick her lower lips until she moans. I make her scream.

Her fingers sink into my hair, which is my favorite part. Women always do that when they're about to cum hard on my face. My day isn't complete until I've had a shot of pussy juice and let's be honest… it's so much better when that pussy is black.

Not like any of my fans could ever know. I play the part well. Hell, I'll even wear the rebel flag once in a while to keep 'em guessing. Fuck fans. Fuck fame. I don't care what they think anymore. *I'm too high to give a fuck. It's not like anyone gives a fuck about me.*

All I care about is pussy — the pussy I have between my lips. The eighteen-year-old digs her fingers into my hair, uninhibited once my tongue spreads her open like a lotus. My cock yearns to get between her legs. I bought her for the night. That means I can do anything to her. *Anything*. But all I want to do is press my tongue between her thighs and bury my nose between her lower lips.

I love the way she smells…

Right before she cums, I pull away from her and kiss her inner thighs. She trembles, uncomfortable with the intimacy. Fuck, I could snort a fat line of coke off those thighs.

I suck on her inner thighs and she moans. She wants my tongue back between her legs but she knows how nasty I'll think she is if she begs for it.

"Spread them wider," I snarl, hoping she feels her absolute submission to me. It's what I demand from all my conquests, even the borrowed ones like Angie Victor. She obediently spreads her legs and I press two fingers inside her. They should have never sent my ass to Hollywood. She moans as I take her with my fingers and groan as I fill her.

"You like that?"

She moans as I plunge them deeper into her.

"I love black pussy, princess. I've had my eye on yours for a while."

I can tell she wants to punch me in the face, but I press my tongue between her thighs while I have two fingers buried inside her and she cums instead. She moans and cries out and I suck every drop of juice out of her black pussy as she bucks her hips against my mouth. Her body is *interest* on a loan.

That shit head Yannick Reynolds borrowed $75,000 for me and two broken toes and a black eye later, he still couldn't come up with the money.

Now I have what I really wanted... *her.* I remove my fingers from between her legs and force her lips apart, thrusting the fingers in. She obediently sucks her juices off them and swallows.

I chuckle and kiss her forehead before murmuring, "You good?"

"Sex," she whispers, "The job isn't done until we have sex."

"Good girl," I sneer, "it was that fucking easy to give your pussy up to another guy, huh? Any STDs princess?"

"You're one to talk," she snaps, "And trust me, it is *over* with Yannick. I'm only doing this to save him from himself."

"It couldn't be because your cunt's absolutely soaked."

"Watch your mouth, white boy."

I lunge for her and grab her arm. She screams and I press her against the wall. Fuck, she's scared. She really does think I'm a total monster. I glance down between her legs and snarl, "Listen. $75,000 gives me the right to cum in there."

"Are you crazy? What if I get pregnant? You're *famous*."

"I didn't pay for you to question everything I say," I snarl, "When I ask you to cum inside you again, you will ask me *which hole*. Do you understand?"

"You're sick," she snarls.

"I know," I whisper, "But you agreed to this, princess. Back out, and I'll break your boyfriend's back tonight."

She says nothing but I can tell I've nearly broken her.

"I want to cum inside you, princess."

"Which hole?" She asks, her voice cracking a little.

"I'm a Southern boy. I like me a taste of black pussy. So that's where I'll cum tonight. Get on the bed."

She lies back on the bed like a good girl, spreading her legs wide and exposing her soaked flower. I strip down faster than I ever have in my life. I haven't been so excited since I lost my damned virginity. I crawl between her legs and line my cock up with her perfect entrance. This girl is the blackest I've ever had, mind you. Such perfect skin I think I'll cum before I get my dick in her.

"Last chance at freedom, buttercup. Last chance before I breed you," I whisper, chuckling as a look of horror crosses her face.

She turns her gaze away from me. I grab her cheeks and force her to look at me. $75,000 was worth something, damn it. I don't just need her consent, although I definitely need that, I need her co-operation. She nods and I slide an inch inside her. She cries out. Fuck. I could pound her and empty myself inside her in ninety seconds flat. I don't have to care about her pleasure. I'm here for that final moment… coating the walls of her tight black pussy with *cum.*

"How the hell did he leave you a virgin?" I snarl, "Fuck… you're tight."

She cries out and pulled me deeper into her. Not so resistant now. Cock has that way with women. It makes them pliable little pets.

"You're tight, black girl. So tight."

I ram the rest of my length into her and she screams. I

pump my hips between her legs, taking her hard. And deep. She moans and cries out to the heavens and screams in the most undignified manner as I thrust between her legs.

"Cum for me, baby. Cum all over that Southern white boy cock... I want that black pussy juice on my dick for the next week."

She cums. Hard. I plunge into her deeper. I can't wait to cum inside her. She is so perfect. So tight. So *wet*.

I pull out of her and groan.

"Turn around babe."

Angie turns around and gasps as I slide my tongue between her lower lips. *Nope. I won't give you what you want, babe. I won't let you forget the night you had Sebastian Jefferson between yours legs.* I spread her lower lips and drive my tongue deeper. Angie moans and wriggles, struggling to get away.

I pin her down and eat her until she cums again. As Angie catches her breath, I slide my cock deep into her. She moans again and I slide back and forth into her tightness until she cries out and soaks my cock in her juices. *Fuck*.

I drive into her one last time and I finish inside her, exhausting myself and spilling every drop of my cum between her perfect black thighs. I pull out of her and say, "Damn. I think you are the best I've ever had, princess."

I kiss her and she kisses me back.

"You have what you wanted," she says, her voice shaking with fear, "Now leave him alone."

I grab her arm as she rushes for her clothes. She looks back at me, terrified but defiant.

"You can't go back to that guy, understand?"

"You need to mind your business," she snarls at me.

"I'm serious, princess," I whisper, "Any guy who would sell you to a scumbag like me doesn't deserve you. You're fucking beautiful. And you were fucking great tonight. Best I ever had, I swear on my mama."

She puts her clothes on and rushes out of my room, slamming my door behind her.

Angie Victor. I don't think I'll ever see that chick again.

1

THE GUY

@Celebz_Leaked

#CANCEL Sebastian Jefferson

Hey Gossipers,

I have some tea from y'all today. Y'all might not believe me but I have ***SOURCES*** *and pictures from my exclusive sources. Sebastian Jefferson, like THE Sebastian Jefferson, SPAT on one of his fans. This shit is crazy.*

These nasty ass white boys are doing too much and their dusty fans keep supporting them. We are done. Remember last year when he refused to take a picture with a fan? Ew. Ew. Ew. Who the hell streams that shitty band's music anyway? 1 Billion views on their last video?

If y'all can get #CANCELSEBASTIAN trending tonight, that would make all the difference.

SPAM THEM! Let them know that we won't let these racist af crusty white boys get away with this shit anymore.

— Celebz Leaked

ANGELINE VICTOR

"WHY ARE you showing this to me, Meg?" I snap, rolling my eyes at yet another stupid clickbait post about Seb Jefferson.

"That's the guy, isn't it," Meg says, "Your baby daddy is the insane but low-key fine white guy who spits on his fans."

"He's not the guy," I lie to her.

Meg has been my best friend too long not to see through my bullshit.

"Yes, it is. It's Callie's..."

"Stop it, Meg. We aren't doing this," I mutter, "Yes. Sebastian Jefferson is the guy. Their band *blew up*. It doesn't matter."

"Are you fucking crazy?" Meg hisses, "It matters. He's rich and you have his kid. You secured the bag. I think you should sue him."

Meg's a divorce lawyer now, and she thinks I should sue everyone. Don't like the music? Sue the radio station. Don't like the coffee? Sue Starbucks. She thinks in lawsuits. She wanted to sue a dating app for setting her up with too many losers. I talked her out of it… Barely.

Meg Nigel's long faux-locs hang away from her face with a yellow head-wrap that looks incredible against her brown skin. When I was younger, I used to want to be as light as Meg, who is still pretty dark. But she's not as dark as me.

She's still folding her arms and waiting for a response to her lawsuit suggestion that I am definitely *not* going to follow.

"I'm not suing him because I don't want him in Calypso's life," I snap, "I don't care if he's rich and famous. That was the worst night of my life. I'm not going back there."

"You said the sex wasn't bad."

"Sure," I snap. "The sex part was fine. But that doesn't change the fact that he's a monster. I was a complete idiot back then. Yannick *sold me* to him for a night. I don't want my daughter knowing that her father is a —

Calypso runs from the swings towards us.

"Mom! Mom, I found a bug!"

She's holding a large green insect with long antennae and I'm trying not to freak out as she turns around and runs toward another kid.

"Callie, no! Put it back! Callie! Don't put it in his shirt..."

Shit. I race for her and pull her away from the little boy she is about to torment with her weird playground bug. I scoop my daughter up and put her on my hips. She's getting big. Five years old is big. She has her own little personality that's so sassy and cute. Until it isn't.

Meg sticks her hands in her pockets and joins us.

"Next time, I'll hold your mom back so you can torture boys with bugs," Meg whispers to her. Callie laughs and wraps her arms around my neck.

"Mommy, can I have ice-cream."

"No, you can't. We need to get you home so you can get plenty of rest before your lesson tomorrow."

"What-ever, lady."

"Excuse me, ma'am?"

"Bye, Felicia."

"Callie?"

"I mean... yes, mommy."

I wonder if she gets that sassy attitude from me. Or from him. Sebastian Jefferson. He doesn't even know that he *has* a daughter. I don't want him to know. He gave me $50 for birth control that night. I pocketed the cash to hitchhike from Los Angeles.

I had enough of the so-called glitz and glamor after my encounter with Seb. Los Angeles was a place that used women up and spat them back out. I was just lucky that my parents forgave me for running away at sixteen. Yannick was thirty-three when he convinced me what we had was love.

I'm not that stupid kid anymore. I don't believe in love.

I slept on Meg's floor for three months before I found a job. Three years of working nights and I started my bar. At least you don't get sexually harassed by your 55-year-old manager when you own your own place.

Back then, when I slept on Meg's floor, I didn't even *think* about my missing periods. I was too busy trying to get a roof over my head and stop Yannick from tracking me down. Six months of stalking me while I was pregnant. Meg went out and bought a gun. I'm more California that way and I couldn't sleep as long as she had it in the house.

At least she was trying to protect me. It worked, didn't it? Here I am with both of them and Meg's talking to Callie about bugs.

When Calypso finally came, my family was *furious.* I wouldn't tell them who her father was. I *couldn't.* I signed an NDA.

But... I was *human,* too. All humans struggle to keep secrets. We either have to tell someone or let the secret hold us hostage until it turns into something else. A heart attack. Cancer. *Secrets kill eventually.*

And Meg was my lawyer, so I could talk to her about the stupid NDA. Now that she's showing me stupid blog posts about him, I regret ever telling her about Sebastian Jefferson. A part of her probably thought I was lying and wanted to use the news story to get me to confess that I got knocked up by a bum or something. The only thing she knows for sure is that Calypso's daddy is white. I rarely go for white guys, but I didn't exactly "go for" Seb. He took me.

Callie's skin is the gentlest shade of brown, lighter than a walnut.

"I'll text you if I have plans, Angie," Meg says, drawing me back into the moment.

"Great. My mom said she could take Callie tonight if you think of something we can do."

Callie sits up straight. "Yay! I want to go to grandma's house. Her food doesn't taste yucky."

I scowl at Callie, who gives me a cheeky grin, and then

kisses my cheek. My mom's Southern cooking might be delicious, but I think vegetables *don't* need sugar in them. Callie and my mom disagree.

Callie offers a sympathetic comfort, "It's okay, mommy. I know you try your best."

Kids can be so harsh. Damn. I wave goodbye to Meg and take Callie to the car. I'm a long way from the girl who had to sleep on Meg's floor. But not far enough. The bar is hard work, and it's even harder doing it all alone as a single mom. At least in Tennessee I have family. I didn't have anyone in Los Angeles.

Calypso's teacher wants to enroll her in a performing arts school and the bar isn't doing well enough for me to pay her tuition.

Callie's really talented. I wonder who she gets it from.

And her tuition? $7,000 a term, three terms a year. $21,000 is way than half my income after tax and bills. I have some money put away, but not enough to commit to a lifetime of tuition like that. If business at the bar picks up, *maybe*.

For Calypso, I'd do anything. I'd never buy new clothes again if it meant allowing her to pursue her dream. To *have* a dream.

My baby girl saved my life. But could I really sue Seb Jefferson for child support? I'd never given him a chance to meet her. He still doesn't know about her.

He's a creep, anyway. What kind of guy buys a girl for a night? A rock star. An asshole. A sin-soaked playboy without a care in the world. The thought of him makes me sick to my stomach. Unlike everyone else in America, I don't care about his sparkling blue eyes or the fact that Rolling Stone called him "the next Cash". Yeah, except Johnny Cash had a soul and Seb Jefferson's a monster.

I haven't needed Sebastian so far. I don't need him now.

Once Calypso and I get home, I lead her through the door and straight to the bath. I need to search her pocket for bugs every time she plays outside. The worst week of my life was when I took her to a boy's birthday party and he had tarantulas the kids could pet. Callie begged for a tarantula for two weeks, much to my horror.

Nashville has more bugs than anywhere else, I swear. And Callie has a way of finding them. Spiders. Cicadas. Horrific centipedes. Yuck.

During bath time, I comb through Calypso's long curls and twist her hair into two cornrows down the side of her head. Her hair is longer than mine has ever been. It's so thick and curly. I should take better care of my hair, but I just wear wigs or braids now and spend my time worrying about Callie.

She always asks for complicated hairstyles that get attention from the kids at school. I'm a wallflower by nature, so this extroverted daughter of mine must be like this because of Seb.

"Okay mocha cookie," I tell her. My heart warms every time I look at Callie's smile. And after bath time, she smells amazing. I just want to cuddle her up. Now that she's getting more independent, I know I don't have too much longer to appreciate her like this — all small and innocent.

"What do you want for dinner? Chicken and salad orrrr do you want to see what grandma's cooking?"

"I like grandma's food," Callie says confidently.

"Cool. Let's get you ready then. I'm sure she'll be happy to see you tonight."

Callie nods, and then she sticks two of her fingers in her mouth, glancing at me nervously.

"Mommy. Are you a lesbian?" Callie asks.

"What?"

Where the hell did she learn that word? She's only five…

"At school Ronnie said if I don't have a daddy it's because I have two mommies and that mommies can be lesbians now."

"Listen, we'll talk about that another time, okay? Tell Ronnie that gossiping isn't nice."

"Oh-Kay."

I call my mom, who is more than happy to have us over. Our place in Nashville's only a few blocks from hers. Seb Jefferson's from Tennessee too, but he's a country boy. You can hear it in his voice. You can't fake that accent. He probably couldn't get rid of it if he tried. When I close my eyes, I can still hear his voice.

Thankfully, I'll never have to see him again. He's too big to come back to our city, too caught up in the Los Angeles grind.

He's probably paying for sex with someone's girlfriend right now. Ugh. Why did Meg have to make me think of him?

My mom takes Callie into her arms as I enter her front door, careful to make an awed gasp at the hydrangea bushes out front as I walk up the front steps.

"Hey mom."

"Hey," she answers, clutching Callie tightly in her arms, "Meg called."

"She did?"

"She said she was coming over to whisk you out of here so make sure I'm ready to shoo you out."

"Whisk me out *where*? I just want to watch Desperate Housewives re-runs and chill. I need some white people mess to forget my problems today."

My mom raises an eyebrow and blurts out, "Meg says you need a man."

"She *told you that*?"

My cheeks gush warmth and I nervously fuss with my wig's middle part. Calypso pretends not to listen, but she's a kid.

They're little sponges and my little sponge listens to everything.

"Grandma, can I show you my performance? I have a lesson tomorrow."

"Sure, mocha cookie. Let's go."

Mom leads Calypso to her living room. Since finalizing the divorce from dad, she's done a lot of work on the place. It's nice. Callie walks to the center of the room without a hint of shyness. That must be him, mustn't it?

I was so shy I barely spoke to anyone when I was a kid. Sebastian Jefferson is... her *dad*. He's performed on stages for millions of people. He must be fearless. Brave. Confident. Like Calypso.

The similarities make me uneasy. Callie clears her throat and taps her foot before giving her polished introduction.

"My song for the audition is called O Little Town of Bethlehem."

I haven't said yes to performing arts school yet, but Callie's voice teacher has been preparing her for the audition, anyway. Mom's helping me cover that expense, but I know it's a lot for her. Since the divorce, she's had to pinch her pennies while watching dad spend all his money on women fifteen years younger than her. I try not to get in the middle of their mess, but I know she loves watching Callie grow.

Callie clears her throat and does her whole bit. She sounds *so* good. I can't believe she's only five. I can't believe she's *already* five. I can remember the night with Sebastian like it was yesterday. I'll never forget it. Not even my mom knows about him. She doesn't care who Callie's dad is anymore, now that she has a grandkid to spoil and trash talk my cooking with.

Mom enjoys reminding me that decent Southern men like a woman who can cook. She cooked for my dad every day for 35 years and he still cheated on her with our neighbor while she had breast cancer. But I keep that thought to myself.

We sit down for dinner after Callie receives all the praise she can handle. Callie finishes eating quickly and hurries off to play with the little ukulele I bought her for her fifth birthday. She seems to have figured out some chords, but she doesn't have the hang of it yet. That doesn't stop her from making up little songs.

"Callie asked if I was a lesbian today," I whisper to my mom so Callie can't hear me over the music.

"Are you?"

"Mom! No. Callie has a *dad*."

"You could have fooled me. I don't know what white boy you let knock you up or why he abandoned his daughter, but he's scum. Lower than scum."

Sebastian *was* scummy, but not for the reasons my mom thought. If she knew Callie's dad was one of Nashville's greatest rock stars, she'd probably say exactly what Meg said. *Sue him.*

"Yeah. You're right," I mumble, hoping she doesn't press me about him.

Meg arrives half an hour later. She's close with my mom and doesn't even bother knocking before she rushes "Aunty Daveena" (my mom). Meg's outfit is *crazy* even for a night out. High go-go boots. Hot pants. A tiny little top.

"Meg, what the hell are you wearing?!"

"We're going to a concert, girl. I'm going to twerk on a white boy and secure the bag. Let's go!"

"I'm dressed like... a *soccer mom.*"

"So? You look hot!"

"I'm *not* going to a concert dressed like this."

"I have a top you could wear!" my mom calls. I flash her a

stern glare and she winks at Megan before running upstairs to get the top and shoving me into the powder room to change. I'm wearing normal jeans and Adidas sneakers. The top is a cute pink halter that I can't imagine my mom wearing to anything.

Once I exit the powder room, Meg grabs me with an unyielding grasp.

"Goodbye, Aunty Daveena!" Meg calls into the house.

Meg never dresses like a lawyer when she's not at work, but I don't think her hot pants and go-go boots will attract the type of successful guy she needs. I keep that part to myself. I'm mostly trying to convince her to slip out of the hot pants and underneath a weighted blanket so we can watch Diary of a Mad Black Woman for the seven hundredth time.

I don't think I can come up with a plan fast enough.

"Bye mommy!" Callie calls, barely looking up from her ukelele.

Meg shoves me into her car like I'm a captive.

"Where are we going?"

"A concert. I told you."

"I don't have tickets anywhere. It better not be country…"

"Angie? Shut the hell up," Meg says. "Get excited. It's a pop-up show, and you're going to love it."

I don't know what my crazy ass best friend has planned, but I don't think I can escape. I'm stuck here with her.

2

THE GIRL

SEBASTIAN JEFFERSON

"I DON'T CARE what some dumb chick gossip blog says about me. We get on that stage and give the best fucking show of our lives. You hear me?"

Mickey fingers his bass guitar and Earl beats out a drumroll. He's always a worse player when he's off his meds, but at least he brings the energy. Mickey's too drunk to do more than nod his head, put on that pink flush and strum. We're only here because I convinced our shit head manager to give us a damn break from the LA grind. We have to justify our stay in the sticks if we want to keep our heads down and out of LA — which all three of us want.

"It's a sick gig tonight. Small. Intimate. The type of gigs we always play in Nashville," I say, knowing it's my role to hype the guys up.

This is my damn hometown and you won't catch me turning down a night in the city for anything. I *hated* Los Angeles. I never want to leave the damned South again. Until our next album drops, we can stay here working and writing and "getting inspiration" as long as we do a few key shows and a few key press interviews.

I tell our manager it'll be easier to stay out of trouble in our hometown. Nashville's always been good to me and it'll be good for Mickey so he can stop his damn drinking and Earl, so he can stay out of trouble with the fucked up women he keeps entangling himself with.

I even got myself a second home in Nashville — somewhere that would have never let a redneck motherfucker like me through the front door ten years ago before I had the tattoos, the electric guitar and the platinum blond hair. Not to mention more money than any man alive ought to have.

Earl keeps tapping out a nervous beat with the tip of the drumstick. Kara fingers her guitar and nods her head. "Sweet crowd we got. We can handle it."

Kara's girlfriend's hanging backstage, waiting for the show to start. She's half the reason Kara wanted to come back to Nashville. You can't find true love in LA and you can't keep true love alive. Nashville has to work for all of us. Now that we've got money and we aren't scrappy little country kids playing in Honky-Tonk bars when we ought to study for the SAT, we all want something LA doesn't want us to have: a happily ever after.

Lord knows a bunch of drugged up, pimped out rock stars are probably doomed from the start. But I'll be damned if I don't give having a good life my best shot after the hell I've been through.

I work the guys up to a frenzy now that Kara's nervous strumming has become an organized, throbbing melody, "And when we're done here tonight, we don't stop partying until we've banged every sweet piece of pussy in Nashville, Tennessee."

Kara whoops loudly, even if we all know there's only one sweet piece of pussy she really enjoys. It's not like our fans know that the iconic southern belle likes women — possessive butch women. We all have our secrets. I know I have mine…

"Let's show Tennessee a good time, motherfuckers," I say.

All these years in L.A. and you still can't take the twang out of my voice. Especially when I say *Tennessee.*

"Woo!" Mickey cheers, necking back a Miller. Times like these I miss burying my face in a bowl full of cocaine and letting go. But I'm 5 years sober from coke, crack, liquor and meth. I have to let the natural high of getting on that stage take me over.

I can't be the guy I was when I hurt her…

I still don't remember her name, but fuck, I'll never forget her face. That dark-skinned, round face. I look for her in every crowd. I double-take every time I see a woman, dark enough to be straight from Sudan.

I imagine the contours of her body, which I can barely remember sober. I just have my imagination. The fantasy of the perfect girl.

The way she gripped me remains permanently etched on my mind. She'd been so sweet. So submissive. She fell into a villain's arms and I used her like a prostitute. She deserved better than cracked-out Seb Jefferson. She deserved better than that punk ass Yannick.

You never stop working the 12 steps and I have unfinished business with Step 8. Make a list of all the people you have harmed and become willing to make amends. I am cursed to live with what I've done forever. She could have only been eighteen…

she had to have been. It kills me to imagine that she might have been younger. That in the throes of a meth bender that involved coercing my producer to whore out his teenage girlfriend to me... I might have done what I did to someone younger.

I never knew what happened to her, and I never saw that motherfucker Yannick again. Mickey does a bump and I fiddle with the chip in my pocket to avoid the triggers. To avoid *using*. Other guys might fuck with that shit and have fun, chill out for a while. I become a fucking monster. I become the guy who fucks a teenage girl after sticking a balled up fifty-dollar bill in her purse.

I *used* women. The more famous I got, the more of them I used. None of them wanted it less than *her*. Goddamn it. What was her name again?

We're ready to go on stage. I can hear the crowd and the natural high starts. Blood rushing past my ears. The thrill of performance. Mickey starts us off on the bass. Earl on drums. Kara on the guitar. The curtains aren't up and I can already hear the sounds of bras pelting at them. My trophies from all the women in America who would die for me. The curtain slowly rises and the heat pulses through me. *The best high on fucking earth.*

"Good evening, Nashville," I croon into the microphone and when they hear my Southern accent, they go *crazy*.

"How many of you believe in astrology?"

The crowd cheers.

"Which sign is the best in bed.... let me hear you scream...."

I hear Gemini faintly. Maybe Aries. I chuckle into the microphone and more women scream. There really isn't a better high than this. It's the only high that could keep me away from the powder. Music.

"I wrote this song *Aries* about a girl I loved... Sorry to all the other signs, but this one goes out to you..."

My baby's an Aries.
I like her red hot hair.
Her red hot tongue and her...
Yeahhhh

Three songs in, and I'm covered in sweat, still high off the music. After our set, we get off the stage and I'm pumped. *We made it.* Our manager steps out of the green room with a shit-eating grin on his face.

There's seriously no explaining how much I hate this guy. But he makes me rich. He makes himself richer, but I'm willing to accept that to be America's Southern heartthrob.

"Get your asses backstage, boys. There are hot and horny women here to meet *Rebel Blood*. Mickey, smile. Cut the crap. Earl, put the fucking lighter away. And Sebastian, try not to *grope* any of the fans this time."

"She asked for it. Literally. For her profile picture. How is that my fault?"

"I saw the damn blog post, Seb. Get your ass under control. I'm warning you. One more scandal and we *will renegotiate* your contract. Keep your ass in line."

I follow Mickey and Earl backstage and glance up, already planning to meet the fans with derision. I hate this part. The part where desperate lonely chicks act like they know you because of your job. I'd rather fuck them than smile at them and act like the guy they wish their boyfriend was. And then I see her. Well, I *hear* her friend first.

"Angie. You are not leaving. You march up to him and talk to him," a loud brown-skinned woman says, a distinctly adult voice over the hordes of high-lilted teenage debutantes desperate to meet us.

My gaze snaps over to the grown women. *Angie.*

That was her name. How the fuck could I forget? Then I see her. The night rushes back to me with all the details I thought I lost to methamphetamine years ago. Angie Victor. She's five years older and damn... she looks good.

She bursts away from the stage area as I make eye contact with her. Hell no. I don't care what my pussy ass manager has to say to me. I'm not letting that woman out of my sight. I follow her through the Emergency Exit.

"Angie Victor!" I call, rushing toward her. It's easy to hurry after women when you're 6'7". Her name rolls off my tongue so easily that my heart nearly jumps out of my mouth behind it. She's here. She's in Nashville. I never thought Yannick would let a girl like her go. She loved him too much and sick motherfuckers like that enjoy breaking a woman who loves that hard.

Her friend stops and stares at me, dumbfounded. Angie turns around. She folds her arms. Holy shit. She's prettier than I remember. Way prettier. Her body's perfect too. And her breasts are *huge*. Meg hurries toward me and says, "Listen, I don't care if you're famous but you need to know that you have a —

"STOP IT, MEG!" Angie screams.

"You tell him, or I will. He can't get away with doing this to you."

"Angie," I say, freezing. Every day in recovery I planned what I'd say to her if I ever saw her again and now she's at my show in Nashville of all places and my tongue turns into a damned cotton ball in my mouth and I feel like I've been bit by a rattlesnake. My blood is cold, and my skin tingles.

"You came to my show. You remembered me," I say. Suddenly, I feel all nervous, like she's the famous one. It's easier to be the famous one. I feel uncomfortable when women throw their thongs and bras at me, but most of the time, all I have to do is stand there. Now, I feel like I need to say something to her so she doesn't bolt, but I'm dumbfounded.

"She could never forget you," her friend Meg chimes in, "Seriously. She can't."

"Meg. Please. Leave us alone," Angie says, sounding seriously pissed off. I remember that look too, and struggle not to smirk.

Meg snorts and then goes back in through the emergency exit.

"Angie Victor," I repeat her name, promising myself to commit it to memory and suddenly feeling like a complete idiot.

"You're the girl," I finish, realizing I sound as stupid as a sheep.

"What girl?" she snaps, "You must have had hundreds of girls by now."

My heart races and I'm serious as a heart attack when I look at her.

"Maybe even thousands. But there's only one girl I'll never forget."

I'm surprised but I know that if I don't think fast, she'll slip through my fingers again and this surprise is heaven sent. One week back in Nashville and I've found her without even looking. Unfortunately, Angie apparently doesn't care much to see me. My comment makes her scowl.

"I'm sorry if I bothered you, Mr. Jefferson. I'm sure you're very busy with all your girls."

She turns to walk away from me, but there's no way in hell I can let her do that. I grab onto her arm and plead with her.

"Angie, wait. Don't go."

My heart pounds at the thought of losing her again. That moment of contact changes everything for me and I know that whatever I do next, I can't let Angie Victor go again.

I'll do whatever it takes to make her mine, even if I have to drag her kicking and screaming backstage. My grasp on her tightens.

3

FORGET ME

ANGIE

"I DON'T WANT to fuck up your life, Sebastian. The show was amazing. You're talented. Just forget you ever saw me."

I mean it. Now that I'm seeing him in person, the horrible night we first met (and had sex) rushes back to me. The things he said to me... and the way I came. I shouldn't have liked the dirty words coming out of his mouth or all of his talking about *black pussy*.

I bite down on my lower lip, willing myself to run away from him. I knew from experience he could overpower me if he wanted, and I'd stupidly sent Meg away.

"Can I get your number at least?"

"No, Sebastian. You can't."

"Okay. Listen, Angie. I'm sorry. I know it doesn't do a damned thing to undo what I did to you that night. But I've changed. And I'm sorry. I'm really sorry for everything I did."

"Right," I snap. "I heard the lyrics to your songs tonight. They're all about sex, cocaine, red heads you want to bang, breasts and money. I don't think you're any different. My friend dragged me out here tonight but it was a mistake."

"Why did you come? If it was such a mistake, why didn't you keep ignoring my existence the way you did the past 5 years?"

"I didn't *ignore* your existence," I huff at him.

How dare Sebastian insinuate that he's the victim of *me?*

"I tried looking for you. I thought about you, constantly."

"That doesn't flatter me, Sebastian. I'm not one of your little fans."

The derision in my voice appears to pierce him. Good. Now that I'm seeing him in person after all this time, I want to hurt the heck out of Seb Jefferson. I want to let him know that I'll never accept his stupid apology. And I'll never tell him he has a daughter.

"Answer the damned question, Angie. Why'd you come?"

"I got pregnant," I tell him. The words come easily because that's the truth.

He lowers his voice, platinum hair glimmering in the evening light, "I thought we took care of that."

"Whatever, Sebastian. I knew you'd react like this."

"You got rid of the kid, right?"

"Yeah. I *got rid of the kid,*" I sneer.

My heart races, but I don't want to tell him the truth. I won't tell him the truth and give him any power over Calypso's life. How could I forget he was such a damned scumbag?

He doesn't want a kid. Who the hell talks about a kid like that? Like something to get rid of. I want to punch the arrogant bastard in his smug face. How many fans will he have without that perfect jawline? What if I made those blue eyes black with a good punch in the face? Where would all of Seb's stupid groupies be, then?

He doesn't seem to notice my anger.

"Then you ain't got anywhere else to be tonight," he said, "Cool."

Great. I've backed myself into a corner. Meg appears again. Was this trifling hoe listening in?!

"She ain't going anywhere!" Meg yells. I flash her another glare and she emerges, shrugging. I scowl at her and she mouths, "Tell him later."

"Perfect," Seb says, "Angie Victor. I owe you a hell of a lot. May I interest you in a drink?"

"I don't drink," I snap at him.

Seb grins.

"Neither do I. But I can't take you for a coffee and I can't take you back to my place."

"There's a juice bar two blocks down!" Meg chimes in.

I turn to glare at her again, but she only winks and yells, "Bye, Angie!"

I snap at her, "You're leaving me?!"

"It looks like you've already got a ride home."

"Meg! Get back here!" I yell, chasing after her, but Meg threatens to tell Sebastian again and I can't have that. I let her go and I stand in the back parking lot, facing my worst nightmare. Sebastian. He's taller than I remember and way more muscular. I guess he's older too and I can see that on his face. He doesn't look like a hungry young man, all money and rage. He looks pensive and... deep. He looked like that while he was singing, too.

His music is awful, obviously, but it's impossible not to bob your head or remember the lyrics. And his voice... His voice makes me forget how much I hate him. But looking at him, our night together comes rushing back to me in painful, disturbing detail. He paid me for sex. He's a monster.

I turn to face Sebastian, loathing all over my face.

"Take me home," I snap.

Wait. I can't go home. Callie's at my mom's place, and I need to pick her up before I go home. Just when I take my phone out to call her and weasel myself out of this nightmare situation, my mom texts me, and I glance down at my phone.

Meg explained. Have a fun night! Callie's already asleep. I'll take her to school tomorrow.

What the hell did Meg explain? Because she sure as shit didn't tell my mother about Seb Jefferson.

I shove my phone in my pocket to hear Sebastian crooning, "That your boyfriend?"

"I don't *have* a boyfriend."

"I don't believe that, Miss Angie," he says. "Pretty girl like you?"

I hate when he says my name. I roll my eyes, hoping he's totally turned off and hoping that he just brings me to my damn apartment.

"I got a vehicle parked at the hotel downtown… it's a bit of a walk if you don't mind," he says.

I try getting rid of him another way.

"What about the band?"

"Want to meet them?"

"NO."

Seb sticks his hands in his pockets and asks, "You ain't keen on Mickey Ford or Earl Wayne Jr.?"

He's handsome. I'll give him that. And he dresses well. Guys in Tennessee don't dress as well as guys in LA, but Seb has that perfect cool that's a little Lynyrd Skynyrd and a little Jim Morrison. Then I remember that scandal with Rebel Blood's website selling teddy bears wearing confederate flag t-shirts and I scowl deeply.

"I'm not keen on any of you good old Southern boys."

Seb sticks his hands in his pockets and if I didn't know better, I'd say he was nervous. Nervous around *me*?

"Let's go this way so we don't get mobbed," he says. His accent is still so strong. I never had a Tennessee accent.

He puts his hand on the small of my back, and I wriggle away from his grasp. Seb doesn't get to touch me. He hasn't earned the right. Even a hand on the small of my back is enough to get me nervous and worked up. Seb's touch is a threat.

"I thought about you all those years," he says, "I suppose you never thought about me."

I bite my lower lip and I know I have to lie through my teeth. How the hell can I tell Seb that I have to think about him every single day because when I look into my daughter's eyes, how the hell can I avoid thinking about her father? I shrug and feel grateful that I'm dressed in a totally not lusty soccer mom outfit. I don't want Seb to think I want him.

"Nope. My friend dragged me here."

"What are you even doing back in Nashville? Did you take my advice and get away from that scumbag?"

"Don't you dare," I snarl at him. Seb Jefferson has enough of an ego without taking credit because I left Yannick Reynolds. *Yannick sold me.* Yes, I left him. I might have been a dumb eighteen-year-old girl back then, but I wasn't *that* dumb.

Seb looks genuinely taken aback.

"I was joking."

"Yeah," she snaps, "I got that. Go ahead, call me a special snowflake."

"You may be special Angie Victor, but you ain't a snowflake."

I hate Seb. I hate his stupid accent and his stupid platinum blond hair. I hate his height. I hate his smile. I hate everything about him. But when I stand next to him, I feel *weird* about hating him. Like all the loathing I've bottled up for him is messing me up. And it's horribly and stupidly wrong.

"Am I taking you back to your place, then?"

"Do people like you even spend time in East Nashville?"

He chuckles and shrugs his big lumberjack shoulders. "I reckon they'd still welcome Seb Jefferson. Even now."

What he means is *especially* now. He can't take five steps outside without a camera flash going off. Right.

"Whatever," I say, "You can take me home. But don't expect me to be impressed by whatever douche bag car you've bought with all your millions."

"I've got several cars, Angie."

"Shut up," I grumble.

If Seb finds my complaints bothersome, he says nothing. What the hell is the point of this? I won't find my happily ever after hanging around Seb Jefferson. He's not Calypso's dad. He's her... sperm donor. And even if I were looking for a dad for Calypso — which I'm not — it wouldn't be a groupie-obsessed drug addict like Seb.

He reaches into his pocket and takes out a little coin. Before I can protest, he opens my hand and sticks the coin in.

"This is for you," he says, folding my fingers around it.

"Great. I don't want it."

I tip my hand into his. Seb's hand closes around mine and he squeezes it shut. Firmly. The contact from his hand makes my chest feel fluttery and gross. He uses women, and I know it. But I can't help the warm and tingly feeling where he's touched me.

"Please, Angie. Keep it."

He walks ahead a little and I refuse to open my hand to look at the weird ass coin he's just given me.

"Seb, I don't want it."

"We're only two blocks away."

"Sebastian Jefferson!"

"Quiet, woman? Do you want people to know we're back here?"

Woman. See? He's a denigrating prick. An asshole. An idiot. And that stupid jawline doesn't work on me and neither does that sexy deep Southern accent. It's overplayed.

"Look at it," He says, and his voice becomes strained. "Please."

I'm not buying his tortured asshole crap.

"Do I look like I care?" I snap.

"Please," he begs again. There's something nice about hearing him beg. It feels like… sweet revenge.

Click here to order the book.
smarturl.it/prettylittlemonster

EXTREMELY IMPORTANT LINKS

Turn the page for a **FREE** book download 📲

EXTREMELY IMPORTANT LINKS

ALL BOOKS BY JAMILA JASPER
https://linktr.ee/JamilaJasper
SIGN UP FOR EMAIL UPDATES
Bit.ly/jamilajasperromance
SOCIAL MEDIA LINKS
https://www.jamilajasperromance.com/
GET MERCH
https://www.redbubble.com/people/jamilajasper/shop
GET FREEBIE (VIA TEXT)
https://slkt.io/qMk8
READ SERIAL (NEW CHAPTERS WEEKLY)
www.patreon.com/jamilajasper

JAMILA
JASPER

Diverse Romance For Black Women

MORE JAMILA JASPER ROMANCE

Pick your poison... Delicious interracial romance novels for all tastes. Long novels, short stories, audiobooks and more. Hit the link to experience my full catalog:

FULL CATALOG BY JAMILA JASPER:
https://www.jamilajasperromance.com/books

PATREON

7 SEASONS OF SERIAL CHAPTERS

NEW serial chapters published WEEKLY on my Patreon.

Read all six seasons of *Unfuckable* (Ben & Libby's story)...

For a small monthly fee, you get exclusive access to over 375 episodes of my first completed serial as well as access to the current ongoing serial, *Despicable*.

Patreon has more than the ongoing serial...

INSTANT ACCESS

- NEW merchandise tiers with **t-shirts, totes, mugs,** stickers and MORE!
- **FREE paperback** with all new tiers
- **FREE short story audiobooks** and audiobook samples when they're ready
- #FirstDraftLeaks of Prologues and first chapters **weeks** before I hit publish
- Behind the scenes notes
- Polls and story contribution
- Comments & LIVELY community discussion with likeminded interracial romance readers.

LEARN MORE ABOUT SUPPORTING A DIVERSE ROMANCE AUTHOR

www.patreon.com/jamilajasper

ABOUT JAMILA JASPER

Jamila Jasper is an Amazon bestselling author of African American women's fiction and romance novels. She writes contemporary interracial romance novels with gut-wrenching plots, titillating alpha male bad boys, and strong female main characters from diverse backgrounds — from London, to Atlanta, to Kampala. In her free time, Jamila enjoys hiking, spending time with her cat and salsa dancing. Use the icons below to find Jamila Jasper on social media. Use the hashtag #JamilaBWWM and post the Jamila Jasper book you read online for a social media shoutout!

facebook.com/bwwmjamila
twitter.com/jamilajasper
instagram.com/bwwmjamila
amazon.com/author/jamilajasper
bookbub.com/authors/jamilajasper

THANK YOU KINDLY

Thank you to all my readers, new and old for your support with this new year. I look forward to making 2021 an INCREDIBLE year for interracial romance novels. I want to thank you all for joining along on the journey.

Thank you to my Patrons.
Join the Patreon Community.

Sydney, Phia, Sharon, Charlotte, Assiatu, Regina, Romanda, Catherine, Gaynor, BF, Tasha, Henri, Sara, skkent, Rosalyn, Danielle, Deborah, Kirsten, Ana, Taylor, Charlene Louanna, Michelle, Tamika, Lauren, RoHyde, Natasha, Shekynah, Cassie, Dreama, Nick, Gennifer, Rayna, Jaleda, Anton, Kimvodkna, Jatonn, Anoushka, Audrey, Valeria, Courtney, Donna, Jenetha, Ayana, Kristy, FreyaJo, Grace, Kisha, Stephanie E., Amber, Denice, Marty, LaKisha, Latoya, Natasha, Monifa, Alisa, Daveena, Desiree, Gerry, Kimberly, Stephanie M., Tarah, Yolanda, Kristy, Gary, Janet, Kathy, Phyllis, Susan

www.ingramcontent.com/pod-product-compliance
Ingram Content Group UK Ltd.
Pitfield, Milton Keynes, MK11 3LW, UK
UKHW040004200726
13854UKWH00001B/37